A
ROSE-RED CITY

Dave Duncan

WEST LOTHIAN

DISTRICT LIBRARIES

191990

A Legend Book
Published by Arrow Books Limited
62–65 Chandos Place, London WC2N 4NW

An imprint of Century Hutchinson Limited

London Melbourne Sydney Auckland
Johannesburg and agencies throughout
the world

First published in the USA by Ballantine Books 1987
First published in Great Britain by Legend 1989

© 1987 by D. J. Duncan

This book is sold subject to the condition that it shall
not, by way of trade or otherwise, be lent, resold,
hired out, or otherwise circulated without the
publisher's prior consent in any form of binding or
cover other than that in which it is published and
without a similar condition including this condition
being imposed on the subsequent purchaser.

Printed and bound in Great Britain by
Anchor Press Ltd, Tiptree, Essex

ISBN 0 09 961920 2

This book is dedicated to
JANET
without whose
encouragement,
support,
and assistance
it would never have been written.

"A rose-red city—half as old as time"

J. W. Burgon, *Petra*

❧ 1 ❦

DANGER CAME TO JERRY HOWARD IN THE MIDDLE OF a clear and languorous summer afternoon. It came without warning and it came by the hand of a friend.

He was in his workshop, happily titling a book, surrounded by tweezers and tools, by punches and gold leaf and the sweet smell of leather and glue. If he raised his head he could look through the double doors into his library and beyond that, through the big windows, watch the passers-by going up and down the sun-warmed cobbles of Fishermen's Walk. On the far side of the walk sat seagulls, posed and preening on the rail—and where else could one find blue seagulls? Beyond the rail, in turn, the harbor shone like glass below a porcelain sky and a breeze as gentle as a maiden's first kiss. Nowhere, he would have said, could he be more content, or secure.

SCAR . . . he aimed a careful L.

A shame to be indoors, yet he was long overdue for some worktime. That morning he had gone fishing with Father Julius, plodding through wet grass and drippy willows and carefully laying invitations to suicide on the trout pools.

SCARLET . . . he reached for P.

Nor had he worked the day before, spending it in a hilarious grape-tramping spree with newlyweds Pietro

1

and Maria and a dozen mutual friends, ending the evening around a roaring bonfire with them and especially with Juanita and—much to their mutual surprise—taking Juanita home to bed.

PI . . . why the hell was X in the M slot?

So now he must work, for he had enough old books on hand, needing rebinding, to keep him busy for the rest of this day and all tomorrow.

And there, perhaps, lay a tiny needle of discontent in his haystack of happiness. Tomorrow would see the start of Tig's boar hunt. He had been invited. He had been very tempted to join—until he had discovered by accident that Killer was in on the plan as well, and very probably the instigator. Any affair in which Killer had a part was certain to be as dangerous, uncomfortable, rowdy, prolonged, and immoderate as possible. There would be unending marches across impossible terrain and bloody battles with inadequate weapons against ferocious, man-crunching animals—lions were by no means impossible if Killer had anything to do with it; there would be sleeping in snow or quagmires, probably during blizzards; there would certainly be juvenile practical joking and hazing, as well as wild orgies of one sort or another, and it would be unprecedented if the party returned intact, with all its members uninjured—indeed, Killer would regard the outing as a failure if that happened.

PIM . . .

In his own opinion, Jerry Howard had long ago proved that he was capable of holding his own in such macho insanities and did not need to keep on proving it at great risk to his physical well-being. Unlike Killer, he did not actually enjoy the process. So he had firmly declined the invitation. Very sensible!

P again.

Juanita was another problem, another tiny prickle in the haystack. No, not Juanita herself. Their brief affair had ended long ago, and last night's rematch had been entirely satisfactory for both. But it had been a one-night stand, and he disapproved of one-night stands. Why, he wondered, could he not, like Pietro, form a lasting relationship with a woman and settle down to the married bliss which should be the lot of any well-adjusted man?

But was he well-adjusted? Be honest! Was he not secretly regretting the boar hunt? Was he, possibly, very slightly *bored*?

Then he saw that he had been staring, unseeing, at *The Scarlet Pimp*, which suggested the amusing thought of shelving the book with the partial title and watching to see who took it down. Before he could suppress the temptation, the outer door of the library opened to admit . . . a friend.

Gervasse had been one of Benjamin Franklin's Parisian cronies and much resembled him. Their generation had believed that obesity was the best indicator of the leisured life of a gentleman; thus he entered a room stomach first and supported himself on a carved oak staff. He was, of course, in perfect health, strong as a smallish mule, cured now of the gout and stone which had tortured him in Franklin's day and had probably formed the subject of many of their conversations. His head was shiny pink, fringed by wisps of pale blue hair, and his cape was a wide expanse of yellow linen, ending in a remarkable overhang at waist level. Below that his indigo trousers swept back in long folds as full as a gown. Short cape and flappy pants were standard wear in Mera and Gervasse's were only remarkable for the quantity of material they had required, but he was an eye-filling sight regardless. He advanced into full view, doffed his blue cap with its feather, and swept a courtly bow.

Jerry had already recognized the thump of the cane on his rug and was around the table, clutching *The Scarlet Pimp* mischievously in his hand. He used it as Gervasse used his cap in a matching bow, although he had never quite mastered the same aplomb in bowing.

Gervasse was flushed and wheezing slightly, as though he had been running. "My dear Jerry!" Wheeze. "So fortunate to find you at home . . ."

"My dear Gervasse!" Jerry replied, sliding *The Scarlet Pimp* unobtrusively onto the big library table. "The pleasure is entirely mine. I shall seek the benefit of your expertise on an intriguing Amontillado which I obtained from Ricardo . . . only . . . yesterday . . ."

Gervasse was carrying a wand.

Gervasse nodded his head in polite acceptance and murmured that he would be delighted to taste a minim of friend Jerry's Amontillado; but he had seen Jerry's eyes lock themselves on the wand, and his own eyes were twinkling. Jerry led him over to the red leather chairs by the fireplace, unable to remove his gaze from that wand.

Outside . . .

Gervasse sank back in the chair, laying his staff by his feet and the wand across his knees and pretending to survey the big room as though he were not already entirely familiar with it, being a frequent visitor, chess partner, and participant in innumerable all-night philosophical discussions from that very chair. Jerry tore his eyes away from the wand and headed for the cupboard where he kept wine and crystal.

So much for boar hunts! Outside! If Citizen Howard had indeed been reaching the beginnings of boredom, then Outside would provide a great deal more stimulation than a boar hunt, even a boar hunt organized by Killer, and possibly an infinitely greater amount of danger.

He poured the wine, determined to show no impatience, but very conscious of his heartbeat and a dry tingling in his throat.

"How many volumes?" Gervasse murmured.

"Three thousand, the last time I counted," Jerry told the cupboard, "but that was many years ago. About a third of them are out at any one time, thank Heaven, or I should have them stacked like firewood."

It was an admirable room, high-ceilinged and spacious, with woodwork shining in a color as close to white as it was possible to obtain in Mera, with four many-paned windows looking out on the cobbles of Fishermen's Walk, and tall alcoves holding a myriad of books, almost all expertly bound by Jerry himself in morocco leather. But Gervasse had not come to admire the city library. He had come with a wand.

"I must return your *Divine Comedy*," Gervasse said.

"Ah, thank you! Most kind! Your health, citizen... and your success."

Jerry put an arm on the mantelpiece and raised his glass, also. "Long life to you, citizen," he said with a smile.

He was not going to ask. Dammit, he was *not* going to ask!

"I have been reading the learned Bishop Berkeley," Gervasse propounded. "Yes, an excellent wine, Jerry, supple on the tongue... I must talk to Signor Ricardo. The matter of the tree that falls when there is no one to hear it—does it make a noise? You are aware of the problem?"

Damnable old tease! "Of course," Jerry said.

"I was wondering—what if there were two men present when the tree fell? One sees it and hears it. The other is deaf and has his back turned. Does that count as half a tree falling, do you suppose?" His eyes twinkled.

"Or a tree falling half way?" Jerry asked, carefully holding his relaxed pose against the fireplace.

Gervasse chuckled and then relented. "I have come, quite obviously, from the Oracle," he said. "I was instructed to bring you a wand—and a message."

Jerry accepted the wand—a three-foot rod of ivory color, carved as though turned on a lathe. It had rings raised at intervals to help the grip and a small sphere at each end. A wand seemed an innocent and totally useless artifact, and yet when he grasped it he felt the familiar tingle of power against his palm and fingers. As always, he was surprised by its weight and its coldness; always, he wondered if it were made of stone. Alabaster? Or marble? Stone should be fragile in such a slender length, and yet he had seen a wand stop a broadsword and had himself once crushed a wolf's skull with one.

He stared at it in silence, fighting down his excitement. Gervasse sipped his wine until finally Jerry met his eye. "A very short message," he said. " 'Take a wagon and a staunch friend and clothes for one.' "

"That's it?"

"That, as you say, is it," Gervasse agreed.

A rescue! Not merely Outside, but a rescue! The

danger needle moved, therefore, up into an entirely different range. He was going to be playing in the First Division.

"Clothes for man or woman?"

"Didn't say."

It hardly mattered in Mera; half the women wore pants, and many men wore robes, and the difference was inconspicuous. Only twice had Jerry been sent a wand, and both missions had been trivial; but he had accompanied others Outside when they had carried the wand and needed companions. Three of those missions had been rescues. He suppressed the memories quickly, especially the memory of a certain fang-filled mouth opening in front of him, of demonic eyes above the fangs, and of Killer's silver-tipped spear coming over his shoulder to slide between those massive jaws in the nick of time. . . .

"And the staunch friend?" Gervasse asked, as the silence lingered.

"Killer." Jerry answered automatically. He drained his glass, still thinking. An astonishingly brief message! The Oracle was usually more specific. And why take clothes? He had never heard of that instruction.

"Ah, yes." Gervasse did not approve of Killer. "I saw him going into Sven's as I was coming down."

"Obviously he did not see you—or at least, not what you were bearing."

"Eh, no." The fat man hesitated and then turned slightly pink. "I assume that he may be interrupted at Sven's?"

Jerry laughed and went to fetch the decanter. "Certainly! He is coaching Sven in Greek wrestling. Why? Did you think he might be doing another sort of wrestling?"

Gervasse enjoyed gossip like a village spinster, while professing to despise it. He turned much pinker and made incoherent noises.

"That's all over, long ago," Jerry said. "Killer collects scalps, that's all."

Time did not matter. He could wait until tomorrow; he could even go on the boar hunt first. Face it—he would not sleep until he did go.

"Old friend, you will excuse me if I be about the Oracle's business?" He laid the decanter beside his guest and accepted protestations that of course he must attend to business. Gervasse would drink half the Amontillado and take the full width of Fishermen's Walk going home. And surely nothing in the next ten thousand years would ever persuade Gervasse to go Outside.

Jerry treated himself to a shave, using a straight razor to force steadiness back into his hand. He took a shower to show himself that he was not rushing, dragged a comb through his yellow hair. He ran up the spiral staircase to the upper room that served as his bedroom and a private retreat on the rare occasions when the library became too public for him. This, also, was large and had an even finer view of the harbor and half the city through its dormer windows. He had furnished it in a deliberate mishmash of styles and qualities as a counterpoint to the formal precision of the library, with a medieval four-poster next to a twentieth-century rosewood concert grand, and chairs from Colonial American to Louis Quinze. Yet the rare visitors admitted to this private place of his invariably commented first on the collection of helmets laid out on the piano—eight of them, from Fifth Dynasty Egyptian to Prussian, all kept well polished, and all authentic. Five had been gifts from Killer, three he had collected himself.

Tossing the wand on his bed, he rummaged at the back of the Victorian mahogany wardrobe, finding and donning his Outside clothes—khaki-green pants, less floppy and a fraction shorter than his others, and a matching cape. His shoulder bag was already packed and ready to grab. He pulled on the green cap and surveyed himself in the mirror; as usual, the outfit made him look like a tall, skinny Robin Hood. This time, though, he could see more stress lines than normal around his eyes, and that was bothersome—would Killer or the others notice those? He adjusted the cap to a jaunty angle and attempted a debonair smile. . . . No, that made him look less scared and more terrified.

He could, he suppose, refuse the summons, but he

knew of no one who ever had. He could not guess what
might happen . . . perhaps nothing, perhaps the worst. He
must ask some of the old-timers and find out if it had
been done; probably the Oracle only issued orders it
knew would be obeyed. Had it sensed boredom in Jerry
Howard? Was that all this was—a shot of adrenaline to
smarten his wits and improve his judgment? Why the hell
should he have to take such risks for the sake of someone he had never met, who more than likely would spurn
what he had to offer? Why—when citizens like Gervasse
were left in peace?

Refuse then, coward.

He retrieved the wand and trotted down the stairs in
his soft felt boots. Gervasse, glass in hand, was standing
by the table, frowning into the *The Scarlet Pimpernel*.

He looked up, unabashed, and asked, "The Mande-
ville *Bestiary*? It's out?"

Jerry was already in his workshop. "Madame Buono,
I think, or Guillamo—check the register." He returned,
shut the double doors, and stuck a note on them: GONE
OUTSIDE—MAKE YOURSELF AT HOME—JERRY.

"Thanks, Gervasse." He paused at the door. "If I'm
more than a couple of days—see to the shelving for me,
will you?" He hated to come back and find hundreds of
homeless books waiting for him.

"Of course, dear boy," Gervasse said. "Glad to. And
good luck." He blinked a few times and sent a concerned
frown after Jerry as he vanished through the front door
and padded down the steps to Fishermen's Walk.

Sven's house was a barnlike hall, dimly lit by high-set
windows, smelling always of wood smoke from the great
fireplace. It was filled with long tables and benches for
feasting; his collection of swords, shields, and axes almost covered the walls. Large, smelly dogs snored happily in the corners, and there was always food piled on
sideboards in case of unexpected famine—a model Val-
halla.

As Jerry pushed through the door from bright sunlight
into cool dimness, he saw that the tables had been
pushed aside. Two large, naked, and oiled men stood

locked together, straining, heaving, and grunting like some monumental sculpture wired for sound—Sven and Marcus. Six or seven others stood around them, cheering, jeering, and commenting; some dressed, some not. The lessons in Greek wrestling were still underway, then, and surprisingly, Killer had his clothes on.

Then the newcomer was spotted. "Wand!" shouted a voice. Sven went hurtling through the air and crashed to the floor; Marcus yelled in triumph; everyone else raced over to Jerry and surrounded him.

Inevitably Killer was first and for just a moment he stood on his toes with his hands out, eyes shining, ready to grab the wand. Then he noted Jerry's battle costume and the gleam in his eye and the shoulder bag. So this was not merely a messenger from the Oracle; the wand was not for him. His eager expression became guarded, his fingers relaxed, and he settled back on his heels, looking then, as he usually did, as though he had been built on the spot by the people who did Stonehenge.

Killer was broad and thick, easily the shortest man present, as well as the youngest. His curly black hair flopped loosely above a face boyishly smooth, yet clouded by a perpetual blue beard-shadow and marred by a red scar on his right temple. At present it also showed a fading black eye and a badly crushed nose. He folded his hands to indicate calmness—the wrists showing below the hem of his cloak were as thick as boots—and he grinned hugely, revealing a ragged collection of broken, missing, and half-grown teeth.

"How many?" he demanded.

"One," Jerry said cautiously. "You were limping."

He sensed the surge of disappointment all around him, but he also noted the wary flicker in Killer's eye.

"Twisted my ankle," Killer said. "I got to you first, didn't I?" It was rare to see him on the defensive. Certainly he had reached Jerry first—but he had been facing the door, and, while his morals, ethics, motives, and sanity were frequent subjects of debate in his absence, no one ever questioned his reflexes. Jerry glanced thoughtfully around the other faces, trying vainly to read their opinions, then turned his attention back to Killer.

"A very short message," he said. "'Take a wagon and a staunch friend and clothes for one.'"

Surprise.

"So?" Killer demanded. No one else spoke. Shortest and youngest, yet the undisputed leader.

Jerry made his decision—not that he had ever doubted what it would be—and shrugged. "You interested?" he asked. Killer rattled the armor collection with a titanic whoop, grabbed him in a life-threatening hug, and kissed him.

Killer was like that.

The others prized the winded Jerry loose and shook his hand warmly, their grips all gritty from the sand used in Greek wrestling. They smelled of sweat and oil and somehow of disappointment, but their concern and their good wishes were sincere, and the unfamiliar attention made him squirm.

Killer squeezed Sven's massive, oiled, hairy arm. "Put off the game till I get back?" he demanded.

Sven nodded and grinned. Because of his size he looked much more ferocious than Killer, but in his case a little of it was bluff. His monstrous red-gold beard opened in a grin. "Get you then," he said.

Killer's hand settled on Jerry's shoulder. "Planning a game of mayhem. Want you on my team."

Jerry tried to suppress a shudder and a sickening feeling in his stomach. "Sure," he said . . . and saw Killer's amusement. "Something to look forward to," he added; Marcus and Tig both laughed. Probably no one but Killer truly enjoyed mayhem, but to refuse would be to resign from his friendship. A boar hunt would be a cocktail party compared to mayhem.

"Ivan?" Killer said, wheeling around. "Tell Will and Aku I've gone? Sven, you handle the fencing, will you? And, Tig, get some tusks for me?"

Tiglath's white teeth gleamed in the middle of the biggest, darkest mass of hair in Mera; normally only his bullet-hole eyes and hooked nose showed in that Ninevehian jungle. "You catch your own," he said.

Killer laughed and turned his own motley tooth-collection on Jerry again. "Let's move!"

"You need to go home first?" Jerry asked. "Anything you need?"

Killer shook his head. Jerry should have known—Killer would shave with a dagger if necessary and either help himself to Jerry's toothbrush or use a twig. He wore unobtrusive gray-green colors on principle, and no one traveled lighter.

"How about your wife?" Marcus asked gruffly.

Killer shrugged. "One of you tell her," he said and led the way to the door.

❧ 2 ❧

A WALK THROUGH MERA WAS NORMALLY A LEISURE-
ly sequence of conversations. The streets were
mostly walkways paved in red granite, liberally furnished with benches and shade trees and planters. They
wound casually among stores and houses and outdoor
cafes, between walls of the same granite or red brick or
pink marble. They jogged unexpectedly up or down
staircases and they constantly offered up familiar faces
as a mountain stream throws out logs.

Although Killer was a head shorter than Jerry, he now
chose to set a murderous pace—obviously to demonstrate that there was nothing wrong with his ankle—and
the other pedestrians, observing the speed, the wand
which Jerry carried, and the sweat which Killer's agony
was pouring down his face, all contrived to reduce their
greetings. They nodded or smiled to Jerry, grinned or
frowned at Killer.

In the bright sunshine, Killer's curls were unmistaka-
bly midnight-blue.

Taking him on as an assistant, Jerry discovered, was
like hiring a hurricane to clean a fireplace. He behaved
himself moderately well in the haberdashers', not inter-
fering as Jerry obtained a middle-size suit of clothes
from the loquacious, gracious Madame Chi—preferring,

12

rather, to corner the little Hittite assistant with the un-
pronounceable name, reduce her to brilliant blushes and
shrill giggles by reminiscing loudly on what the two of
them had been doing three nights back, and extract a
promise that they would do it all again, and more, as
soon as he returned.

But then their path led down Jeweler's Lane to West
Gate and the stables, and that was another matter. He
began by enrolling the farrier and two grooms for his
mayhem team, which would surely leave the place short-
handed for several days afterward. He rejected with obscenities several geldings suggested by Wat the Hostler,
insisting that they had all been overworked that morning,
and without consulting Jerry at all, he demanded to see a
certain little bay mare which he well knew was Wat's
current favorite.

"That one's reserved!" Wat snapped.

Killer pointed at the horse trough.

Wat glanced around in the vain hope that his men
would interfere. "You take good care of her, then," he
growled—rumor claimed that Killer had once held him
underwater for fifteen minutes.

Killer ordered Rab the stableboy to lead out the mare
and went over her like an art expert examining a suspect
da Vinci, from teeth to tail, from ears to shoes, ending
by feeling her legs very carefully, also fondling Rab's legs
in passing. Finally he announced that the mare would
pass and he would take the mare then, and Rab when he
got back. Rab smirked as though that were an honor.

Killer then turned his attention to the problem of
transport, mocking Jerry's choice, insulting Wat's, and
making a halfhearted, semihumorous attempt to convince Jerry that a Roman racing chariot would qualify as
a wagon. He quickly made his own selection and at-
tended to the harnessing himself. Jerry had only to jump
aboard as Killer drove the vehicle out of the yard, with
the best wishes of the hands ringing in their ears.

All along Wall Road pedestrians leaped to safety, and
obviously the next stop would be the armories. "You get
guns, and I'll get blades," Killer said. "What else do you

need?" He hated firearms with a passion, but that had not prevented him from becoming one of the best marksmen in Mera.

Jerry was hanging on to the backrest with one hand and his cap with the other. "You're the expert. You make me feel like a first-timer."

Killer scowled and shook his head. "This is your war, friend. The Oracle picked you. You know why, don't you?"

"My century, I expect," Jerry said. "Or because I speak English."

"Maybe," Killer said, steering between two scampering old ladies. "But you know what I want when I ask you along on my treats?"

"Someone who speaks Greek?"

"Sometimes," Killer admitted. "But it's usually because I want brains. Sven and Aku and the others—and me—we're muscle men. You're a thinker. You read books. You mix with the philosophers. So maybe the Oracle wants brains this time? I say again—what have we forgotten?"

Jerry was annoyed to discover that praise from Killer was an enjoyable sensation. Between that self-analysis and the hectic jiggling of the journey, he failed to achieve any world-shattering insights into their needs before the wagon came shuddering to a halt before the doors of the twin armories. "Weapons should do it," he said.

The Armorer (Firearms) was one of the very few people in Mera whom Jerry disliked—an intimidating, taciturn, mysterious man from somewhere uptime from him. He scowled on hearing the Oracle's vague instructions and handed over a couple of Lee Enfields. The British Army, he said, had spread them all over the world, and they had stayed in use in some places for a century—they would fit almost anywhere or anytime. Unconvinced and unsatisfied, Jerry took them back down to the wagon.

Killer was pulling a tarpaulin over swords, bows, arrows, javelins, shields, and daggers, but at the sight of the Lee Enfields he exploded. The *improbable* things weighed more than he did, he said, and couldn't hit a charging dragon at ten paces, and what sort of ammunition? They hadn't given him the new stuff with expanding silver bullets? Wait there, he commanded, and hobbled off into the Armory (Firearms).

Jerry climbed up on the bench and prepared to feel inadequate, but he was hailed at once by Grace Evans, who had noticed the wand and wanted to touch it, because she had never had a chance to handle a wand before. Given that opportunity, Killer certainly would have contrived an obscene misunderstanding. Joe LeFarge and Gary came over to offer best wishes, then others. By the time Jerry had disposed of them all, twenty minutes had gone by, and he realized he had better be checking on his deputy's progress. At that moment a one-man arsenal came shuffling out the door and proceeded to load the wagon with two laser pistols, two Uzi submachine guns, a Gatling, and showers of ammunition—an incredible burden for one pair of arms.

About to throw the Lee Enfields in the gutter, Killer changed his mind, secured the tarpaulin, and climbed up beside his friend. He wiped his forehead with the hem of his cape and licked blood off his knuckles.

"You're loaded," he said. He laid his leg on the splashboard and pulled up his pants. The ankle was purple and swollen like a great fungus—it was a miracle he could walk at all. "You'd better find another helper, Jerry," he said.

Jerry was stunned. "When did you do that?"

"This morning," Killer said. "I took a shortcut out a window."

There might have been an outraged husband blocking the doorway, of course, but that was unlikely—the husbands were part of the fun. An outraged wife was another possibility, but probably he had merely wanted to speak to some passer-by and had not bothered with stairs.

This morning? "Then the Oracle knew of it," Jerry said. "If it had said a cautious friend, or sensible . . . but it said staunch, so it knew I would ask you."

Killer smiled very briefly and boyishly. "I thought I could manage, but I see I'm not fit for duty, Jerry."

"What happened to the armorer?"

Killer grinned and licked his knuckles again. "Not too much," he said innocently. "But he got to the bayonet rack before I could catch him. I had to disarm him first. It slows me, Jerry."

Jerry spared a sympathetic thought for any man unfortunate enough to annoy Killer when he wanted to test himself; probably the armorer had received injuries which would have crippled him anywhere but Mera.

"If there was going to be fighting," Jerry suggested, "then the Oracle would not be sending me, certainly not me and only one other. If you'll risk it, then I will."

Killer thumped a hand down on his companion's knee. "I bring danger, Jerry. The legions have it in for me now. We've counted; there are always a hell of a lot more around if I'm there. I've won too often; they smell me and they flock. You've got a lot better chance of sneaking Out and back quietly if you don't have me with you."

That was news, and lip-biting news, too, but it would be cruel to let Killer talk himself out of this now. It must be hurting him to try, and he would hurt deep if he succeeded. The Oracle had known of the ankle. There was one problem about Killer . . . but one did not impose conditions on him, so it must wait.

Jerry was about to snap a curt, "Let's move," because that was his style, but then he remembered that Greeks liked speeches. He said, "I would face Asterios himself and all the legions of Hell with you at my side, Achilles, son of Crion, rather than one solitary demon with anyone else. Now move your baby buns out of here."

Killer smiled shyly and wavered, then shook his head. "I shouldn't," he said. "I just wanted to see you well fitted out. Let's go and get Sven . . . or Ali?"

Jerry was surprised, but he decided to have one more try. If Killer truly believed he was incapacitated, then nothing would change his mind. If he was merely being extra cautious out of loyalty to a more cautious friend, then there was one sure persuasion.

He said thoughtfully, "Well, I understand. Going Outside with only an amateur like me must be pretty scary. . . ."

"Giddyap!" Killer roared, and the wagon lurched forward.

Good! That was settled. Now for the other problem.

"Killer?"

"Yes, Jerry?"

"Keep it Platonic?"

The fragmented teeth flashed, and the hand was withdrawn from Jerry's knee. "Spoilsport," said Killer.

They rattled out through North Gate, and instantly the hoof and wheel noises were lost in the grass of the wide meadow that fronted it. The land dipped gently before them and then rose again into scattered clumps of trees. Killer drove straight forward, heading for those long shadows, knowing that he would find a road. The little mare pricked her ears and trotted as eagerly as a puppy on an outing.

Killer mumbled a short prayer to Hermes.

There were four ways out of Mera. North Gate was for danger—the Oracle had not needed to specify.

Jerry twisted round to admire the view—the pink granite walls and above them the rose-red little town, flowing gently up its hill to the house of the Oracle at the crest. The strange and unworldly collection of variegated buildings with walls of wood, red brick, and warm stone, roofs of shiny copper or matte-red tiles, somehow contrived to blend together into a friendly and beautiful place. Westward, the evening sky was golden as the sun prepared to depart and do its duty elsewhere.

Jerry tossed Killer's discarded shoe into the back and found a scrap of twine in his bag. He bent over and fastened the wand loosely across Killer's ankle, and Killer muttered thanks.

The wagon swung around a copse, down a glade between two others, and soon there was bare earth beneath their wheels and a narrow road winding through trees.

"You want to drive?" Killer asked.

Crazy! Killer knew horses inside and backwards, and he did not. So it was a hint, Killer trying very hard to play the unfamiliar role of loyal subordinate instead of giving orders. Jerry should have thought of it on his own.

"No," he said, and clambered over the backrest to sit on the bench behind it, facing the rear.

The road had twisted—or reality had—and the sun was on their right. The trees grew thicker and became a spruce forest, thick and black as sable. A layer of needles muffled the sounds, and the air grew heavy with gummy scent—cool, moist, and dark. Jerry dug out one of the Uzis and loaded it with a clip of Mera's own ammunition, silver-coated bullets. He himself was not convinced that silver was necessary, but Killer and many of the others swore by it.

Then the surface had changed imperceptibly, and the light. The temperature had fallen; the trees ended without warning. Jerry found that he was gripping the backrest as though it were a dangerous snake, and his head was swinging around constantly. Gravel beneath the wheels, grasslands in all directions . . .

"Dawn or dusk?" he asked, and hoped that it was the bouncing of the wagon that made his voice shaky. Let it be dawn!

"Dusk, I think." Killer flicked the reins lightly, and they began to move faster. "Dusk and bad weather."

A gravel road winding gently across moorland—it could be anywhere or anytime, except that this much gravel must have come in trucks, so twentieth or later. No fences, no trees—indeed, no vegetation except grass, thistles, and low scrub waving eerily in a rising wind. Clouds hung low and ominous. The land rolled gently, and the road wound around in the bottoms, never providing a view. Jerry began to feel claustrophobic. Why couldn't it have been a nice, cheerful dawn?

"Jerry?" Killer said, leaning his head back. "You don't have to play mayhem if you'd rather not."

Now what? "I know that," Jerry said cautiously.

"You could be referee," Killer said.

Jerry laughed; that was a trap for newcomers. He said. "Never! I'll play for you and hope for a quick concussion."

Killer chuckled and did not reply.

Jerry pulled out the other Uzi and loaded that also, found the javelins—hopefully an entirely unnecessary

precaution, but there could be several legions of demons
behind those hills. More and more he was conscious of
how much an amateur he was at this. Killer was the expert, and the band that had been at Sven's house was the
nucleus, the regulars. People like him were enlisted now
and again for special cases. Why, this time, had the Oracle chosen to send the wand to him?

The landscape was bleak, unfriendly, and sinister.

Killer was whistling happily.

Dusk certainly; the light was fading into an inflamed
sore in the west, the sky turning black, the wind getting
stronger. Puffs of dust watered his eyes, and his cloak
flapped. He should have brought some warmer clothes;
Killer reveled in discomfort. A few spots of rain . . .

"White," Killer said. "Still tingles."

Jerry glanced at the back of Killer's head, but the light
was too poor to see if his hair was still blue. No white
and no black in Mera—to the regulars, the wands' turning white was the first sign of being Outside. "How's the
ankle?"

Killer said it was better, but even a wand would have
needed longer than that to cure it.

More bouncing and shaking . . . flatter country . . .

"We're here," Killer said at his right ear, and Jerry
twisted round to look.

The land was flat as ice, but now the light was too
poor to make out distance. Straight ahead along the
roadway, a solitary brilliance beckoned. There were no
other lights anywhere; one light in a world of darkness.
Jerry swung back to being rear gunner.

Then Killer pulled up, bringing stillness and silence.
Only the wind moved. The light was ten minutes' walk
ahead, a blue-white glare from a high pole—some sort of
fluorescent from after Jerry's time—shining down on a
cottage and a barn surrounded by hedge. The road ran
straight to the gate—no arguments about destination—
and Killer was untying the wand from his ankle and
would be asking for orders.

Inside the yard the road led directly to the barn, the
cottage set on the left side, a small outhouse between
them. The whole yard was bright as day, but no lights

shone in the windows. The wagon might be heard, even in this wind, and they would be walking ducks for watchers in the cottage. Steps leading up to the porch meant a raised floor inside and sightlines higher than the top of the hedge. They could leave the wagon and walk —but not on Killer's ankle. He could have Killer cover him from behind the hedge as he went to the door—but there was nowhere to tether the mare except perhaps to a gatepost. She surely was not gun trained and on this pool-table landscape she could be gone for ever.

Killer passed back the wand, and there was still a slight tingle in it. Jerry scrabbled for a laser pistol and checked the charge—no reading. That meant no later than early twenty-first, and electric lights meant the guns would run. Good; swords were a bloody business.

"Where to, boss?" Killer asked.

"Straight down their throats," Jerry said. "Or am I being stupid?" Killer's reply was directed to the mare.

At the gate Jerry jumped down and opened it, then stepped aside as Killer ran the wagon in, flashed past the cottage door, and wheeled around like the expert charioteer he was, so that he was facing out again; and nobody had opened fire. . . .

Jerry walked up the steps and hammered on the door with the wand, stood to one side as he had been taught, and felt every pore tighten up, making his skin feel as if it had shrunk on him. He waited. There was firewood stacked on the porch and more nearby. Then he turned the handle at arm's length and pushed the door away into blackness.

"Anyone home?"

He had a flashlight in his bag to use—if the battery was still good—but he had left it in the wagon. He reached round the jamb and found a light switch. The room was empty. He crossed it in quick strides, checked the two doors beyond, and found two bedrooms. Unless there were old ladies under the beds, the cottage was deserted. He went back and told Killer, who jumped off the wagon, stumbled, cursed, and then went in a fast half hop, half skip to check the outhouse and then the barn.

Rain began to splatter on the porch roof.

The piano was a surprise—a battered walnut upright. He hadn't seen an upright piano in . . . more years than he wanted to think about.

This was more a vacation cottage than someone's home; half of it a living room-kitchen, the other half split into two bedrooms, one large and one small, a dresser and bed in each. The main room held the piano, a table with four chairs around it, a sofa, and an armchair in front of a black iron range that would double for cooking and heat. The light came from a naked light bulb, but two oil lamps suggested that the power was unreliable, and he wondered where it came from—he had seen no power poles. The rain was getting louder, and he ought to be helping Killer. The icebox held three large steaks, six eggs, about a pound of bacon, milk. . . . He was not expected to stay here for long.

The wagon rumbled forward until it was level with the porch. Jerry ran out, told Killer to stay where he was, and started to unload the weapons. Killer climbed into the back and passed the swords and javelins across to him. Jerry carried them in and heaped them on the sofa. He went back out, and Killer threw him a wadded bundle which was obviously his own clothes—he was standing naked in the growing deluge. Then he passed the Lee Enfields and the Uzis; the Gatling and the lasers stayed where they were, obsolete and premature, respectively. Killer handed over the Gatling ammunition and, after a second's analysis, Jerry took it—the Gatling was still deadly and it would be lying in the wagon in the barn.

Then Killer drove the wagon to the barn. Jerry started tossing more firewood up from the main pile onto the porch, his Meran clothes shielding him from the downpour. Killer had not stripped to keep his clothes dry—he was enjoying a cold shower, which was fairly typical. A true Greek, he was never really happy with his clothes on. He was also a show-off.

Jerry went back into the cottage and gave it a thorough inspection. The furniture was all old and second-hand, the upholstery shabby, with the flowers long faded on the chintz. The sofa was lumpy. One bed, obviously, would be for the person they had come to meet, the potential eater of that third steak. The second bed... well, probably Killer and he would be taking turns at guard duty anyway, but he could survive on that sofa if he had to. Both bedrooms had bolts on the doors. He tried a few keys on the piano, and it was in tune. He found a bucket, a tin basin, and a stack of three large towels, so the Oracle had even foreseen the rain.

When Killer came limping in, Jerry was busying himself with the stove and pointed to the towels. Killer was shivering, but he shook his head and picked up the bucket.

"I'll get that," Jerry protested, angry at his oversight. "Where's the well?" But Killer had already gone.

He returned with a full bucket of water, bolted the front door behind him, and surveyed the room carefully as he dried himself. Rain was thundering on the roof now, dribbling noisily from the eaves—a hell of a night.

Before he got dressed, Killer made his own inspection of the cottage—and it made Jerry's effort look like a quick glance. He even crawled under the beds. He peered in, behind, and under the icebox. He poked in all the drawers and cupboards and under the rugs. He glared suspiciously at the piano and asked what the devil that was.

Jerry told him, and he pulled a face—Killer disliked anything more complicated than pan pipes. He sniffed at the oil can and hefted it for quantity; he tried all the switches and grinned childishly as the lights went on and off. Then he frowned at a small box standing on a shelf over the table, beside the lamps, matches, soap dish, and two empty cooking pots.

"That's a wireless!" said Jerry, who had missed it. He turned a knob, and it came to life at once, surprising him; but he could find nothing but static.

Killer grinned and picked up the wand from the table and walked across the room. The static grew quieter.

"How did you know about that?" Jerry demanded.

Killer chuckled, pleased at catching him out in his own time frame. "I've seen them before, but smaller.

Besides, a lot of that technical stuff gets fouled up by the wands."

Of course Killer had been Outside hundreds of times, not a half-dozen like Jerry. After some knob-twisting, Jerry found a badly garbled voice gabbling quickly, something about a President addressing a Congress. So it was not a wireless, it was a radio, and he knew which continent he was on. He turned it off.

Killer pulled on his pants.

"It's all fake," he remarked casually. "There's never —ever—been horses in that barn. I tasted the floor to be sure. The biffy has never been used. There's no junk lying around the yard or under the cottage, and, even in my day, peasants collected junk. In your century, they're nutty about it. This place has been created for us, specially."

The room was shabby, and the furniture old—but there was no dust on anything. Jerry should have noticed that at least.

Cool shivers danced along his spine. So they were in the borderlands. Technology would work, if it was not downtime, but faerie would work also, at least near the wand. Jerry had discussed this situation many times with Gervasse and the other philosophers, and none of them knew what to expect. Either the wands created bubbles of their own power within the reality of Outside, or this was a transitional condition on the outer limits of Mera's influence. Only the Oracle knew and it would never say. The worst of both worlds, then, an unholy mixture. The enemy might come as flesh and blood, armed with firearms or with claws and fangs; the guns would hold them off, if they were not too many. The wand was still tingling, so it would have power against the disembodied legions of hell if *they* came—unless, again, they were too many or too strong or clever—but what of the in-between, Asterios himself, or his equals or senior deputies? Jerry almost wished that he were back in Mera, playing a nice game of mayhem.

"Well?" he asked. "Are we ready for whoever is going to come calling? Anything I've forgotten?"

Killer tugged the cloak over his head and gave his

curls a final rub with the towel. "How do you turn that
high light off?"

Jerry thought, then looked around for a circuit box,
but the master switch did not turn off the yard light.
"You don't," he said.

Killer shrugged. "You shoot it, then, if you have to,
but we'll probably want it on, not off. Need to get more
wood in. Close the drapes. Move the sofa over there and
the chair there. All the windows look good and solid. I
found no gaps in the hedge, and it has prickles. We can
see the gate from that window. Hide the weapons around
the place so we can lay our hands on them. There's
enough oil to keep one lamp lit just in case; we'll keep it
down in that corner and sit in the dark so it's safe to
open the drapes—" Killer scowled. "What are you grinning at, Jeremy, scion of Howard?"

He was grinning at the transformation in his companion. Jerry himself was very conscious of the stress, of
the cold, naked feeling of Outside, the vulnerability. The
skin on his face felt tight, and he kept wanting to twitch.
Perhaps he did twitch. But in Killer the stress was coming through as a cool professionalism, a vastly more
adult approach to the world than the juvenile posturing
and rowdyism he affected in Mera. What mercenary
leader would not jump at a chance to hire Killer? He was
the enlistment officer's dream, the ideal recruit: a
twenty-year-old with four hundred years' experience.

But the concept of measuring a man by the length of
his service was totally foreign to Killer's thinking, so
there was no way to explain that.

"I was just musing, Achilles, son of Crion," said
Jerry, "that I'm proud to be your friend. Mera would be
a duller place without you . . . but I like you even better
when you're mortal."

Far away in the grasslands, barely audible over the
rain, something howled, lonely, haunted, and unworldly.

❧ 3 ❧

"ARE WE NEARLY THERE, YET?" ASKED LACEY. "For Heaven's sake!" stormed Ariadne, "that's the nine hundred and ninety-ninth time you've asked me!"

Then she thought, *Give me strength*, took a deep breath, and said, "Sorry, darling. Mommy's very tired. Yes, I think we're nearly there and I'm sorry I shouted at you."

Tired was not adequate. Exhausted, fatigued, frazzled...there were barely words for this sandy-eyeballed, concrete-in-the-bones feeling. She wanted to close her eyes and sleep for a few years, and a cold car would be quite comfortable, thank you; but she had Lacey and Alan with her, and the metronomes in front of her were wipers, and she must not sleep.

She had been driving for fourteen hours.

Lacey was sobbing and trying to make it a silent sobbing, which was worse than the furious bawling that Alan had indulged in until he had faded away.

"Soon, darling," said Ariadne. "Remember I showed you the sign at the turnoff? Hope, it said. We're going to a place called Hope. That's a nice name, isn't it?"

Lacey sniveled and probably nodded in the dark.

Except that there seemed to be no Hope. She had

25

given up trying to reach the border that night—the coffee had done no good and the hamburgers had merely allowed Alan to have his third attack of car sickness and make the car stink even worse. Okay, maybe the coffee had helped for ten minutes or so, but then her eyelids had started folding up again, the rain had gotten worse, and the cold fact had soaked in—she wasn't going to make the border that night. Then a sign had said HOPE NEXT TURNOFF, and that had sounded like what the marriage counsellor ordered; and she had taken the exit to Hope.

And she had seen the lights of Hope, dammit, through the dark and the rain—it had been only a mile from the highway, probably less. She had stayed on the road these last twenty minutes and more. There was no Hope!

She had done well to get this far. None of them would have believed she was capable of it—withdrawing the money without Graham knowing, staying dried out for three whole months, getting to know the kids again, teaching them to trust her, buying a car, having her license reinstated, picking Lacey up from school and Alan from day care when Maisie was having her hair done. She had planned it all by herself, and none of them had suspected what she was up to. She had been born in Canada and so she could claim to be a Canadian; once she got her kids across that border, it was going to be the Devil's own fight for those two to get them away from her again, if they ever found her. She had done very well, and only this expletive rain had stopped her from making the border in one big rush. They were probably still checking all the motels within a hundred miles of home, and here she was, almost out of reach.

Swish-swash, swish-swash...even on high, the wipers could barely keep up with the rain. It filled the headlight beams with silver dashes and furred the roadway with a silver mist, and if it hadn't been for the rain she'd be a hundred miles farther ahead, safely over the border. But Hope had dissolved in the rain and washed away. The last forecast she'd heard had promised sun and high temperatures for the next three days, and chance of precipitation, zero. Why could she never bet against odds like that? This was the sort of rain for monsoon places, the tropics, not the sort of anemic drizzle she'd expected in North Dakota—or possibly Minnesota, she wasn't sure, but not yet Manitoba.

The radio was silent now, after thirteen hours of Lacey twiddling knobs, pressing buttons, and jumping from one shrieking rock station to another, from country to western and back again. That was one small blessing from the rain: it had finally soaked into the aerial or something, and suddenly all they'd been able to get had been static, a strange, waily sort of static, and even Lacey didn't want to listen to that. Al had gone to sleep in the back, after fourteen hours of bawling and vomiting, and that was not a small blessing. Lacey was drooping into the corner and might even go to sleep soon, too. Then she could keep driving and might even make the border—if it was still open at this time, whatever time it was. The digital clock on the dash had started dancing around on its own, too, going backwards at times, and leaping all around the day. If the rain was getting into that, then maybe the whole obscenity car was about to rust solid and stop dead.

If it didn't, she would. Even talk from Lacey would be better than driving them all into a ditch. Except the country was so flat that the ditches looked almost safe; hard to say for sure when all she could see was a bright mist in the headlight beams and outer space beyond that in all directions.

"When we get to Hope, we're going to get a nice motel, honey," Ariadne said. "With soft beds and all warm. Won't that be nice?"

Lacey, probably, nodded.

"You talk to Mommy, honey. Help keep me awake."

"What do you want me to say, Mommy?"

"Whatever you like."

The road started to wind, unexpectedly, after a thousand miles of checkerboard straightness, and she slowed down, aware that she was cornering badly and that driving in this state was crazy. What was there to wind around on land this flat? Couldn't they even build a straight road?

How long since she had seen another car?

"Where are we going to, Mommy?"

"I told you, dear, we're going to Canada. We're going to have a nice place to live, you and Alan and me, and Mommy's going to teach piano."

"Will Daddy come and visit us?"

Not if I can help it. "I don't know, darling."

"Will Maisie come and visit us?"

Over my dead body! "No, honey, not Maisie."

Thunk! Bounce. *Thunk* and re-*thunk*...the damn pavement had ended, and she was driving on gravel. That settled it—she was lost.

"Will Peggy come and visit us?"

"No, dear, but maybe we can get you another pony to ride." Wanted: two-bedroom apartment, willing to accept ponies. Large balcony essential.

She was lost. She didn't know which way was north or west or east or straight up, and there wasn't anything to see. She came to a four-way junction, and all four roads looked exactly alike in the rain; there were no lights anywhere. She had driven off the edge of the world. Keep straight on, then.

"Don't want another pony. Want Peggy." More suppressed sobbing; the kid was as pooped as she was.

Then there was a light, a single star through the water-slicked windshield. Star of Hope? A very small Hope, then. A farm, obviously—this great waste of blackness must be one of those super-size, mechanized farms that the magazines told about. That was why there was only the one light.

"See that light, honey? Over there? I'm going to drive in there and ask where we are, because I think we've taken—"

"We lost, Mommy?" Panic!

"No, dear. But I think Mommy took a wrong turn and I'll stop and ask the lady at the farm."

The light was about a hundred yards back from the road, and she braked carefully—this was no gravel road, this was mud—slowed down to a crawl, and turned very carefully into the hundred-yard driveway. The car continued to turn after she told it to stop, apologetically slid backward off the driveway, and came to a complete halt.

Ariadne ran through her restricted collection of obscenities under her breath. She dropped the gear shift to L and stepped on the gas. The wheels said, "*Mmmmm!*" and the low corner sank appreciably lower. She tried R, and it sank lower still.

She turned off the motor and then the lights, and there was nothing except the dark roar of rain on the roof.

She stretched and rubbed her eyes and then looked over the seat. Alan was still out cold, a marble cherub under his rug with his thumb in his mouth and one arm around his teddy. In sudden panic she recognized the silence and looked at Lacey, also fast asleep, face pale in the darkness. She must have dropped off about thirty seconds before this unspeakable ditch grabbed them.

The rain roared on.

If there was nobody home at that light . . .

Ariadne checked her watch, and it was only nine o'clock. Well, they wouldn't be in bed yet, and she couldn't have been driving for fourteen hours, although she was almost certain it had been later than nine in the coffee shop. Now, did she dare leave the kids alone? If they woke up with her gone, they'd be terrified. But to wake them up and drag them along that soggy road in this rain would be more cruel still. She had a raincoat, somewhere in her grip in the trunk, but almost nothing for them, just what they'd been wearing . . . and Alan's indispensable teddy, thank the Lord.

She would have to leave them, be quick, and hope that they stayed asleep. Alan was comfortable, and even Lacey had settled into the corner in not too bad a position. The first thing would be to get her raincoat and a decent pair of shoes out of the trunk, then run down to that house and ask if they had a tractor. Even if they charged her fifty bucks, it would be worth it.

She opened the door quietly and was engulfed in icy water—she had forgotten the wind. She put her foot down and sank into mud up to her ankle; pulled it up and no shoe.

By then she was half-soaked and already starting to

shiver. *Oooo*—that rain was cold! Purse? Money? Well, there was no one else on this road, so she slid her purse under the seat.

She pushed the door shut quietly, lost the second shoe, and gave up on the raincoat idea. She started to hurry along the road toward the light, shielding her eyes with one hand, and giving silent thanks that the surface was so muddy that the rocks hardly bit into her feet at all.

A coyote howled a couple of fields away.

It was great to be out of the putrid car, and the cold shower was reviving her. This was no mechanized superfarm, though, just one barn and a tiny house; perhaps they did it all with transistors. The yard was half-flooded, puddles shining silver in the glare from the high mercury-vapor light, and the light itself was emitting a high-pitched whining.

Puddles, deep enough for her heart to sink in. There were no lights in the house. Well, if no one was home, she would break into the barn and spend the night with the kids. Gratefully she stumbled up the steps onto the little porch, out of the rain. Lights sprang up in the windows in great welcome floods. The door opened before she could touch it, and there was a man standing in the doorway.

She saw what he was holding out to her at the same moment as he said, "Did you by any chance come to borrow a towel?"

Then she was inside, standing in electric brightness beside an old iron range, feeling a delicious glow from it, rubbing her face with the towel, and conscious that she was soaked through and dripping all over the linoleum, but the towel was big and soft and very welcome.

"I've just made some tea," said the man. "You like tea?"

"I adore hot tea," she said. "Cream and sugar, if you have them, but it doesn't matter if you don't—just tea will do." She looked around the room. Not a farmhouse at all, she saw now, it was a weekend cottage, all cluttered with old furniture, Contemporary Salvation Army, but a reassuringly normal sort of place, and the man looked fairly safe and sympathetic.

He was about her own age, tall and spare, with a concerned and friendly expression on an ascetic sort of face. He had yellow hair, not a usual sort of blond, and he wore it combed straight back and oddly short at the sides, but he was well dressed—green slacks and a checked shirt with a green wool sweater. He looked more like an engineer or an accountant than a farmer. She felt herself relax slightly from the tension of being a woman alone and vulnerable, because he did not look like *The Mad Rapist See Page 4*. Civilized. Potentially useful.

Then a second man walked out of one of the other rooms, limped across to the door she had just come through, and shot the bolt—and also shot her heartbeat up about twenty points, because there was a likely Mad Rapist if she had ever seen one, certainly not the sort of kid you would want to follow you to the subway.

His nose had been hammered almost flat, and he had a red scar over one eye. His knuckles were purple and skinned—this one was a bruiser, a tough. His clothes were all right, jeans and a shirt, but half the shirt buttons were undone, and the sleeves folded up to the elbow to show off the forearms. He was barely taller than she, bull-necked and heavy, probably a body-building freak. Then he smiled, and half his teeth were missing. She backed up a couple of steps and almost knocked the tea cup out of the tall man's hand.

"Ah!" he said. "Sorry—my name's Howard, Jerry Howard."

"Ariadne Gillis," she said and held out a hand.

He looked slightly surprised and shook it; soft hand —no farmer. He was uneasy, and she suddenly became aware that her blouse was soaked and clinging. It wasn't the sort of blouse that was supposed to cling—he could probably read the maker's name on her bra strap. He held out the cup with a shy smile.

"You're very welcome, Miss? Gillis. You picked a bad night to come visiting."

She had her back to the kid. When the Howard man

shot a sort of warning glance over her shoulder, she turned around once more.

"This is my friend Achilles Crionson, but he prefers to be addressed as Killer. Don't let his appearance scare you, though. . . . He's trying to give it up—hasn't killed anyone in weeks."

"You are welcome," said the kid, standing too close. He took her hand and held it . . . and held it . . . he was giving her full eye contact—a heavy-lidded, arrogant stare, challenging her to break away first—inquiring, inviting, offering . . . *Jeez*! This one was bad news, God's gift to women, arrogance in spades—superstud, at your service. She felt herself blush before those steady black eyes and saw the satisfaction. *Lady*killer?

She pulled back her hand and dropped her eyes to the tea cup and took a shaky drink, hot and sweet. The kid did not step back, so she did, turning once more. to the older man.

"Look," she said, "I've gone and put my car in the ditch at the end of your driveway. I know it's a terrible night, but if you have a tractor and could . . ."

Howard shook his head; he was drinking tea also. "No tractor."

"Telephone, then?" she asked, heart sinking. He was going to suggest that she stay the night.

"And no telephone. We do have a horse, but I wouldn't try pulling out a car with a horse in this weather at night." He was almost as uneasy as she was. "We do have a spare room, Miss Gillis, and it has a big, strong bolt on the door. The plumbing is as primitive as it could be, but Killer and I were just about to cook up some steaks and we have a spare steak. . . ."

"No, I can't . . ." she said. Not stay the night with Mad Rapist around—she fancied she could feel heavy breathing on her back. If she couldn't, he was thinking it.

Howard tried a smile, and it was as reassuring as his companion's smile was disturbing. "Come here," he said, laying his cup down on the range. He led her over to one of the two doors and threw it open on a room with a single bed with clothes laid out on it—jeans and

blouse, bra, gray sweater, a bright yellow raincoat with a
hood, shoes and socks. . . .

What . . .? How. . .?

Howard rattled the bolt on the door. "Solid," he said.

"But I can't impose on you like this," she protested.

He gave her an odd look, turned pink, and stuttered,
"It's a spare room. Killer and I sleep next door."

She didn't believe that. Killer had been sending her
signals; and so had this man, although much more dis-
creetly and unintentionally. They hadn't been reacting to
her the way gays did. There had been interest—frank
come-and-get-it lust in Killer's case. This Jerry was
lying, hoping to put her at ease, but making himself uncomfortable at the same time.

"It's very kind of you, Jerry," she said. "But I have
my children with me, out in the car—"

"*CHILDREN!*" He stared at her as though she had
said she had the Russian Army along. His eyes went to
the kid's, and the kid returned a huge grin, showing
those shattered teeth.

"Children?" repeated the older man, still stunned.

"Yes, children," Ariadne said. "You've seen them
around—like small people. The storks bring them."

Howard was still staring at Killer, and Killer was still
grinning back at him. Why this reaction to children?

Then Howard seemed to pull his wits together. "We'd
better get them in here, then," he said. "How many,
Miss—Mrs. Gillis?"

"Oh, please call me Ariadne," she said, wondering if
he was always so formal. A shy man? "Only two. Lacey
is seven and Alan almost three. They were both asleep
when I left—" Then she had a sudden fit of shivering.

Howard took two strides over to the chair, grabbed up
the big bath towel, and in two strides had brought it
back. "You get changed before you catch pneumonia,"
he said. "Then we'll go and get the children." He pushed
her firmly into the bedroom and closed the door before
she could argue.

Sensible man, she thought as she stripped and
wrapped the towel around herself and started rubbing.
Crude but cosy little room, with plank walls and almost

filled by the bed and a dresser, but at least there was a rug to stand on. She heard voices; the door behind her had swung itself ajar. She had very good ears. . . .

". . . heard of children turning up on a rescue?"

The kid laughed. "No. But I warned you that the Oracle wanted brains. Got any ideas?"

Rescue? Oracle? She finished drying and inspected the garments on the bed; the jeans were a perfect fit. There was a comb in the hip pocket, but they were all brand-new clothes. What was going on here? Oracle? The bra was right, too. Was Graham behind this? He couldn't be, and it wasn't his style . . . but it looked as though she had been expected. It sounded that way, too.

"She won't come without her kids, obviously."

Come where?

"Then take them."

"But we were told to bring clothes for one."

How could she have been expected? She had not known herself where she was going and, now that she had got here, she didn't know where she was. They must have confused her with someone else, been expecting a woman whose name they did not know . . . a woman her size?

The voices got more distant, and the rain noise on the roof almost covered them; she could only make out that there was arguing. Then Howard said, ". . . and you cover us from here," and that seemed to be the end of the matter. Good job he was in charge and not that other one.

There were sensible shoes her size—and very few women took a four—and rubber boots. No complaints about the organization. She stepped back into the main room, and Howard was wearing a big yellow slicker like hers and rubber boots, also. He was holding an oil lantern.

"What side of the border is this?" she asked as she thunked across to him in the boots.

A curious hesitation . . . "What side did you want?" he asked.

"I was heading for Canada."

He nodded and exchanged a meaningful glance with his companion. "Then you have reached safety," he said. "You are running from someone, aren't you?"

She had nodded before she knew it. "Is it so obvious?"

He smiled that comfortable, shy smile. "Killer and I were sent here to help someone in trouble. You look as though you qualify... Ariadne. Please regard us as friends and as on your side—whatever it is. Okay?"

"But... but it was the merest chance I got here...."

He nodded in agreement. "I know that and I'll explain later. Meanwhile we have to bring your cubs into the ark. How far is it?"

"The end of the driveway."

"How... yes, all right." He turned away to the door, and the kid sniggered at some secret amusement.

Howard opened the door.

Hoooooooooowl....

He swung back to study her. "They're still a long way off," he said, as though expecting her to start having hysterics, then looked over at the kid again, who was hovering near a window.

"They might frighten Al," she said, "but Lacey knows about them. Still, I'd like to get back..."

He didn't move from the doorway, blocking her path.

"Knows about what?" he demanded. His eyes were narrow—with worry?

"Coyotes," she said.

"What the devil is a coyote?" Howard demanded, and again looked at his companion. She turned in time to see the kid shrug.

Two grown men in the very middle of the continent and they didn't know coyotes? She smiled politely at the joke, and it wasn't a joke.

"Wild dogs," she said. "Between a fox and a wolf. They howl a good fight, but they're quite harmless. I rather like the noise—wild and lonely. I'm surprised you haven't heard of coyotes, Jerry."

"Killer and I are strangers in these parts," he said, obviously embarrassed. "How harmless is harmless?"

"Totally," she said. "Unless they get rabies, I suppose. And they'll take a dog for sport, if they get one."

He nodded. "I'm going to assume they're rabid. Let's go rescue Alan and Lacey."

❧ 4 ❦

THERE WERE ODD THINGS GOING ON—NO DOUBT
about it. She hoped it was just the bone-deep fatigue, the weariness that felt like a plastic bag over her
head. She hoped it was just that and not an attack of
D.T.s coming on. Please not that—it had been months!

First the roadway; she was sure that she'd skidded off
just after the turn, but when they had gotten to the car—
and it had been farther away than she'd thought—there
had been no sign of the junction. The driveway had kept
straight on through the trees. Those trees—spruce or
fir—she couldn't remember those, either. Had she really
been driving in her sleep, or close to it? There had been
fence posts, but no trees. Now there were trees and no
fence posts, very thick, dark woods in fact, showing in
the glow of the lantern.

Lacey and Alan had been still asleep, thank the Lord.
They had wailed and fussed at being wakened. There had
been no way to keep them covered by the raincoats, so
they had both been soaked and chilled and weepy by the
time Jerry and she had carried them up to the cottage.
And the howling was certainly coming closer. Coyotes or
not, her scalp had prickled at the sound, and she had
been glad to get to the porch. Even Killer's horrible grin
had been almost a welcome sight.

36

Then there were the clothes. She'd taken the kids into the bedroom, stripped them off, and wrapped them in towels. She was sure that she'd thrown her raincoat down in a corner, but when she looked for it, it had vanished. She could not recall taking off the boots, and those had disappeared also; she must be punchy with fatigue. Then Jerry had tapped on the door and handed in a couple of green ponchos, suggesting that they try those—and they had fitted very well and made Lacey laugh, and Alan had laughed with her, not sure why.

Clothes—when she went back out to the main room, Jerry was working on supper at the range. He'd taken his shirt and sweater off, and was wearing a white tee shirt. He blushed quite pink at her look of surprise, and, although she had started to trust him, some of her first uneasiness came rushing back. Some sort of prolonged striptease? Perhaps it was hot beside the stove, although the rest of the place was cool. Then she saw that Killer had done the same, although he had put on one of the sleeveless things they called muscle shirts, which he certainly had not been wearing earlier. He did have more right to wear it than most. He saw her looking at him and gave her that sleepy inviting look again and then grinned as she turned away quickly.

Odd things going on, but she didn't feel D.T.-ish, just impossibly weary and tired, too tired even to feel very worried now. She was so totally at the mercy of these men that she might as well just trust them. There was nothing she could do except scream, and nobody to hear—and so far they seemed to be helpful, sympathetic, and well-meaning.

"Sorry I can't offer you a drink, but we seem to be running a dry ship." Jerry was peeling onions with a butcher knife and had a pan of potatoes boiling on the range. She felt another surge of relief, another notch loosened on the belt—if there was nothing to drink, then she needn't worry about that.

"Maybe the kids would like some milk?" he suggested.

Of course they would.

She wondered why the furniture was put the way it

was, with the sofa facing the front door and the armchair beside it facing the bedrooms. Who wanted to sit and stare at doors? Then Killer had pulled up a wooden chair in front of the range and he had Lacey on one knee and Alan on the other, like his-and-hers elves in their green ponchos. She had never seen them take to anyone that fast before; certainly not Alan, who was a suspicious little devil. Killer and Lacey were chattering away as though they'd known each other for years, while Alan clutched his milk in two hands and cultivated a white moustache.

"Why is your nose funny?" Lacey was asking.

"It got banged," Killer said. He spoke to her as though she were an adult, and Lacey was responding to that. "But it'll get better soon."

"Who banged it?" she demanded, frowning.

"A friend of mine. We were playing with big sticks. He banged my nose, and I banged his head. I banged harder than he did."

Lacey thought about that. "Then what did you do?" she asked. Jerry caught Ariadne's eye and smiled.

"I put him over my shoulder and carried him to the hospital," Killer said. "He got better, and we went off and had a party."

"You bad man?" Alan asked.

"Very bad," Killer said. "Grrrrr!"

"Grrrrrrrrrr!" Alan replied in great delight and innocently tipped the rest of his milk over Killer.

Ariadne swore loudly and grabbed up a towel which was lying on the counter.

"No problem," Killer said softly. "I'm waterproof." He wiped the shirt with the back of his hand, and a few last drops ran down his jeans and fell off. Puzzled, she went and sat down. Waterproof undershirts?

Lacey had been studying him. "Did the tooth fairy give you money for all those teeth you've lost?"

"No," said Killer. "Did the tooth fairy give you money for the one you lost?"

"She gave me a quarter."

Jerry giggled and wiped onion tears from his eyes. "Lacey, if the tooth fairy gave Killer money every time he lost a tooth, then she wouldn't have any money left for good people like you. He's very careless with his teeth, is Killer." He paused and then said, "Killer? Show us your beautiful smile again. Ariadne, take a look at this."

Killer grinned up from the chair, and Jerry used his big knife like a pointer, as though he were demonstrating on a dissection. "See there? And there? New teeth coming in. See that? Broken tooth, but it's rounded, not rough. It's healing. Those two are still jagged because he only broke them yesterday. They'll all be back to normal in a couple of days—unless he gets kicked in the mouth again first, which he usually does."

Such things were just not possible. She stared at the teeth incredulously, avoided Killer's mocking eyes, and turned to Jerry. "He . . . his teeth heal?"

Jerry nodded and went back to his cooking. "His nose will be straight as a ruler inside a week. I hate him to hear me say this, but it's quite a handsome nose when it gets the chance."

She shivered and fetched a chair and sat down by the range, not too close to Killer and his burdens, and stared at the chinks of firelight. Heal teeth? Maybe it wasn't she who was having D.T.s. Lacey examined Killer's teeth, and he growled and pretended to bite her fingers.

"The scar doesn't change," Jerry remarked. "I never found out why. Why is that, Killer? Why that one scar?"

Killer shrugged. "No idea. I've had it as long as I can remember. Perhaps since I was born."

Killer was a puzzle. He seemed barely more than a boy, but now she could sense a strange *solidity* in him that was far from boyish. Incredibly she heard her own voice saying, "And when was that, Achilles? When were you born?"

He frowned at her, and she raised her eyebrows—this time she would make the challenge.

He accepted, held her gaze with some amusement, and said quietly, "I'm not sure. In the sixty-ninth Olympiad."

Huh?

And Jerry was looking very thoughtful and, perhaps,

pleased, as though she had wormed a secret out of his friend. "In Thespiae, right?" he demanded.

Killer hesitated and nodded.

"A city renowned for its shrine to Eros?" Jerry asked, baiting him.

Killer glanced at the children and then said, "Damned right," with a grin, implying that 'damned' was not the word he had in mind.

"Famous for its fighting men, also?"

Killer's face went crimson with sudden anger, and the tall man was instantly wary, almost nervous. He said, "Sorry—shouldn't pry. It doesn't mean anything now, Killer."

What doesn't? They were talking on their own band, these two.

"It does to me," Killer growled and then switched on his smile for Lacey—to heck with adults! "Shall I sing you a song, Lacey?" he asked.

"What 'bout?" demanded Lacey and airily handed her empty glass to her mother.

"About the place where I live," Killer said. "It's a very nice place. It's called Mera. It's the place where the sun always shines, and there's lots of good things to do and nice people to do them with, and nobody ever gets sick or grows old. Okay?"

"'kay," Lacey said.

And in a surprisingly fair baritone, Killer sang:

Oh come with me to Mera then, and I shall take
  you Maying,
To wander in the morning on the meadowland of
  spring,
With crocuses, anemones embroidered on the pas-
  tures
And foamy clouds of blossom where the lark
  ascends to sing.

When noontime comes to Mera and the hawk
  above the haystack,
When sunlight stands as pillars in the forest's
  shady dells,

We'll dine on cream and berries by the leafy woodland waters,
And lie among the hyacinths, the mosses, and the
bells.

As evening gilds the cornfield comes the time to
lead you homeward,
By vineyards and by orchards, while the swallows
fly away,
To feasting at the fireside and the happiness of
company,
To satisfy and consummate and plan another day.

There was silence. Perhaps this kid wouldn't be so bad
on the subway after all—certainly he would scare away
any other muggers. Was that why he was here now?

"That's very good, Killer," Jerry said. "Whose is
that?"

"Clio's," Killer said without looking up. "See, Lacey?
Mera is the land where wishes come true. What would
you wish for, Lacey, if you lived in Mera?"

"Peggy," said Lacey. "He's my pony."

"Isn't that a girl's name?"

"He's a boy!" Lacey insisted. "It's short for Pegasus,
'cos Pegasus was a pony with wings, but Peggy doesn't
have wings, but I pretend he does. I would wish that he
did have real wings."

"I going to get a pony *soon!*" Alan announced.
"Daddy promised when I'm three."

Killer looked doubtful. "You're too little to ride a
pony."

"Am *not!*" Alan swung around and appealed to higher
authority. "Mommy! You tell Killer that I ride gooder
than Lacey."

She hadn't heard of the promise, but it sounded credi-
ble, and his birthday was only a few weeks off. On her
money, without alimony, the only rides the kids would
get would be on buses. "He's very good," she said.
"Quite fearless."

Alan said, "See?" belligerently.

"Okay," Killer said. "The wings might be too big a

wish, but if you come to Mera you can both have ponies, and there are lots of grassy places to ride them." He looked around at Ariadne and put on his sleepy look. "And what would Mommy wish for?"

He had been talking at her all along, of course, and Jerry was watching.

"Peace and quiet," she said.

"But there are lots of exciting things to do there," Killer said, "and nice people to do them with. You should let me take you there and show you."

Not likely!

"And how does one get to this Mera?" Ariadne asked. "What airlines fly there?"

"Supper's ready!" Jerry said firmly. It wasn't, quite, but he made them get the chairs around the table, while Killer carried Alan gently into the bedroom and laid him down, already asleep. Lacey was sleepy also, but insisted that she wanted some steak and made sure that she sat next to Killer.

Ariadne was feeling surprisingly better—perhaps it was the tea, or the coffee which Jerry had now produced, or perhaps it was an odd feeling of relief. She actually had an appetite, and the steak was good. She had reached . . .

"You did say that this was Canada?" she asked.

Jerry hesitated. "I don't know," he said. "All I said was that you had reached safety and you are among friends. . . . I'm not quite so sure of the safety now, though."

The howling sounded again, closer—real howls, not the yip-yippy stuff coyotes usually did. But of course coyotes could howl, too. Jerry and Killer exchanged glances, and their tension was obvious. They didn't know coyotes and they didn't know which side of the border they were on and they could heal teeth? There was no more conversation until they had finished eating.

Jerry tossed the dishes into a bowl and said loudly that they could wait until morning. Then he eyed Ariadne and said, "Do you feel up to playing a little music for us?"

"Yes, Mommy!" Lacey said, sensing another excuse to stay out of bed longer.

Ariadne looked thoughtfully at Jerry. "What makes you think I can play?"

"Can you?"

"Yes."

"Well?"

She shrugged. "Yes. Once I could." No need to poke old sores.

He smiled mysteriously. "There had to be some reason for that piano. Killer and I arrived about an hour before you did. We've never been here before, either." He nodded to indicate Lacey. "I'll try to explain shortly. But will you play for us? It's well tuned."

She shook her head. "I'm too tired." He could tell that it was in tune. . . . "You play something."

He smiled and carried one of the chairs over to the piano.

"I'll go check on the mare," Killer said and limped toward the door. He did not seek out the raincoat that Jerry had worn earlier, just left in his jeans and muscle shirt. She wondered where those raincoats had gone, for there were no closets in sight, only two small cupboards by the range.

Jerry looked up from his seat by the piano and laughed.

"He doesn't enjoy harmony," he said. "Anything closer than an octave is a discord to Killer. Ariadne, don't let him scare you. He does take no for an answer."

So this was a private word, was it?

"Off to bed, young lady," she said. "Mommy'll come and give you a kiss in a minute. Don't wake Alan."

Lacey stomped grumpily into the bedroom, shutting the door with a bang.

Jerry hesitated, a worried look on his angular face. "This is difficult. . . . I am going to tell you a very strange story. You will probably conclude that I am utterly crazy. Just believe that I don't get violent, okay? I'm guaranteed harmless."

She could believe that. "Is your friend?"

"Killer?" Jerry said, and chewed his lip. "Yes. He's

promiscuous as a goat, an Olympic-class lecher and proud of it, but he does take no for an answer. He won't force you, because he's too certain that you'll yield on your own. So just say 'No' firmly. You'll have to keep saying it, but it'll work."

"You implied earlier that he would prefer you."

He blushed scarlet. "He'd be quite happy to get either of us, and happier to have both. He's a Greek and he has all the bad habits of the Greeks of his day, polished by four hundred years of practice. He's not serious at the moment, because he's on duty. You should see him when he is serious. I've been saying 'No' to Killer about once a week for forty years."

There it was—four hundred years, forty years—he'd associated himself with the line that Killer had been shooting. She couldn't think of a sane reply to such insanity. Jerry, sensing the tension, suddenly grinned, revealing a sense of fun under the formality and the odd shyness.

"Of course, you could try saying 'Yes' and see what happens. He wouldn't bother you afterward—not for a while, anyway."

"No, thank you," she said firmly. "He's either too young for me—or much too old."

He chuckled. "One lady of my acquaintance insists that Killer is a unique experience. Like being run over by a slow freight, she says, every wheel."

The rain continued to drum on the roof unceasingly. She perched on the arm of the sofa. "The sixty-ninth Olympiad?" she said.

The yellow-haired man frowned. "I shouldn't have pushed that; he's never been that specific before. Give or take a year, Ariadne, Killer was born in 500 BC."

She just looked at him. There was nothing to reply to that.

He shrugged. "Okay, I warned you! I don't mean that he's twenty-five hundred years old. Time in Mera doesn't run with time Outside, but he's been there about four hundred years, as well as he can estimate. I was born in 1914. I've lived in Mera for forty years more or less, which makes me about seventy. I don't know what

year it is here, now, but I suspect I'm close to being on
time . . . but that's just coincidence. I have been a long
way downtime on some trips Out."

"You've dropped a couple of years," she said, as
calmly as she could.

He sighed. "I've had broken legs heal in three days in
Mera, and obviously—obviously if you believe us—we
don't age. You saw Killer's teeth, Ariadne; if those were
faked, then we've gone to a lot of trouble to fool you,
haven't we?"

She shook her head, too confused to think.

"Were there trees on that road when you came in?"
he asked. "We got here right at dusk, and there wasn't a
tree in sight, just a hedge. Now there's no hedge but a
forest. It's faerie—magic. It has to be, Ariadne."

"I'm punchy," she said. "I'd been driving all day, and
now this. . . . I can't think straight."

He nodded sympathetically. "Go off to bed, then. Bolt
the door. *Don't* open the window. Don't even open the
drapes if someth . . . someone taps on it. Killer and I will
be out here, so take whichever room you want, with the
kids or the other. Come and get us if you need anything
—we shan't be sleeping. Warn Lacey about the window.
Use the pots under the bed, I'm afraid—it isn't safe to
go out now."

"Why?" she demanded. "Not just coyotes?"

Jerry shook his head. "It's all part of the Mera thing.
There are . . . opposing forces. They can't attack Mera itself, or they haven't so far, but they try to prevent anyone else getting in. We come to 'rescue' you, as we call
it. You admitted you're running from someone. . . ."

"Yes."

He nodded. "And we shall offer you the chance to
come back with us. If you come, you will be invited to
stay. You can refuse either offer. Nobody's forcing you,
neither here nor there. But the other side doesn't want
you to have the chance and they would love to get their
talons on Killer and me—especially Killer. If those are
coyotes out there, they sound more like wolves than
wolves do. Before dawn there may be worse. So, 'Watch
the wall, my darling.'"

There was something very likable about this diffident, soft-spoken maniac, unless fatigue was rotting her judgment. "Kipling," she said. "'Watch the wall my darling, while the gentlemen go by.'"

He smiled, pleased and surprised. "You win a cigar! Try this, then:

Where falls not hail, or rain, or any snow,
Nor ever wind blows loudly; but it lies
Deep-meadow'd, happy, fair with orchard lawns
And bowery hollows crown'd with summer sea ..."

She nodded; Tennyson on the death of Arthur, the departure for Avalon. "Does King Arthur hold court in Mera, then?" she asked.

He took the question seriously. "There was a man who could have been the source of the legends, a leader from sixth-century Britain. He trained Killer."

"Was? He died?"

Jerry's face grew even more serious. "He came Outside on a rescue—like this—and failed to return. The other side got him."

She laughed. "I think it is certainly bedtime, Mr. Howard, when you start the fairy stories. Play me one little piece."

He lifted the cover. "I'm not much good—I haven't played in months, so this may be terrible. And I'm better with a score."

He wasn't terrible, he was a very good amateur, but she could tell that his fingers were rusty. Then she got caught up in the music.... He stopped with a discord and a muttered oath.

"Sorry. I'm not sure of the next bit. Like it?"

Like it? "It's marvelous! Incredible! What is it?"

He was surprised by her enthusiasm, then his face lit up. "It's Killer's teeth again—another piece of evidence. It was written by one of my friends. A bunch of us were sitting around my room one night, and he'd been playing for us—doing take-offs on Sibelius, Wagner, and Copland and tying us all in stitches. And then he played some of the stuff he writes now, using twenty-third-century rhythms, which are incredibly complex, and I asked him to play a little of the kind of music he used to write, before he was rescued. He improvised that—improvised it! Next day he wrote it down for me."

"Who?" she demanded, feeling her hands starting to shake, seeing the understanding in his eyes as she fought down that terrifying recognition.

"You would know him if you saw him."

"No!" But she had known the music, the inevitability of the music, as characteristic as handwriting, the sensation that whatever came next was preordained by God, the utter mastery. And it was not one of the known pieces. . . .

"No!" she shouted again, rising.

Jerry stood also, smiling triumphantly. "Yes! That's it, Adriadne! The key! There's always something to convince someone who's going to be rescued. That's why the piano . . . that music has convinced you, hasn't it?"

"No! No!"

"Yes! He was rescued from a slum in Vienna. You've heard the story of the unmarked grave, the funeral that no one went to? What year was that, Ariadne Gillis?"

"Tell me?" she whispered.

"1791," he said. "Correct?" He smiled at her.

It was true, then. This man knew a piece of music that only Mozart could have written, but which Mozart had not—a posthumous composition? The cottage wheeled around her and then steadied. . . .

Jerry Howard's green slacks and tee shirt had vanished. He was wearing a pair of very floppy gray-green trousers, the same color as Lacey's poncho; he was bare-chested and he was holding a long white rod in his hand. Her own outfit had changed into a sleeveless cape and loose pants like his, in the same gray shade as before, but not the same clothes.

She staggered, and he grabbed her and held her up.

Killer entered in a gust of wind and rain and slammed the door. His jeans had become floppy pants also, matching the poncho that Alan was wearing. Although the trousers were dry, his bare chest was soaking.

"Well!" he said and came limping around the sofa. He looked from one to the other.

"She believes us," Jerry said, releasing her.

Killer grinned and came too close once more. "Come with me to Mera, then," he said, quoting his song. "Come with me to Mera, pretty lady?"

She shook her head. A four-hundred-year-old juvenile delinquent? "I'm not sure if I do believe. . . ."

Jerry took her arm and led her to the chair. "Belief isn't something you decide consciously," he said. "It's there or it isn't. You believe. That doesn't mean you have to come with us, or stay there if you do. But at least we can talk about it."

The climate must be good there, she thought inanely —they both had superb tans. Good for the kids? Far beyond Graham's reach, then, it would be the ultimate sanctuary.

"Avalon?" she whispered.

"Avalon," said Jerry, kneeling beside the chair. "The Islands of the Blessed, the Fortunate Isles, Shangri-La, Elysium, Brasil, Tir na nOg, the Land of Youth . . . it's been around a long time, Ariadne. It's in all the legends, of all lands and cultures and times. The place where wishes come true."

And they would take her there? She had been fleeing to Canada, stealing her own children so callously stolen from her, seeking freedom, peace, and a life free of fear. Now he was offering all of that, plus immortality? She must be going crazy. D.T.s again! And yet . . . that earnest, gaunt face, the obvious concern . . . surely she was imagining all this?

"What happened to your shirts?"

Jerry looked puzzled. "We gave our capes to the children. I don't know what you saw. These are Meran clothes. They provide a local disguise."

"But you had shirts on and then tee shirts and now nothing!" she protested.

He smiled. "I only saw Killer with a cape and then Killer bare-chested. Tee shirts? I suppose that was the best the pants could do without capes. You believe now, so you are not deceived."

"Play that music again!" she demanded. It seemed like the only straw of sanity in this hayfield of confusion.

He smiled, went back to the piano, laid the rod thing across his lap, and played again, fumbling to a halt as he had before.

She got up and went over, and he yielded the chair to her. She played it through...then back to G-sharp... first theme in the left hand, now? Second theme inverted? "No!" she said, "too complex. That would come later, near the recapitulation?"

He was beet red. "And I was trying to impress you!" he said. "You're professional!"

She suppressed the childish pleasure. "I'm a mother."

"But you're first class!" he spluttered. "Concert pianist?"

She spread her hands. "Reach was my problem, Jerry. I probably could never have made the grade." Pregnant, she had not been able to reach the keys.

"I think you would have," he protested. "But come to Mera, and I'll give you the score—a Mozart holograph."

She smiled and was about to say something when wind rattled the bedroom door. Killer was there in two steps, a stumble, and a curse. He had a submachine gun in his hand, and she had no idea where that came from, unless he had pulled it up from between the sofa and the chair as he stumbled. He hit the door with a massive shoulder; it was bolted. He stepped back and hurled himself against it, staggering to catch his balance as the door jamb was shattered by the bolt and the door flew open. Then she and Jerry were there also, the window was open, and the children were gone.

❧ 5 ❧

FOR A MOMENT THERE WAS NO MOVEMENT, NO AC-
tion, only a whirl of thought. The window was wide
to the night and rain, the drape streaming like a flag. The
bedclothes were rumpled, the children's clothes hung
wet on the footboard, a teddy bear lay on the floor by the
dresser—all stark below the naked light bulb swaying on
its cord.

Then Killer shouldered the others back and pulled the
door closed—they were too visible through that window.

Jerry had screwed up. He should have heard something, but he had been so caught up in convincing Ariadne that he had not been listening. The first time he
had been given a rescue to do and he had screwed up.

Or had he? He had been told to bring clothes for one,
not for a mother and two children—perhaps this had
been foreseen. Was Ariadne expected to desert her children to go to Mera? What kind of woman would ever do
that? He did not think she was that sort of mother, and
so the mission was doomed to failure if the children were
lost. Realization dawned that he very much wanted Ariadne to come to Mera, he wanted to show it to her,
introduce his friends to her, and take her riding and
swimming and doing all the million other things that a
man and a woman . . . and that also. Perhaps it was only

pity, but perhaps it was the start of love? That was crazy. He had known her barely a couple of hours and only this morning had been admitting that he couldn't form a stable relationship with a woman. Maybe he hadn't found the right woman?

But who—or what—had taken the children?

Killer?

He had been gone a long time, seeing to the mare. He could have gone round the back of the cottage and... but why? Because he, too, had seen that the children were an extraordinary problem, a break in the pattern? Had he faked a kidnapping?

No—Killer was livid with fury, the scar a brilliant curl above his eye. Killer had screwed up also, he had been outside and so he should have heard or seen something. Killer did not take kindly to failure. Killer never took to failure, ever, on any terms. He was speechless.

To pursue an enemy of unknown essence into a dark night was virtual suicide: anyone or anything might be waiting out there, the children nothing but bait, the Merans the targets. It was a mad risk, insanity, and Jerry was the boss, he held the wand.

"Yes! Let's go!" he said. He saw the lightning flicker of expressions on Killer's face—astonishment, doubt, and then a wild joy—and Killer had vaulted the sofa, bad ankle forgotten, and was out the door.

Jerry pulled the other Uzi from the cupboard by the range. "Stay here!" he shouted. "There may be shooting. Sit on the floor or lie down, but don't go out!"

Then he was down the porch steps, instantly drenched by ice water, under the purple glare of the high hissing lamp and an easy shot for a marksman anywhere. He ran for the driveway, tucking the wand in his belt like a sword to leave both hands free for the gun. Puddles shone everywhere; there would be no footprints, but the driveway was certainly the best bet. Then he saw two monstrous red eyes flash ahead of him and a faint white glare on the trees beyond—a car or a truck starting up. It was at least a quarter-mile away, he had no chance of catching it, and it was too far to shoot. With the kids in there he dared not...

Where was Killer?

He ran anyway.

Outrun a car? It was hopeless.

Then Killer went by him in thundering explosions of mud and water, the mare's eyeball and teeth showing huge and white with terror at this accursed burden stretched along her back: a half-naked man riding her with no saddle or bridle, only four centuries of practice in every sort of daredevilry imaginable. He was using the gun as a whip. Horse and rider vanished into the darkness ahead, intermittently visible as a black eclipse of the receding taillights.

Jerry ran. He was out of the yard light's reach, stumbling and squelching along an unknown muddy track, steering by a vague shadow of himself ahead and those dwindling lights. He saw Ariadne's canted car appear and dematerialize again as the new vehicle shot past it.

What could Killer do? Even on this mudpit of a road, the car could outrun the horse. If he dismounted she would be gone—and how could he dismount anyway with an injured ankle? He surely daren't try to shoot from horseback. . . .

Crack! He had.

The taillights vanished, trees appeared suddenly to one side and then vanished in the unmistakable and expensive noise of car crash. Then there was only silence.

Jerry continued to run.

Running in cold rain was a strange sensation and probably quite efficient, but he was gasping and slowed almost to a trot by the time he came within sight of the car, sprawled across a shallow ditch, radiator wrapped around a tree. It was even larger than that monster vehicle Ariadne had been driving. The inside lights showed occupants . . . stupid to show oneself like that. . . .

A yellow flash and a flatter *Crack*! and he remembered the yard light behind him. He hurtled into the ditch and rolled in icy mud. *Stupid yourself*, he thought. Well, they weren't going anywhere, so he paused to catch his breath and wonder where Killer was. The car lights had gone out, and the world was the bottom of a tarpit in a cellar.

Now what did he do? How could he get them out of there? He dared not shoot into the car for fear of hitting the children. If he tried a blast over their heads, they could shoot at his flashes.

He started to shiver.

Hooves approaching—Killer returning! After the shot, the mare would have gone from mere panic to insanity, yet somehow that incredible character had managed to turn her. But now he was heading back into ambush. He must be warned, and a shot from Jerry's gun ought to do it . . . too late . . .

The brakelights flashed ruby over the expanse of watery road. The mare shrilled in terror, visible for a moment—riderless—and then gone. An instant later she splattered past Jerry, heading home to the barn, if she could continue to keep all four legs unbroken on such a rampage.

Someone in that car had brains, using the brakelights like that. And where was Killer? He might have fallen off the mare a mile down the road and snapped his neck. That did not sound like him, but the next move must obviously be Jerry's. He rose and started to approach, conscious of thudding heart and cold rain and still-too-fast breathing—but also aware that he was well muddied and invisible as long as he stayed in the ditch.

Something howled in the woods, the sound dying away in a curdling chuckle.

Too damned close; his hair stirred.

If these intruders with the car were human—a reasonable but not certain assumption—then they must also be wondering what that howl was. Surely no one could believe that noise had come from a wild dog? If they were human, how had they found Ariadne? If they weren't . . .

If they weren't, then he was too late to save the kids.

Another howl, long and evil and much, much too close for comfort—*and on the other side*.

Then a yammering roar ripped the silence of the night. Streams of tracers blazed above the car roof and Jerry's head, making him dive flat again. A full thirty-two-shot clip, he realized, coming from the trees on the far side.

Killer had solved the problem, taken cover in the woods. Probably Jerry would have thought of that himself in a week or two.

Darkness and silence.

That had given the chorus something to think about also.

The interior light came on, then one headlight, glaring off into brown tree trunks.

Surrender!

"Who are you?" That was Killer's voice, from the far side.

A less distinct shout, from a window. "I am Graham Gillis. These are my children."

Aha!

"Throw out your gun."

Jerry crossed, out of Killer's line of fire. "I'm on this side," he yelled.

Evidently the gun—a gun—had been thrown out, because Killer's voice shouted, "Then all of you get out on the far side." Away from the gun, of course.

There were three of them, plus the children; all swaddled anonymously in rain clothes, one very tall and one short, probably a woman. Jerry emerged from the darkness; the whole play was being staged in a dim reflection off the trees. The big one was holding—probably— Alan, and the shapeless huddle next to the small one would be Lacey. Then Killer came hobbling up from the far side, very slowly, bent double, very lame, using his gun as a cane.

He did not wait for Jerry's decisions this time.

"Names?" he barked.

The big one replied. "I am Gillis. This is my wife, and this is my driver, Carlo."

"Right," Killer said. "He will carry the girl. Mrs. Gillis, you will carry the baby."

"And I?" demanded the big man, perhaps wondering if he was to be shot out of hand.

"You're going to carry me," Killer said.

"Go to hell!" Gillis snapped, and Killer knocked him down with the gun, then beat him with it until he got up.

"You will carry me," Killer repeated, and the big man

tried to jump him. The gun barrel rammed into his mouth. That was enough argument. Killer was no small burden, but Gillis led the way, staggering like Sinbad under the Old Man of the Sea, who now had the automatic from the car.

Jerry followed behind the procession, carrying both Uzis, wondering what sort of a muck up he would have made without Killer along. They left the car light on, and he walked much of the way backward, expecting to be attacked from the rear at any moment. The gun play had announced their location—if there had been any doubt —but the howling had stopped, and that was not a good sign.

In the comparative safety of the yard light, Jerry handed a gun to Killer, who was standing on the porch watching the rest of the procession file inside and looking mightily pleased with himself. The mud on his face and chest was streaked to a thin gruel by rain, but he had obviously come off the horse hard, with a fine collection of bruises and scrapes. Jerry headed to the barn.

The mare was back in there, steaming and audibly shivering from terror and cold; badly in need of attention that she was not going to get. He shut the door, returned to the cottage, and was surprised to find Killer still on the porch, leaning against a post, his bad foot raised, apparently watching what was going on inside—but leaving himself an uncharacteristically easy target against the light. Probably he was calculating that the next attack would not be from firearms.

"What's happening?" Jerry demanded.

"Sounds like domestic bliss," Killer said. He put a hand on Jerry's shoulder as he was about to go by. "I landed your fish, scion of Howard, didn't I?"

"Yes, you did. Thanks, Killer."

The grip tightened. "Thanks you say? Thanks? I rode that horse with no bridle. I shot out the chariot wheel from her back. I turned her and got her safely home. Thanks?"

The little bastard loved to brag and he had lots to brag about now—a Hollywood stunt man could not have carried all that off in forty takes, and certainly not with a bad ankle. Nobody else could have, not in Mera, not Outside.

"Is that all you can say?" Killer demanded wickedly, still squeezing Jerry's shoulder.

He could say that he thought Killer had come of his own free will and had done what he did because his self-respect had been wounded. But what of Jerry's self-respect, was it not his mission? He could say that he thought Killer had come out of friendship—but his friendship had included diving off a runaway horse into pitch darkness, holding a gun, and onto a sprained ankle; and Jerry Howard could never do that for a friend, even in Mera where he would be risking only a few days' pain, and most certainly not Outside.

So that got him back to the evaluation he had made a thousand times before: that when you sorted out the diamonds and the dirt inside this Achilles son of Crion and you pushed away the dirt—the masochism and gratuitous cruelty, the bombast and the puerility, the lechery and perversion—you were left with a few precious stones. Very few, but very precious; and in the midst of those, great and shining like the Koh-i-Noor, was the loyalty which promised that Killer would do anything for a friend, *anything whatsoever*. So Killer's friendship was worth a lot more than Jerry Howard's, and that conclusion was intolerable to him, as Killer had known it would be.

He should have guessed that one day it would become inevitable.

"You're a good friend to me, Achilles," he said hoarsely. "And when we get safely back to Mera—you and me and Ariadne and her kids—I'll show you how good a friend I can be to you."

Killer's eyes widened. "A promise, Citizen Howard?"

"A promise," Jerry said bravely. "Anything you want."

Killer had not expected quite that much. He sighed blissfully. "And the pretty lady will be grateful also," he said. "What a happy little fellow I am going to be."

"You bastard!" Jerry's anger blazed. "You keep your horrible hands off her."

Then he saw he had fallen into another trap—Killer was looking up at him with infinite devilry dancing in his eyes. If anything was more fun than seduction for Killer, it was seducing another man's woman and letting him know it. "So?" Killer said. "My cold friend Jerry has at last found himself a lady he cares for? Truly the Oracle knew what it was doing."

Jerry was too mad to argue; Killer's pursuit of Ariadne would be utterly implacable if he thought that Jerry cared.

"But that's her business," he growled. "Let's go in."

"Do let me lean on you, dear boy," Killer said in an affected tone . . . but Jerry had never known him to ask for help before.

"You really mushed that ankle this time?"

Killer chuckled. "Oh, I saved the ankle pretty well," he said. "Trouble is, I broke the other leg doing it."

Jerry put an arm around him and helped him into the cabin.

The little place seemed very full of people, and Alan was having a screaming tantrum, not helping matters at all. A big pile of leaky raincoats and slickers dribbled by the entrance, and the room smelled stuffily of wet people. Jerry deposited Killer on the sofa, then slammed the door, and shot the bolt.

"Over there!" he ordered, waving his gun. "Take the wooden chairs and put your backs against the wall. Ariadne, you can sit in the big chair if you want."

He had the gun; he was obeyed. Then he took stock. In the center, Killer was sitting on the sofa with gun handy and his legs up, facing the captives at the end of the room, but in a good position to cover the main door at his side.

Ariadne had slumped down in the big floral armchair behind Killer's head, but it had been turned so that she also was facing the prisoners. Obviously she did not feel that she belonged with them, but she did not seem to be associating with Jerry and Killer, either; she was a third party of one now, shrunken and dejected.

The newcomers sat in a row between the range and the kitchen counter with its bowl of dirty dishes—a bad first impression for visitors! There were no windows within easy reach, and the table was in front to discourage sudden jumpings.

Gillis, in the middle, loomed even larger than Jerry had expected—as tall as he, and as thick as Killer— a swarthy, fortyish, heavyset man. His black wavy hair was going thin in front, his black eyes were glaring furiously from under heavy brows. His lips were swollen and bloody, and he had a bad bruise where Killer had gunwhipped him. The blue pinstripe suit looked strange to Jerry, but that must be what a successful businessman wore these days, for it was undoubtedly a good piece of tailoring, with very narrow lapels and no cuffs on the pants. A necktie, for Heaven's sake—hadn't the world got rid of those yet? Gillis was studying his captors carefully, probably just realizing that Jerry was in charge now, that Killer was the action man and would not be the negotiator, if there was negotiating to be done. He looked to be an arrogant, domineering man.

Having both parents present to compare, Jerry could see that Lacey's straight blond locks came from her mother and Alan's dark curls from Daddy. Yet Lacey was probably going to be tall, as her father was, and Alan shortish like Ariadne, and he was surely going to inherit his father's bull shoulders.... But Jerry was badly out of practice at evaluating children.

The second man was much younger, about Killer's nominal age. Carlo was a swarthy, hollow-chested youth with long brown hair all mussed by rain and a hard day. A curious mixture of races showed there in the high cheekbones and narrow features combined with thick lips. He was not unlike Luis, who had come from twenty-first Venezuela; but Luis was a jovial, easygoing type, and this kid wore a very resentful stare that looked as though it might be his normal expression. His black leather coat could contain all sorts of curiosities, but the jeans were too tight for anything but himself. With a weapon he might be dangerous, but even Jerry could snap him if he was unarmed.

Then there was the woman—the second Mrs. Gillis, presumably, but certainly young enough to be his daughter. Taller than Ariadne, she had fairer hair than her predecessor's honey color, and her figure was fuller—a great deal fuller, if those were real—and the straining sweater was pink cashmere. Perhaps it was not fair to judge a person's intelligence on first sight, especially at gunpoint, but Jerry had a strong suspicion that the second Mrs. Gillis had not been chosen for brains; her qualifications were more the sort that Killer would appreciate. She wore tailored pants in lime green, all splattered with mud now, and those made Jerry think of lady golfers. Perhaps that was formal dress these days.

Jerry could read rage on Gillis, contempt and wariness from Carlo—not fear from a kid his age? The woman was scared, of course, but even so there was an insipid vagueness about the round, doll-like face.

The most interesting thing about the second Mrs. Gillis, though, was that she was clutching the screaming Alan, while Lacey was standing close, with an arm around her, staring at her mother across the room.

Gillis was a rooster; he would start blustering at any moment. Carlo—a donkey, stubborn and likely to kick. The woman—a dove, perhaps, good for cooing and not much else. Ariadne, he had thought of as a canary, small and golden and full of song. . . .

Jerry made sure that Killer had his eyes on the visitors and then looked at Ariadne, whose pearly gray Meran cape and pants made her seem much more properly dressed to him. The haunted look that he had noticed when she first arrived was redoubled now. She was hunching her shoulders and hugging her arms around herself, making herself smaller than ever, and staring nowhere with haggard eyes. He remembered the flash of hope that had come with belief in Mera. Now it had gone, and he longed to know what those delicate features would look like when it returned, when he had her safely out of this mess. He suspected that they would fill with a very sparkly sort of fun and humor, for there had been hints of humor, even in her troubles. *Like small people. The storks bring them*—feeble in itself, but a good attempt under the circumstances. Certainly she had nothing to laugh at now, with her children so obviously clutching at The Other Woman. This was going to be an interesting session.

He had just finished his survey, then, when Alan stopped his wailing. "There, there," and, "Tush, tush, tush," muttered the girl, rocking him. She might be a dumb blond and might look more like the teenage babysitter from next door than a mother, but she wasn't doing a bad job with Awful Alan.

Jerry wandered over to Ariadne's chair and laid his Uzi on the floor, then collected the pistol from Killer and headed back to the edge of the table, facing his captives and staying out of Killer's line of fire. He pulled the wand out of his belt—but of course they would not be able to see that.

He was bone tired, but also jittery with tension, a nasty combination, and he wished he could feel as calmly relaxed as Killer seemed to be, broken leg or not. Killer had much, much more experience in this sort of thing, of course, and it was a long time since J. Howard had exercised command. *Carry on, Squadron Leader!* It wouldn't hurt to let them see that he was nervous—they might heed his warnings more—but if he started to fall apart, then all was lost. He must keep control. He braced himself and tried to put authority into his voice.

"I give the orders," he said. "My name is Jerry Howard. My friend affects the name of Killer." Carlo's lip curled and Gillis' brows dropped. "He has earned it! The first order is this: Until morning, no one leaves, the door stays closed, as do the windows. You are not even to touch the drapes, or look out. Is that absolutely clear? I shall shoot anyone who touches a curtain."

"You would shoot a child for looking out a window?" demanded Gillis.

Jerry waved the automatic. "I might have no choice; we are in a very dangerous situation. I will explain, but you are not going to believe me. That doesn't matter. You only have to believe that I believe, because I have the gun. There is evil out there." He expected a smart-aleck reply from the Carlo kid, but he didn't get one. "You heard those howls in the woods?"

"What the hell were those?" demanded Gillis.

Jerry shrugged. He was quite sure that he had heard wolves earlier, but by the end they had been something else, and he suspected hyenas—a much nastier killer than the lion, which had had a better press. But talking about hyenas in North Dakota, or wherever these people thought they were, wasn't going to get him very far. The main thing was that the foe had recognized the Uzis' firepower and held back—which meant that something bigger was on its way.

"'What the hell' is the correct question," he said. "The supernatural is loose here, tonight."

Gillis snorted. "What kind of a shakedown is this? You got the kids back. What else are you after?"

"Shut up!" said Jerry. "We only wanted to restore Ariadne's children to her, and the only reason I am keeping the rest of you here now is that it is too damned dangerous to throw you out in the rain. If we're all alive in the morning, then you are free to go. I know you don't believe in ghoulies and ghosties, but by morning you will."

Their expressions said that no, they wouldn't.

He shrugged. "Perhaps I can demonstrate a little, because I am going to search you. Mrs. Gillis' purse, if you please?"

The big man scowled and lifted his wife's handbag from the floor. Jerry edged cautiously around the table and reached out with the wand, hooking the handles and pulling it from Gillis' hand. The three newcomers gasped simultaneously, for it must be seeming to float of its own accord. Jerry swung it around, walked over, and laid it in Ariadne's lap, seeing Killer grinning hideously at the juvenile prank.

"Just check for weapons," Jerry said. He noticed that little Lacey did not seem surprised, so she could see the wand and therefore had believed what Killer had told her. It was ironic that those who did not believe in faerie and Mera would see magic, while those who did believe would not.

"Nothing," Ariadne said in a dull voice. Her pallor was incredible, and she must surely be reaching a breaking point. He returned the purse on the end of the wand, dropping it at its owner's feet.

"Your jacket, Mr. Gillis?" Jerry said. "Stand up and remove it slowly, please."

The big man folded his arms. "Look, Howard, if that's your real name, you're in big trouble. I have legal custody of those children, so you are abetting a kidnapping. Your accomplice fired on our automobile and then used automatic weapons. You're holding us here at gunpoint, and federal—"

"Your jacket!"

"How much is she paying you?"

"She—Mrs. Gillis—isn't paying me anything," Jerry said. "Where I come from and where I'm going, money is of no use at all."

"True, because you're going to jail."

Jerry smiled. "Nice try, but not so. Now, your jacket or I shall have to unchain Killer again. *Keep your hands in view, Carlo!*"

Warily Gillis rose and removed his jacket. Again Jerry fished for it with the end of the wand, and the big man watched carefully, trying to understand the trickery. There was nothing of interest in the pockets except a little flat thing with numbered buttons that looked like some sort of calculating machine, and Jerry quietly pocketed that out of general interest. . . . It probably wouldn't work in Mera, though. No, the curiosity was the shoulder holster now revealed on Gillis; the automatic had been his. Did respectable businessmen go around armed in this time frame? Not a rooster, then, a gander—less noisy, but vicious.

Jerry tossed him the coat, made him stand up and turn around, carefully ran the end of the wand up and down his legs; he detected no suspicious bumps.

So far, so good.

"Now, Mr.—is it Mr. Carlo, or is that your first name?"

"Excretion of an unclean animal!" Carlo snapped.

There was a puzzled silence, broken by a snigger from

Killer. Jerry grinned to himself; in whatever language that obscenity had been phrased, the wand had translated it literally. Carlo bit his lip and seemed to shrink slightly, puzzled and shocked.

"Your jacket."

Stubbornly Carlo mouthed something, but silently. Jerry began to tense. "Killer? Can you part his hair at this distance without pushing his eyes apart?"

"Three times out of ten," said Killer, aiming the Uzi.

This was a bluff, because if the cottage was truly faerie then it was likely bulletproof, and there could be ricochets, and violence itself was dangerous. But the bluff worked, and the leather coat yielded a professional-looking switchblade. A driver? Not a donkey, a weasel —sneaky and dangerous. Jerry demanded that he remove his boots and throw them over and then checked him with the tip of the wand before deciding that he had now disarmed his captives. The second Mrs. Gillis was obviously concealing nothing on her person except possibly foam rubber.

He went and sat down wearily on the arm of Ariadne's chair. The prisoners were disarmed and also shaken by his party trick with the wand. To his eyes, the wand was brilliant white now, making the icebox look gray. . . . Killer had noticed and was grinning. Killer grinning always meant trouble for someone, even if only himself. The forces were building.

"Now," Jerry said, "I shall try to explain the precautions—"

Two sets of heavy boots came thumping up the porch steps, then stamped on the porch itself as though to shake off mud. A massive fist knocked imperiously.

"Open up!" boomed a deep male voice. "This is the FBI. We have you surrounded—come out with your hands up."

6

"**N**OT A WORD!" JERRY HISSED, POINTING THE gun straight at them. "Not a whisper, or I shoot!"

Gillis beamed triumphantly, and his wife smiled. Ariadne had uttered a sort of sob and clutched at Jerry's arm.

"Open up!" the voice roared again.

Still watching his prisoners, Jerry rose and moved around to the door. He laid the wand over the bolt, a symbolic bar binding door and wall, and shouted, "*I know you for what you are. Begone!*"

There was, of course, no reply, and he walked back to his seat on the arm of the chair, still watching them.

The minutes passed. . . .

Curious—the Gillises had been pleased and relieved, but the Carlo youth had shown something else: fear or anger. Now they were starting to frown, and he was visibly relaxing.

"I think that should do it," Jerry said at length, "until the next try."

"Who was that out there?" Gillis barked, a scowl darkening his heavy features. Not the FBI, obviously.

"There was nobody out there."

The black eyes narrowed, and then he looked at his

64

companion, Carlo, at his wife, and then back at Jerry. "Bull!" he snapped. "I've seen better conjuring tricks at the Rotarians' Christmas Party. I don't know what scam you're trying to pull, Howard, but it isn't going to work on me, no matter how many accomplices you have out there."

With just three of them—he and Killer and Ariadne —it would have been easy. But now there were eight, and Killer was immobile—too many sheep and not enough sheep dogs. Killer twisted his head round to smirk at Jerry and then turned back to his guard duty; he could see the dangers, and the smirk said that the Oracle had wanted brains. The sensible thing would be tie them all up and gag them, but that would be violence and dangerous in itself.

"Demons," Jerry said. "We had the flesh-and-blood monsters, and our guns scared them away because flesh can be destroyed. Now comes the pure evil, the disembodied legions of Hell."

Mrs. Gillis paled and started to whimper; her husband put a comforting hand on her knee and glared at his captor.

"Perhaps you'd like to put Alan on the bed?" Jerry said. "Poor little tyke, he's had a rough day."

She looked at Gillis for orders, and he nodded without really taking his attention off Jerry. "That's a good idea, Maisie," he said.

Well, now he had a name for her. He opened the bedroom door and left it open after this Maisie had returned to her chair. Alan was as limp as wet leather and looked as though there would be no sound from him until morning. Lacey scrambled up to take his place on Maisie's lap, huddled in her poncho and almost as pale as her real mother was.

"Guns would be useless against what's outside," Jerry said. "But there are rules. They can not come in unless they are invited."

Gillis was disbelieving and furious, the Carlo youth disbelieving and contemptuous—but Maisie wavered slightly.

"What happens if they do get in?" she asked. There

was a trace of gold chain at her neck, which might mean a crucifix; perhaps she could believe in demons.

Jerry shivered involuntarily. "Eight unmarked bodies. The coroner would probably attribute the deaths to carbon monoxide poisoning." That was the best possibility. A crazed bloody-orgy was another. Worst of all would be eight cases of demonic possession loosed on an unsuspecting world, time bombs of evil to be detonated later.

"Bull!" Gillis roared. "Don't listen to him, Maisie. You're frightening the child, Howard. What is the point of this?"

"The point is that I am deadly serious!" Jerry snapped. "Unless each of you will give me your word that you will do as I say, I am going to tie you up and gag you. Now, will you listen?"

"Go ahead, then," growled the big man.

"There are demons outside," Jerry said, "but this cottage is demon-proof, and they can enter only if they are invited—but they decide what's an invitation." Belief would be almost impossible to get in this century; perhaps that was why there were so few Merans from technological cultures. "They have very liberal definitions of what constitutes an invitation. It need not be specific. If one of you had said, 'Oh, good!' just now—that would have been an invitation. Any one of you can do it with one word. That's why you must not say anything—by the time you work out what you've said, it's too late. We know the names of a few of the major demons and to pronounce one of those names—even in a command to go away—would be an invitation."

Gillis snorted.

"You're awfully heavy for Maisie, now, dear," his wife muttered to Lacey, and he turned his attention to the child, lifting her over onto his own lap. That was more important than demons, obviously.

Jerry sighed wearily. "The only words it is safe to say are the ones I used: 'I know you for what you are. Begone.' If you hear a voice you know calling to you, try that first."

He glanced down at Ariadne, and she looked up at him with a blank, hopeless expression. There was no rope to tie them all up, although bed sheets might do. Would they hold still for it under Killer's gun?

"Demons flock around me," Killer said cheerfully.

Stupid little braggart—he couldn't help. "They are also scared witless of you," Jerry snarled. "At least, so Tig says. When you're in the party, the demons are a hell—pardon the expression—are a lot more circumspect, so he says."

Killer smiled, flattered but very pallid, and it took a lot of pain to show on Killer's face. The wand could help, as it had somewhat helped his ankle while they were in the wagon, but he would refuse to accept it at this point—Jerry was the Oracle's choice. That was one of the unwritten rules of the field men.

"And why must we not look outside?" Gillis asked.

"Because you may see your grandmother with a plate of cookies for you," Jerry said. "Or a baby drowning in a puddle. As the night goes on, we shall hear people we know out there, calling us. If you are so stupid as to peek out, you may see anything imaginable, anything that just might persuade you to open the door or utter a foolish word."

Maisie was looking to her husband.

"Don't believe a word of it, honey," he said. "Lacey, the foolish man is just trying to scare us. He had friends out there making funny noises. What do you want of us, Howard?"

"I want your word that you will not look out, approach the door—even an approach might do it—or reply to anything you hear. Your solemn word, or I tie you up."

Gillis shrugged. "I promise. Humor him, Maisie. One of Ariadne's drinking friends, I suspect."

The woman said, "I promise." Jerry looked at Carlo, who shrugged and mumbled, "Sure."

"Very well," Jerry said. "I hold you to it at gunpoint and I repeat that I am serious. Ariadne, you believe me?"

She nodded in silence.

"She also believes in pink elephants," Gillis said.

Jerry rose. He would love a cup of coffee, but there

was probably only enough coffee left for one pot, and the water supply was getting low, too. That thought immediately gave him a torrid thirst, and he walked over to the water bucket, which had been placed in a far corner by the piano, where it would not be kicked. As he passed a window, something tapped on the glass to catch his attention. He ignored it, angry at the crawly sensation it gave him. The water was lower than he expected, and he decided not to mention coffee. As he passed the window again, a kitten miaowed.

Enough coffee for three, enough food for three ... again he wondered if the recovery of the children had been an error. Perhaps Killer's success had been so superhuman that even the Oracle had not anticipated it.

"How long is this farce going to last?" Gillis demanded, squirming. Those were not the most comfortable of chairs.

"Till morning," Jerry said. "The darkest hour is just before the dawn. If we survive that, then Killer and I are leaving. We are going to take Ariadne and Lacey and Alan with us. You will be free to leave also."

Ariadne turned to stare at him incredulously. Obviously she had not thought that the rescue was still available.

Gillis straightened his heavy shoulders. "I have legal custody of those children."

Jerry shrugged. "That is of no interest to me. I am taking them beyond the reach of law." And the Oracle might roast him for it.

"It's very quiet out there," Killer said uneasily. He had sat through sieges before. Jerry had not, although he had heard the stories often enough. "They're usually chirping and gibbering by now."

He had not worked it out—with so many innocents present, trickery was a better tactic than terror, but to act too soon after the failure of the FBI ploy would make them suspicious. So the enemy would play a waiting game.

The rain had stopped at last; there was only a steady drip from the porch roof. Jerry asked what time it was. Gillis said it was two fifteen.

"Then my watch has stopped," Maisie said crossly. "I have eleven thirty."

Carlo had uttered only a couple of obscenities since he sat down, but now he said, "I have five after five."

The three captives looked at each other in surprise, and Jerry grinned: the faerie was fouling up their watches. It normally did not effect clockwork, so they must have something more sophisticated.

"How did you find me?" Ariadne demanded.

"Direction finders," Gillis said.

Jerry wondered what those were and decided not to ask.

"The Devil's own dance you led us, too. You sure had trouble finding the spot, didn't you?"

She pulled a pouting face as though she didn't want to reply, then said, "I got lost. I didn't plan this, Graham. I was heading for Canada."

"Canada?" Gillis scoffed, and Carlo laughed aloud. "You never did have much of a sense of direction, did you?"

She dropped her eyes, a woman mauled in too many fights to accept another.

"Your juvenile plotting has been fun to watch," Gillis went on, baiting her. "Of course Mike told me when you applied to withdraw that money . . . and Charlie, when you bought the car. So Carlo went around there before you took delivery and fitted the beepers on it. Alan's teddy is bugged also, which is how we knew which room they were in."

It was pathetic to see so large a man picking on so small a woman. She showed no anger, but her tone festered with contempt as she replied.

"You were always so clever, Graham—I can't think why you ever married anyone as stupid as me."

"You weren't stupid until the drink rotted your brains," he said. "Smart enough to get yourself knocked up by a smart young lawyer with good prospects but not enough working capital to stand a paternity suit. And I admit that I didn't know you had a couple of henchmen lined up. Where did you find these two?"

She waited so long to answer that Jerry had decided

she would not, then said, "Right here, when I arrived. I went in the ditch and came here to ask for help. Mr. Howard and Mr. . . . and Killer . . . have been very helpful and friendly, and that makes a wonderful change from dealing with creeps like you, Graham."

Domestic bliss, as Killer had said.

"Bull!" Graham retorted.

Jerry squirmed and wished he would stop using that word.

The big man persisted. "Are you saying that two complete strangers would pull off what these two did for the sake of some waif wandering in from the storm? How much of my hard-earned alimony are you paying them?"

"Nothing."

Graham scowled disbelievingly. "What's your motive, Howard? If she isn't paying you, who is?"

They had hours to kill yet, and there was no harm in telling the truth—it had been around for centuries, disregarded as myth and legend by those whom it did not concern. Besides, he had to be sure these captives would obey him, and they might be more inclined to do so if they thought he was a raving lunatic.

"I was sent by an organization of which you have never heard," Jerry said, noticing Carlo raise his eyebrows. "Killer and I are field men. From time to time we are instructed to contact certain persons and offer them sanctuary, and your former wife is such a person. How or why she was chosen is not my business."

"Sanctuary?" the big man echoed. "Asylum? Where?"

Jerry tried to make himself more comfortable on the arm of the shabby old armchair. Ariadne edged over to one side; he took that as an invitation and moved down to sit beside her, perched on the front of it.

"We call it Mera," he said, "although it has had many names. It is a land of happiness and perpetual youth."

The two men exchanged glances, and Carlo rolled his eyes.

"I am about seventy," Jerry said, "and Killer is well over four hundred. You are not going to believe me, but as I said before, you only have to believe that I believe; and Ariadne is interested . . ."

Sitting under the stark glare of the bare light bulb, he told them of the sunshine city of Mera, where every day bore the scent of warm flowers and the sea; of its streets and squares and winding alleys, quietly bustling with many people brought from all times and all places to live and be happy in its timeless peace. Between the bare plank walls, the plywood ceiling and the drab linoleum floor, he sketched its beauty, the shining reds and pinks of marble and sandstone, granite and brick: buildings of many styles huddling below the house of the Oracle. His voice droned on in an ominous quiet—no wind or rain outside, now, only a gentle dripping onto the porch.

He told of the tiny harbor outside his window, sparkling blue under the summer sky, providing haven for little ships of all nations and ages: smoky old tramp steamers from nineteenth-century London, triremes and quinquiremes from Corinth or Mycenae, gilded galleys from Byzantium and chubby medieval cogs from the Hanseatic ports of the Baltic. He told how he would wander down there some days and talk with the sailors—Chinese unloading silks, who believed they had sailed their junks to Zanzibar, Arabs carrying coffee, as they thought, to the Andamans, Yankee whalers loading water at Lahaina, caravels from Spain trading in the Indies, brigantines, schooners, and argosies. He watched the skepticism become incredulity, the incredulity grown into trepidation. He was amused and content that it should.

He told of South Gate, leading to the farmlands, the vineyards, and the ranches; of vistas of wheat, of rice paddies planted by Asians, and tulip fields tended by Dutchmen; he described the creaking old waterwheels, the miniature hamlets, the orchards that could have blossom in the morning and bend under fruit by nightfall, or vice versa. He told how Merans living in the city could relive a rural past by helping bring in a harvest or trying their hands at plowing with oxen—and how Killer was partial to sweet-scented haylofts containing sweet-natured milkmaids.

"Damn right!" Killer said. "Nothing like 'em."

He told them of the wild lands beyond West Gate, where he had teased trout with Father Julius the previous morning and where Tig would find his boar to hunt, the open spaces and the forests, the hills and the streams, backed by misty ranges where only the setting sun could go. He talked of hiking and boating and riding.... "Peggy!" said Lacey sleepily.

And now he was leaning back, squashed together with Ariadne in the chair, and he had his arm around her, and she did not seem to mind.

He told them also of North Gate which led back to reality, where the Oracle sent out its rescuers, where someone like Killer might go to test out a firearm for the armorers. He described the first time he had been sent a wand and how horrified he had been to venture Outside alone; how he had walked out into a grove of trees and then fog and found himself in nineteenth-century London, strolling among trees in Hyde Park. He told how he had obeyed his orders and headed for the slums of Limehouse—and been amazed and astonished to see his reflection in store windows dressed in top hat and tailed coat, although he was conscious only of wearing his usual Meran garb. He told them how he had found the abandoned child where he had been told he would find her and had delivered her safely to Dr. Bernardo's orphanage ... and then sadly returned to Hyde Park and thus to Mera, weighed down by guilt and sorrow that he should have no greater succor to offer among such suffering and that he should be so extraordinarily blessed.

"Why that one, Jerry?" Ariadne asked. "What was special about that child?"

"I have no idea at all," he said. "I don't even know her name. Just a girl, one among thousands."

"That you in there, Jerry?" called Tig from the yard.

"Not a word!" he bellowed, leaping to his feet in terror, seeing the heads all turn and the mouths start to open. He slammed the wand across the door and roared out his conjuration once more. "Not a word!" he repeated. He fetched the fourth wooden chair with hands trembling and sweat on his face and sat down beside the door. That had been very, very close.

Even he had almost answered.

"Now," he said, when he had his breath back. "We'll take it one at a time. Mr. Gillis, who did you hear?"

The big man's eyes narrowed. "It's Joe, from the office."

"No it wasn't Joe. Mrs. Gillis?"

"It was . . . it sounded like Mother," she said, looking puzzled, hesitant to contradict her husband, who gave her an astonished look.

"Carlo?"

The boy's face had closed up tight. He said nothing, but his lips moved as he mouthed another obscenity at Jerry. The kid had hardly spoken six words all night, yet he looked far from stupid—perhaps he was older than his skinny form indicated.

"Lacey? Who did you hear?"

"Gramps," she said. She was close to tears, frightened by the tension.

"Ariadne?"

She bit her lip and said, "None of those, anyway."

"Killer?"

"Clio," Killer said, and he was looking astonished.

"I thought I heard Tig," Jerry said. Killer snickered.

Would this convince them? "There you are, ladies and gentlemen. We all heard a very familiar voice. I heard it ask if I was in here. Had I answered in the affirmative, then that would have been as an invitation. *Have I got it through your thick heads?*"

Gillis was giving him a long stare. "You have puzzled me, Howard. I can guess how you could have done the other, but I don't see how you could have pulled that trick—four or five different voices . . ."

"Thank you," Jerry said. "You are being honest with me and with yourself. Now, please, will you all go along with my story for now? If I'm a raving maniac or if I'm from a fairy world—in either case, please go along?"

This time he got a nod from Gillis and a shrug and a nod from Carlo. He was hoarse from talking and weary from the constant vigilance; they sat in silence for a while, cramped and uncomfortable all in the stuffy and shabby little room.

"Mr. Howard," Maisie said solemnly. "Have you taken thought for your immortal soul?"

Now there was another pail of snakes.

He decided to slide along the boundary between lying and speaking true: "Yesterday morning, Mrs. Gillis, I went fishing with Father Julius, who is a good friend of mine in Mera, and who has lived there more than a thousand years. He is an elderly man—he seems frail, although he can outwalk me easily on the hills—and he is a most saintly, gentle, and devout man of God. He was an abbot in twelfth-century Burgundy. You could not find a more holy or a more studied priest, full of lore and love. We have talked often and at great length about my soul and his and of all the souls in Mera."

She smiled in relief and nodded.

He hadn't given her Father Julius' opinions, though, and Ariadne at least had noticed that omission.

"Just how do you leave here tomorrow, Howard?" Gillis demanded. "And how do we?"

"We have a horse and cart," Jerry told him. "It is never far to Mera. You will like a ride in a horse and cart, won't you, Lacey?"

The wan little girl nodded. She had put her thumb in her mouth when her parents started savaging each other, and it was there still, small enough comfort for a divided child from a divided marriage.

"And we?" Gillis asked.

"I suggest you wait about twenty minutes after we have gone and then start walking. The countryside will have changed by then. It can't be far to somewhere. The demons very rarely attack by day, and you are not their targets. Doubtless they have other chances to get you," he added, smiling at Maisie.

"Jerry?" Killer said faintly. "It's getting dim in here."

Jerry looked up and, true enough, the bare bulb was an orange glow. The light had been dying away without his noticing.

He muttered his thanks and jumped up to organize the oil lamps. One had been glowing on low in the corner for hours. He turned it up, and now it was brighter than the electric light. He placed it on the table, lit the other, and put it on top of the piano. He looked in the icebox, and everything was thawing in there.

"Howard?" It was Gillis again. He was beginning to show stress, his bruises dark and his swarthy face livid in patches around the eyes—but he had been standing up to the strain better than any of the rest of them, a strong man. Even the inscrutable Carlo was fidgeting now. Jerry returned to his chair by the door.

"You are going to take my ex-wife," the lawyer said, "and my reaction is—good riddance. But you are also taking my children, and that I object to very much. Why?"

Jerry looked at Ariadne, saw terror in her eyes before turning back to her ex-husband. "Because, regardless of what any real-world court says, I will not separate a mother and her children."

"But you do not know her history?"

"I care not. She is their mother."

Killer, he could now see, was unfocused and shivering. Either the pain was throwing him into shock, or he had internal injuries. Jerry was on his own.

Gillis bared his teeth. "Unfortunately. She is also an incurable alcoholic. I have shelled out thousands for cures for her, and they never last. I tried removing the liquor—she bought more and hid it. I took away her money—she sold her jewelry, including heirlooms from my mother. My ranch is a long way from town; I disabled her car—but nothing works."

The idea of alcoholism being curable like a disease was new to Jerry—but medicine must certainly have progressed since the forties.

Gillis continued his address to the jury. "Not only did the courts award me custody, Mr. Howard, but they have restricted her visiting privileges. She can only see Alan and Lacey when I am satisfied that she is sober. She terrifies them otherwise, falling around and slobbering over them—"

"I am not interested," Jerry said, not daring to look at Ariadne. "Why certain people are chosen for rescue and the great multitude is not I do not know. Only the Oracle knows and it does not say. I myself was perhaps the easiest rescue..."

"We are talking about my former wife!" Gillis snapped. "And about my children. I tell you—it is impossible to keep her dried out for more than a month or two. She will steal, lie, do anything. She disappears on binges for days, even weeks. She was recovered like trash from the gutter on several occasions, not knowing where she had been or what she might have done. You are returning these children to her care?"

The stuffy little cabin was silent, except for a faint crackle from the wood stove. Jerry now glanced at Ariadne and then turned away quickly. He looked at the second wife and saw a frown of disapproval.

"Mrs. Gillis," he said, "does not your religion talk of mercy?"

She bristled—and in a soft, round, gentle girl, it seemed ridiculous. "To those who confess and truly repent, mercy is granted," she said primly.

"Then perhaps Mera is one form of mercy?" Jerry said softly. "Many who are rescued are saved from imminent death—I have seen bodies brought in, scarcely more than corpses, barely breathing. Within two or three days they are as healthy as I am. Cancer, typhoid, turberculosis... what else, Killer? Bubonic plague, sword cuts—nobody dies in Mera, nobody is sick. I don't think alcoholism will be much of a problem there."

Gervasse would have drunk half the Amontillado, but no one could call Gervasse an alcoholic; his mind was needle sharp, his health flawless, and his personality irresistible. There was nothing wrong with Gervasse.

Again there was silence in the shimmering light of the oil lamps, except for muffled sobbing from Ariadne's direction.

"*She is not worthy!*" Gillis shouted.

"*Who are you to say?*" Jerry roared back at him and angrily took hold of his temper. He should be a proper professional and not became emotionally involved with his client, Ariadne. "Have you any further charges to lay?"

The big man folded his arms, his face red now, his bruised lips tight shut. "Is that not enough?"

"No!" Jerry said. "If that is all you have against her, then I say that she is more worthy than I was!"

A very long silence ensued.

He hadn't intended to say that.

At last he turned and looked at Ariadne. The hope was back. "I also have sinned," he said. "I was not sent to be judge, or prosecutor, or defense counsel. I shall take you to Mera as I was instructed and deliver you to the Oracle, and there you will make your decision."

She nodded without speaking, pale cheeks shining.

He turned back to Gillis. "I may be making a mistake; I was not specifically told to bring the children. If I am wrong, then they will be returned safely. I am certain of that. Many do not choose to remain after they have spoken to the Oracle. It always promises that they can return, and we have never caught it out in a lie or an error."

"Returned to me?" Gillis asked. "Or sent back with her?"

"I don't know."

The light bulb was barely a pink glow now.

It was very still outside, silent. What would come next?

"Mr. Howard, sir?" The voice came from Carlo, and Jerry turned to him in some astonishment until he saw that the "sir" was not intended to convey respect.

"Mr. Carlo, sir?"

"You don't get older in Mera?"

Jerry shook his head, moving the kid up about six notches on the scale. He could tell what was coming next, and Gillis had missed it.

"How about children, then? Do they get older? Or stay children?" He had a soft voice with a beat to it that Jerry could not place.

"I don't know," Jerry said. "Killer, you're an old-timer—do you know?"

He was asking because he was worried about Killer, not because he expected an answer—he had already had Killer's answer earlier that evening.

"No," Killer grunted.

"There are no children in Mera?" Carlo asked, eyes gleaming with triumph.

"I have never seen any," Jerry said.

He could not force himself to look towards Ariadne.

Lacey drifted off to sleep in her father's arms. He must have been extremely uncomfortable, but he did not suggest laying her down. Carlo and Maisie fidgeted and squirmed. She turned very pink and said she needed the ladies' room. Jerry sent her off to a pot in a bedroom and made Ariadne stand guard over her.

Killer insisted he was fine, but did not speak unless questioned.

Endless night—surely they must be at the north pole and this was still only December?

No sounds or signs outside. What was going on? Why didn't the enemy try something more? What—who?—no, *what*—were they waiting for? Had the message been passed in Hell? *We have Achilles son of Crion in our realm, he is injured, and his only companion is incompetent.*

Come and get him . . . Lord Asterios.

No, he must not even think that name.

The cabin was stuffy and hot, but Jerry could no longer resist the thought of coffee. He took the pot over to the water bucket, and nothing scratched or miaowed at the window, but as he came back he thought he heard a chuckle outside, too quiet for the others to hear.

He threw another log in the wood stove and put the pot on top.

Then Carlo straightened. Then Maisie. Then he heard it also, faint sound in the distance. Now they were all staring at the window, all hearing it.

"What's that?" Maisie demanded nervously.

"You tell me what you think!" he replied, his scalp crawling with the rising tension.

"Sirens!" Carlo snapped, his eyes narrowing.

"No—it's a mob!" Gillis said, stirring uneasily.

Jerry said, "Just remember it's a trick. I hear hounds."

The distant noise carried him back to his childhood, his grandfather's farm, and standing on a stile with the old man holding him, looking out at the misty morning hills of Dorset. And the hunt poured over a distant skyline, the men in their red coats, the horses, a faint horn call . . . and the white foam of the dogs in front, streaming down the hill and giving throat. He could hear that baying now. Damn them, digging around in his mind!

No, these were bigger than foxhounds—wolfhounds or mastiffs, killers.

They were coming closer.

"Remember!" he shouted. "It's a trick! Whatever happens, don't speak!" Too shrill . . .

He grabbed up the wand—and thought for an instant that Maisie's eyes started to follow it—and *where* had he put the automatic?

Who was being hunted? Who rode to these hounds of Hell?

Much closer, now, a huge pack was baying and belling up the driveway, surely almost into the clearing and the glow of the yard light. The temptation to look out was a knife being pushed into his back. Hounds—a romantic noise to a child, hideous terror to the quarry. . . .

Footsteps slapped in mud, stumbled up the steps.

The door rattled as someone fell against it, and the noise of the hounds rose triumphant, as they closed on their prey.

"Jerry!" It was Juanita. Oh, God! "Popsicle, let me in!" No one but she had ever called him Popsicle—he wasn't even sure what it meant. *"Popsicle! Let me in!"* Her voice rose to a scream, and his attention wavered, as he thought of the soft, cream-smooth body he had held in his arms and of the teeth of hounds. . . .

Carlo leaped to his feet and dived to the window above the counter, pushed aside the drape, and looked out.

Jerry jumped for him.

Then there was a leg between his legs, and something struck the back of his neck. The floor leaped up and battered him breathless, while all the lights of heaven flashed inside his eyeballs. He was rolling under the table and had dropped the wand, and someone was screaming.

He had never made a faster recovery, scrambling to his knees, throwing the table away bodily, finding the wand. Killer was on his feet—one foot—and locked with Carlo in a parody of Greek wrestling, Carlo yelling incoherently. Jerry lurched upright and smashed a blow of that heavy, cold wand—gleaming horribly white now —at the youth's head. Carlo and Killer went down together.

The bolt on the door moved. Maisie was screaming—everyone was screaming.

He slammed the wand against the door as it began to open.

"I KNOW YOU FOR WHAT YOU ARE. BEGONE!"

He had his shoulder against the door, and for a long moment it was as immovable as the Himalayas. The wand blazed, and his muscles and joints creaked with the strain. Then it gave way and slammed shut, and he slid the bolt.

Saved.

He leaned a damp forehead against the wood for a moment to catch his breath—and regain control of himself, for he had very, very nearly crapped his pants with terror. Saved. Then he swung round in fury to find Carlo and beat the shit out of *him*.

At his feet lay Killer, face down in a fountain of blood, with six inches of pointed steel protruding from his back.

And on the other side of the door something started to laugh.

» 7 «

I CAN'T HELP YOU UNLES YOU WANT ME TO HELP YOU,
Ariadne. You must know that all this isn't really happening? I can help you if you want me to, but you must
ask me. It must be your decision. Tell me that you want
me to help you. . . .

The voice was that of Dr. Waters, the only one who
had ever been able to give her any real help in St. Luke's
Sanitarium. She had heard his voice start very quietly
and then get louder. Jerry had said he was hearing
hounds, but she had known that it was the voice of Dr.
Waters. It grew louder and more insistent, ever more
sympathetic and caring, begging her to let it help her.
The effect was hypnotic. She had recalled what Jerry
had said and tried to remember that it was a trick, that
she must not ask for help, because that would be an invitation, but it was so very hard to believe that Jerry was
not the hallucination, hard not to believe that Dr. Waters
was standing outside the door of her room, standing in
the corridor and talking to her—because it sounded just
like Dr. Waters.

Then suddenly he had rattled the door handle and
shouted that she must answer *now*. She had been going
to tell him to come in when she saw Carlo leap for the
window and knew that they had both been tricked. Then

everything seemed to happen in slow motion: Jerry
jumping for Carlo, Carlo doing some sort of Kung Fu or
Judo and Jerry flying off sideways, Carlo grabbing up the
butcher knife from the bowl of dirty dishes and heading
for the door, Killer bounding up from the sofa to block
him, the two of them swaying in an embrace with Carlo's
hand bringing up the knife, and then Jerry striking him
down with that white stick that he had kept close by all
evening—and managing to shut out the horrors and get
the door closed once more. . . .

She was already kneeling by Killer when Jerry turned
around and looked down and the laughter began.

Blood . . . torrents of it . . . together they rolled Killer
over on his side and stared at the handle protruding from
his abdomen.

"Pull it out!" Jerry snapped, because it was on her
side, and somehow she found the willpower to grip that
bloody handle and pull. It came out quite easily. Jerry
eased Killer over on his back and laid the white stick on
him.

She jumped up and ran for the bedroom and yanked a
sheet from the bed; something was giggling helplessly
outside the window. She raced back into the kitchen and
around the sofa again with the sheet and knelt down beside Killer; she started folding the tangle of bedsheet into
a pad.

Killer's eyes had opened, but his face was already
almost as pale as the sheet. He was looking at Jerry,
twitching and trying to speak.

"Oo . . . that one hurts, friend," he said.

"Just relax," Jerry said. "The wand will hold it."

He shook his head as she offered the bedsheet. There
was someone laughing outside the door; Lacey was
screaming in the background, Maisie was holding her
and gabbling prayers. Killer grimaced and then grabbed
the wand with both hands; Jerry's face was the bleakest
she had ever seen, but he seemed to be waiting for the
wand to work a miracle—or else for Killer to die.

She glanced around—Maisie was taking Lacey away
into the other bedroom, with Alan, and Lacey's hysterics were becoming quieter. Carlo was sitting up, rub-

bing the back of his head and obviously still only half-
conscious. Graham was as white as any of them, standing by the table and staring down at the casualty—he
was convinced now. No one could disbelieve, with that
demonic laughter outside; it sounded like a dozen of
them screaming with mirth. She could visualize comic-
strip devils with horns, hooves, and tails, all bellowing
with laughter, slapping one another on the back, and
staggering around in helpless mirth: she wanted to clap
her hands over her ears and scream at them to stop.

"Jerry?"

"Don't speak, Killer. Just wait."

Killer's lips moved and then he said, "Jerry? You
there?"

"Yes, I'm here," Jerry said.

"Tell Clio she did well."

"You tell her yourself," Jerry snapped. "We'll get you
back to Mera all right. I have a promise to fulfill, remember?"

Killer's eyes were closed, but he smiled and said
sleepily, "Then it was not always Eros?"

"Of course not!" Jerry said loudly.

Killer's smile died away, and he seemed to become
unconscious, his hands tight around the wand. If he was
still bleeding, it did not show; but there was too much
blood to be sure. Jerry bent down and put an ear on
Killer's chest for a moment, then straightened up.

"He's alive," he said. He, too, was smothered in
blood.

They all climbed to their feet at the same time—Jerry,
Carlo, Ariadne—and their shadows swayed around the
walls.

Carlo looked confused and dazed. Jerry stepped over
to him and grabbed him by the front of his shirt.

"You bastard!" he said, and struck him hard across
the face with his gun. Carlo staggered and would have
fallen had the other man not been holding him. "Bloody
bastard!" He struck him again.

"Cut that out, Howard!" Gillis barked, and Jerry
pointed the gun at him.

"You keep out of this!" he said. He was about to

swing the gun again when the bolt on the door rattled and moved slightly. Jerry rushed over to it, letting Carlo collapse on the floor.

He pushed the bolt back hard with the butt of the pistol and it stayed. Jerry wiped his forehead and turned to look at his victim. "If it wouldn't bring in the demons, I would kill him. If Killer dies, then I shall kill him for certain—if I can get to him before they do. Violence brings them. . . . Take him in that other room and tie him up. Gag him. Move!"

Graham always knew when to back off, and this was one of those times. He bent down, took hold of Carlo, and dragged him away. Jerry took a spoon from a drawer and knelt down to hold it over Killer's lips. The laughter outside was louder, as though more demons were joining in.

Ariadne sat down on the sofa and started to shake uncontrollably. The laughter! She should go to Lacey, but Maisie was probably doing as good a job as she could, and she was all splattered with Killer's blood. Jerry tossed the spoon away, listened to Killer's chest again, and then stepped over him and sat down beside her on the sofa.

Graham came back, took the lamp from the piano, and returned to the bedroom. She heard linen being ripped.

"He may be all right," Jerry said. "The wands have power to heal, and it has stopped the bleeding."

She tried to speak through chattering teeth. "He needs a hospital."

"He needs Mera!" Jerry ran a hand through his pale hair, leaving it streaked with blood. "I've heard of this, though—the wand put him into some kind of coma; his heart beat is very, very slow, but it seems to be steady. Aku was saved this way once. I think it can hold him till morning."

The blood had not stuck to the wand, and the wand was glowing white.

Then he looked at her and suddenly put an arm around her. "Thanks, Ariadne. You were the only one who kept her head. God! I shouldn't have battered the kid like that . . ."

It was very comforting to be held. No one had held her like that in a very long time; there was no sex in that embrace, merely human contact and mutual comfort.

"You can't turn off the sound effects, can you?" she asked, her voice a little steadier. "It sounds like a sitcom out there."

"Whatever that is," he muttered. "No. This is the chirping and gibbering stage, I suppose. They know they won't fool anyone now, so they'll try to drive us crazy."

She shivered and cuddled closer to him. His grip tightened.

"He's tied up," Graham said, behind them. "I can't gag him—his mouth is bleeding too much. He'd choke."

Jerry stood up and gestured with the gun. "Right. Back in there, Gillis. You're next."

"I'll behave, damn it!" Graham said. "I believe you now, Howard."

"Move!"

She sat and shivered with her hands over her ears for a while. It was impossible to drown out that laughter—bellows and shrieks and giggling and chuckling, all around the cottage. *Drive us crazy* . . . it wouldn't take long. If Lacey was still shrieking or Maisie still praying, she couldn't hear them.

Then the shadows danced and Jerry returned with the lamp. He put it on the piano again and came back to her side. They sat together and looked down at the motionless figure of Killer, lying on the floor like a corpse laid out for burial, clutching the wand.

"I've really loused up," Jerry muttered. She could barely hear him over the gibbering. It was more a gibbering now, less like human laughter, more like a cage of apes. "I'm sorry, Ariadne. You deserved to get to Mera, and frankly our chances aren't too good any more."

"I can stand the noise if you can," she said. "We're none of us going to be inviting that lot inside." Strangely, she was feeling better than she had done earlier—backs-to-the-wall syndrome?

"True," he said . . . but there had been a hesitation there.

"Give me the bad news, then," she said.

"No—you're right. We can wait it out."

"Tell me, Jerry, please. I'd like to know the worst."

He turned and smiled at her, and almost she thought there was admiration there. Who had given her admiration since . . . since Noah's flood?

"Okay!" he said. "It's just about hopeless, though. You saw that door? I had to force it shut and I thought I couldn't."

She nodded. "So?"

"It's the third wave," he said grimly, watching her face carefully. "First the flesh and blood. Then the disembodied. But now . . . it's as though it takes them time to gather their forces, and now we must be nearing the darkest hour. Dammit, this night can't go on for ever! *Why are they so strong? What's bringing them?*"

"What's the third wave?" she demanded as calmly as she could.

"The in-betweens. Griffins or sphinxes or basilisks—the monsters that aren't one thing or the other."

"Vampires and werewolves?" she said. "Stakes through the heart and silver bullets, like the old stories?"

He nodded. "That's it. We do have silver bullets, truly. A silver bullet through the heart will kill most of the in-betweens, but I have an uneasy feeling that we're going to get something big, really big. Maybe an anti-tank gun with a silver shell would do it." He studied her and then blurted out, "You're a brave woman, Ariadne!"

"When you've spent as much time in hell as I have," she said, "it begins to lose its terrors."

He put his arm around her again, this soft-spoken, lanky man with his fair hair and bare chest, now dark with his friend's blood. "I had hoped to rescue you from that hell of yours," he said. "But I doubt that I'm going to make it. I should have liked to have shown you Mera, Ariadne. It's a wonderful place. You deserve it."

Deserve it? She thought of the strange beds she had wakened in a few times—sometimes with smelly old men asleep in them beside her, sometimes with nobody there except hallucinations. She thought of gutters, of being mugged, of the drunk tank, of begging total strangers for small change. Deserve it?

She shivered. "No I don't! Those things that Graham said about me were true, Jerry. If ever there was a fallen woman, it was me. I don't deserve Mera, and perhaps that's why your demons have done so well. It wasn't fair of your Oracle to send you and Killer after one like me."

He turned his head away from her and looked down at Killer, his face shadowed. Something with claws rattled across the roof, and they ignored it.

"I told you that I wasn't worthy of Mera, either," he said. "I've never talked about it and I shan't now . . . but I often think that many people in Mera . . ."

His voice died away, and she said, "Why is he called Killer?"

Jerry chuckled. "Oh, I named him that; a pun on Achilles, is all. He loved it and insisted on it after that. He's very childlike, is Killer, in many ways. He comes from a childlike culture. The early Greeks were a bunch of squabbling brats. Even the great philosophers who came after were sort of childlike, weren't they? Asking questions like kids? The showing off and the fighting, the love of nudity and the homosexuality—they're juvenile traits. Even their gods were a gang of quarrelsome, horny perverts."

"I'd never thought of that," she said. The racket outside was getting quieter, or else she was finding it easier to ignore.

He nodded to himself. "I don't suppose they were all as bad as Killer; he's an extreme case. People don't change in Mera, Ariadne. They may get younger-looking as the wrinkles disappear, as hair and teeth grow back, but their natures don't change after they get there. I arrived as a thirty-year-old and I'm a thirty-year-old now. I don't have Killer's adolescent wildness, but I'm not a seventy-year-old, either. You can learn things, but you don't change. Killer is a boy with four hundred years' experience. I was thinking last night what a superb guerilla fighter he would make with those qualifications."

He was mourning his friend. She thought that Killer

would mourn a friend sincerely also, but not in quite the same way. His friendship would be much more easily granted than Jerry Howard's, so Jerry's would be a deeper, more precious, and more vulnerable thing.

"You talked of Father Someone, who was an old man?"

"That's true," he said. "And there was a Chinese mandarin rescued just after I was—Shi-liu. About the same age as me, from the Tang Dynasty. He's aged steadily and looks his seventy-or-so years now; I expect he'll stay that way from now on." He smiled at her surprise. "His culture respected age, so that was how he wanted to be. Father Julius is much the same. He sees himself as an elderly shepherd guarding his flock, so his appearance didn't change. My good friend Gervasse looks like Benjamin Franklin. Not all societies worship youth. And there are limits, even in Mera. A woman or a man rescued in old age never gets truly youthful—but they're all strong and healthy."

Things were howling up and down outside, gurgling howls dying away in chuckles. Something was tapping persistently on the door.

She must keep the conversation going, it kept her panic down.

"Tell me about Killer," she said. "Why was his birthdate so important to you?"

He shook his head and frowned, and for a moment she thought he would not tell tales about his friend. Then he gave a slight shrug. "It's guesswork. He's a Thespian."

"You mean an actor?"

Jerry smiled. "No. Drama was invented by a a man named Thespis, which is why actors are called Thespians. It also means a citizen of Thespiae, which was a city northwest of Athens. Do you know any Greek history?"

"Not much," she confessed.

"Thermopylae?" he asked. "You must have heard of that? 480 BC. After Marathon, it's the second date in European history; not counting fictional dates like the founding of Rome."

"Persia?" she said doubtfully.

"Right. The Emperor Xerxes invaded Greece and he was held up at the pass of Thermopylae by the Spartans. They died to a man defending the pass against impossible odds, and even then, the Persians only won because of treachery by other Greeks."

He fell silent for a while, and she suddenly realized that in Mera history would be very real. Probably you could find eyewitnesses to most of it, to the Black Death or the Crusaders; meet people who had fought in the great battles. Killer? Born in 500 BC, and Thermopylae was in 480, when he would have been about twenty.

"There was one Spartan who missed the battle," Jerry said. "He was sent away—under orders—so he missed it and did not die with his friends."

"Killer?"

He shook his head impatiently. "No, he was a Thespian, not a Spartan. That one Spartan was so over-whelmed by shame that he killed himself. Can you imagine that, Ariadne? It wasn't his fault that he survived, and any of us would be happy and relieved, and our friends and relatives would congratulate us, but to the Spartan it was a disgrace he couldn't bear."

Maisie suddenly appeared, silently, a shadowy figure looming in the uncertain lamplight. She stood there, looking down at Killer and fingering her beads.

"The children are both asleep," she said. "Or else un-conscious . . ."

"Thank you, Maisie," Ariadne said. "Thank you very much. I have all this blood on me—I thought I would frighten them if I came."

Maisie nodded, still looking at Killer. "Is he dead?"

"No," Jerry said, looking up. "The wand will save him."

She nodded again doubtfully. "That was what you used to lift my purse, is it? It was invisible?"

"You can only see it if you believe in Mera, because it is a part of Mera," Jerry said. "You can see it now?"

Obviously she could, but she didn't say so. She crossed herself. "Graham and the other man?"

"They're tied up in the other room," Jerry said. "You come and sit with us."

She muttered something about the children and wandered back to their room; she was clearly in shock.

The gibbering . . . they must keep talking. "You were telling me about Thermopylae."

"Yes," Jerry said. "The Spartans had a very good press, as we would say nowadays. Mention Thermopylae, and everyone thinks of Sparta. But a thousand Greeks died there, defending Greece from the Persian horde—three hundred Spartans and seven hundred Thespians."

So there it was. The man lying at her feet might have fought at Thermopylae, the second date in European history. And incredibly, she could believe.

"Only a thousand men, out of all Greece," Jerry growled. "Some had gone over to the enemy, but do you know where the others were that day? At the Olympic games! No, I'm serious. You see why I think of them as children?

"Thespiae had the shrine of Eros," he continued, "but it did not have as good publicity as Sparta did. If we come out of this alive, Ariadne, you must never mention this conversation to Killer!"

"No. Of couse not." He was trusting her. She had forgotten what trust felt like.

"So I'm guessing," Jerry said. "I think there was one Thespian who survived, one of the seven hundred. I just can't imagine Killer running away—although I suppose that's possible, and it might explain his insane courage now, constantly proving himself—but I speculated that his scar was a wound from Thermopylae, that he awoke among the carnage and wandered away. The Thespians as a whole were not as bloody-minded as the Spartans, but Killer certainly was—he wouldn't be able to stand the shame, either. I thought the scar was his mark of Cain. . . . But now he says that he's had it since childhood, so I was wrong on the scar."

"The date fits," she said.

He nodded and suddenly forced a laugh, breaking the spell. "Probably he just missed the battle because he was worshipping Eros with someone else's wife. He'll never tell us, that's certain."

He was telling her that Killer had a dark secret and he had said that he had one himself. Was he hinting that her shame was her passport to Mera?

As though he had read the thought he said, "There are many people in Mera who will not discuss their past, Ariadne. Only the Oracle knows."

"That wand," she said. "It's glowing!"

He did not reply, and she looked at him and saw fear in his face.

"Why?" she asked. "Why is it so bright?"

"What is a wand?" he replied. "I don't know. Killer believes they have spirits in them. I tend to think they are machines, that the Oracle charges them up somehow with power, with faerie, like batteries. When they're working really hard, they shine like that."

"Keeping him alive?"

"Certainly." He glanced uneasily around the shadowy room. "But it's also keeping this cottage in existence, because this place isn't truly real. The faerie is holding the daemon out . . . and the demons' power is growing. Can't you feel it? The air stinks of sulfur."

She wished he hadn't said that. He was more frightened than she was, because he knew more. This time she put her arm around him.

"Can the wands overload?" she asked.

"Maybe," he muttered reluctantly. "Or run out? If they do, then that might explain the rescues that fail— the ones where nobody returns. It must be taking a lot of faerie to keep Killer alive."

The light flickered. He pulled out of her hug and jumped up. He grabbed the lamp on the table, muttered a curse, and went to inspect the one on the piano.

"We're almost out of oil!" he shouted. Then he strode over to the oil can, picked it up, and shook it. There was no sound. "It was half full!"

They stared at each other in mutual dismay as the lamp on the piano guttered out.

❧ 8 ❧

JERRY WAS FRANTICALLY POKING AT THE WOOD STOVE, trying to make it burn brighter—and the pile of firewood had already shrunk horribly, revealing the hilt of a sword which had been hidden behind it.

She felt a strange calmness, a sort of inevitability that was probably an effect of shock, like Maisie had. She wandered over to the room where the children were and looked in. Maisie was kneeling by the bed, praying, the words undistinguishable under the gibbering and obscene mutterings from the window. Alan and Lacey—she thought she could make out their shapes, little bundles on the bed in the gloom, but she couldn't be sure and she couldn't go and give them a farewell kiss because she might waken them, and that would be the most unkind thing to do right now. Perhaps they were innocent enough that demons would have no hold over them . . . but werewolves? *Good-bye, darlings. Mommy is very sorry she got you into this*.

Then she looked into the other bedroom. The youth was sitting on the floor, leaning against a wall, visible in the stream of light from the doorway, and tied up with strips of bedsheet. One eye followed her angrily; the other was half closed by swelling and his mouth equally puffed on the other side, smashed by Jerry in his fury.

Something was gnawing loudly at the window frame, making harsh rasping and tearing noises.

Graham was squirming around on the bed, also bound, and with a gag over his mouth. She leaned over him.

"If I take off the gag, will you be quiet?" she asked, and he nodded strenuously.

She fumbled for a long time with the knot. What had she ever seen in him? Her mother had asked her that. "He is a man who knows what he wants," she had answered. Silly little bitch—she should have trusted a mother's instincts, because a man who knows what he wants can easily become a man who will do anything to get it; charm becomes a weapon and charisma corrupts. Then the gag came loose....

"There," she said.

"Untie me, Ariadne! Don't leave me tied up like this!"

She had never heard him beg before and despised herself for the momentary pleasure that thought gave her.

"It isn't going to matter soon," she said and noticed how flat her voice sounded. "The oil has all disappeared from the lamps. Jerry thinks we're going to be attacked by monsters."

"No!"

"Maisie is praying like a conclave of cardinals," she said, "and I'm sure she won't forget you. I just wanted to tell you that I didn't mean to get you into this. You're not blameless, Graham, but you didn't deserve this. Not quite this . . ."

"Oh, that's very comforting," he sneered. "I would have been more careful if I'd known that D.T.s were infectious."

Why couldn't they just talk together, like human beings?

"Evil is infectious," she said. "Which one of us was the vector, Graham?"

"It was my fault, was it?" he snapped. "Nothing like a wino for self-pity."

He would never admit an error—he never had. "No," she said. "In the end I was much more at fault than you;

all those things you said tonight were true, except that you blamed only me for Lacey. If that was where we went wrong, then you were as much at fault as me... and you were the one who pushed for an abortion." That would hurt him.

"Always that!" he snarled. "I was waiting for it.... All right, for that I'm grateful. I love her—and see where you've got her?"

What else had been his fault? Plenty, she thought. The long absences, the strange friends, the sudden incredible prosperity—feast after famine—and then the steadily growing realization that a young lawyer couldn't possibly be making this much money by honest means....

"How about Alan, then?" he said with a sneer. "If we're going to chew over the old bones, he was all my doing, wasn't he?"

"If you mean that you virtually raped me that time, yes," she said. "I suppose you get the credit for Alan." That was a night she would never forget; even now she got cold shakes at the sight of a cowboy hat. She had left him, taken Lacey and gone... and that had perhaps been her last chance for sanity and sobriety, the last ray of sunset before the dark and the storm. He had tracked her down to her sister's cabin, a cabin not unlike this one, and they had had a most glorious fight. Shredded and tattered, she had gone off to bed, and he had stayed in the chair and finished the bottle....

She could still remember the crash as the bedroom door opened, him standing there, ready for her, his intent obvious, his mind made up... and the cowboy hat. Looking back at it, the cowboy hat should be funny, but the events of that night had never ripened into funniness. He had arrived wearing western dress, having come from some ranchmen's affair or other, and all night long they had screamed and argued, and he had never taken off that hat. Even when he finally came roaring into the bedroom to slake his lawful lust, he had still been wearing the hat—nothing else, just the hat. No, somehow that was not funny, even now. Too much pain, too much humiliation. She had left again with Lacey before dawn, before he awoke, and had stayed away until she had realized that she was again pregnant. . . .

He broke the silence. "Well, at least he looks like me," he said. "To begin with I worried, but I had the blood groups checked—which doesn't prove anything, but didn't disprove anything—and we're a rare type, he and I. And the little beggar does look like me."

Obviously he still wasn't sure. She could try once again.

"I suppose this is a deathbed repentance, Graham, so I'll assure you again that there is no doubt. I was never unfaithful to you."

He snorted.

"Not consciously, then. When I was on a bender . . . but that came later, after Alan. No, he had to be yours."

Pause, as though he were gathering ammunition, but then he said, "All right, deathbed repentance. Maybe all of it wasn't a hundred pecent your fault. Ninety-five, maybe, but not a hundred."

"My, you're gallant!"

"Go back to your demon lover, then."

"He's a better man than you'll ever be." But that was just going to start the shouting and tearing again. She stepped backwards and almost fell over Carlo.

"Who is this character?" she said. "Where did you get him?"

"Just a friend," Graham said, suddenly cautious.

No, not a friend. An electronics expert with a switchblade, one of the new generation of all-rounders.

"What's his speciality?" she asked, curious.

"Revenge," said a distorted whisper from the floor.

"Meaning you'd better not get between him and that Howard man tomorrow," Gillis said. "If the devils don't get him, then Carlo will."

Not very likely—Jerry Howard could handle that little punk. It didn't matter now, anyway.

"If this is good-bye, Graham," she said, "then good riddance." Nice exit—he hadn't had a reply ready for that. She went out and closed the door on the chewing noise coming from the window—maybe both men would be gnawed to death by werebeavers before morning, and she wasn't sure she cared.

Jerry had created a good blaze in the stove; a cheerful glow and crackle were streaming out its open door. The noises outside were dying away—was that a good sign or a bad sign? He was back on the sofa, checking out the guns, two of them submachine guns and two that looked like hunting rifles, with small clips for six or so bullets. She went around in front of him and looked down at the barely visible shape of Killer and the wand in his dead-man's grip, shining brightly as though fluorescent.

"He's still alive?" she asked.

"No change," Jerry said, snapping a gun back together. "I suppose he could stay that way for quite a time, if the opposition left us in peace."

She stepped over Killer and sat down next to Jerry, moving a couple of guns to do so. "Show me how they work," she said.

He looked at her in surprise. "You've shot before?"

She picked up one of the rifles, grunting at the unexpected weight. Pointing it over Killer at the door, she worked the bolt rapidly, spraying cartridges. "I lived on a ranch—the gophers' nemesis, I was."

"Wonder woman!" he said.

"Those Uzis are beyond me, though," she said and laughed at his astonishment. "But I've read enough magazines in doctors' waiting rooms to recognize them."

"Killer would approve of you, I think," he said. "Or maybe not . . . he thinks a woman's weapon is a feather duster."

"Clio? That his wife?"

He nodded. "You noticed the message? That she did well, not that he loved her? She is supposed to keep house and be there in his bed if he comes home early." There was an acidity in his tone that she had not noticed before when he spoke of Killer. Why did they always come back to Killer? She wondered about this Clio.

Then he showed her quickly how to fire and reload the Uzis and the others, Lee Enfields. "Stick to single shots," he said. "Automatic fire only when things are absolutely desperate." The walls might be bulletproof, he said, and cause ricochets.

Then the second lamp faded away, and they were sitting in the fire's glow. The two front windows showed up as pale rectangles, for the high yard light was still working. Shadows crossed and re-crossed the drapes, inhuman, indistinct, humped shapes.

They fell silent, Jerry hunched over with his face in his hands. That would not do.

"And who is in Jerry Howard's bed when he comes home early?"

He lowered his hands and smiled at her. "Jerry is."

"Bachelor?"

He nodded. "Bachelor. Not a virgin, but not a Killer."

"In forty years?"

The light was too dim to see if she had made him blush.

"I catch a fish once in a while," he said, "but I always throw them back. I'm too fussy."

"What specifications do you have, then," she asked, "that are so hard to fill?"

It was growing very quiet outside.

His teeth glinted in the flickering light—perfect teeth, of course. "Not tall," he said, "because I'm very insecure and need the advantage. A blond, naturally—but not too blond because then other men would chase her too much, and, as I said, I'm insecure. Musical, because I like music; interested in literature, because I have thousands of books for her to read, and I like to read in bed."

"Is that all you do in bed?"

He sort of spluttered—she had figured him as shy—and if she were serious, she would never dare push him like this, but it was keeping their minds off the other things. There was nothing they could do; talk was all they had.

"Sometimes I get madly passionate and chew a girl's ear," he said, "or read Keats to her. They like that."

She said, "I suppose if they're all five or six hundred years old, it would be dangerous to excite them too much?"

He was responding, eyes shining with enjoyment by that dancing firelight behind her. "And what specifications have you drawn up for Graham's replacement?" he asked.

Queen's gambit accepted. "An older man," she said.

"Good thinking."

"Musical, of course. Well read."

"Good on Keats?"

She sniffed. "You know what you can do with Keats?"

"We'll leave him to Killer," he said, and they laughed together in graveside humor.

"So you have marriages in Mera?" she asked, and he nodded. She pondered. "Surely sex must be a problem, though? It usually is, isn't it—people are like that. Can any marriage last for centuries? Don't couples tire of each other?"

He leaned back wearily. "It's surprisingly rare. I suppose there's a lot of cheating; I don't know. Well," he added in a softer tone, "I do know—I've done some. But with no disease and no pregnancies, Mera is a great place for love-making." And before she had to think of something else to keep him talking, he said, "It's the place where dreams come true."

"What do you mean by that?" she demanded, intrigued by his tone.

He turned his head and smiled at her. "Things are possible in Mera that aren't possible elsewhere. The angles of a triangle don't add up. . . . Have you ever read Homer?"

He was a Greek freak. "A little; in translation, of course."

"You must come to Mera and read the original," he said. "If you know the *Odyssey* or the *Iliad* . . . Killer can quote great chunks of them at you, by the way, they're his bible. He can't read, but Clio can; she reads him bits, and he memorizes them. Of course he knew a lot of them before he ever left Greece; it was how he was educated. He likes Hesiod, too, because he was another Thespian. What I'm going to tell you makes more sense in Killer's view of it—which is Homer's view—than it does in

mine. In Homer's world, if a friend dropped in to visit
you—Mary Smith, say?—well, in Homer, you could
never be quite sure that it really was Mary Smith or actually the goddess Athena in disguise."

"Listen!" she said. The yard had gone absolutely silent; even the faint chewing from the window of Graham's room had stopped.

"No, don't listen," he sighed. "It's just a trick to make
you jumpy. Let's get back to Mera. . . . I don't know what
it's like for girls, but most boys—men—see a good-
looking girl once in a while and think, 'wouldn't it be
lovely. . . .' Then they go home and pester their wives, in
most cases. . . ."

He had left this world forty years ago. "It's not un-
known nowadays for ladies to think that way," she said.
"If we see some tall, blond . . . er . . . bare-chested type?
Not rare at all, actually, these days."

"Thanks," he said. "I'll remember that, if I can. But
in Mera, the dreams come true."

"Huh?"

He stared in sudden silence down where Killer lay,
only the pearly trace of the wand showing. "Take Killer
as an example. A horrible example, perhaps, but an example. I've told you how promiscuous he is. So he takes
a fancy to, say, the Mary Smith we mentioned, and starts
pestering her. She tells him to . . . vanish. Fair enough,
but one day when Killer makes a pass, she responds.
Great—he has another stamp in his album. But Mary
Smith may know nothing about it!"

"Jerry! How?"

He chuckled. "Killer's explanation is that the goddess
Aphrodite took pity on him and assumed Mary Smith's
form. I talk about wish fulfillment, but what does it matter? Of course, the truth may be that Mary Smith did
actually fancy a tumble with Killer and is lying. Who
knows?"

"But . . ." The idea was too numbing to take in.

"I suppose there are limits," he said. "You probably
couldn't have two husbands without the fact being obvious, but truth in Mera is very much what you believe.
Reality is relative. There is no black and white in Mera,

literally. If I get you to Mera, Ariadne, I shall probably
have an affair with you, at the very least, whether you
know it or not!"

"You get me to Mera, Jerry Howard," she said, "and
you needn't put the goddess Aphrodite to any trouble on
my behalf."

They sat and looked at each other for a while in silence, and then he sighed and got up and put more logs
into the stove.

There was a murmur outside, a sound like a great
crowd. Jerry must have heard it also, but he came back
and sat down without mentioning it.

"What is bringing them?" he muttered to himself.
"Why so much, so many?"

"Killer's words?" she said. "He talked about Clio and
then he said something about Eros. 'Then it was not
always Eros?'"

He cleared his throat harshly. The noise outside fell
and then came back, greater, like an orchestra tuning up
or . . . or a crowd waiting for the teams to emerge? Jerry
started to speak loudly, as though trying to drown it out.

"It happened a month ago," he said, "and this is just
one example out of many, over the years. I was heading
home of an evening and was hailed unexpectedly by
Lopez—another friend. He asked me in for chess, and
we sipped wine and smoked Havanas and played chess
until we were too drunk to remember what colors we
were. Lopez is so black he's blue in Mera, so that took
some doing." The noise was growing, and he was raising
his voice over it.

"I staggered home at last, crawled upstairs, and found
Killer—asleep."

Even dim firelight was bright enough to show his
blushes.

"So I went downstairs and read a book for a while. I
think I was holding it upside down, but it didn't matter.
There were two glasses and an empty wine bottle there.
In a little while Killer came down and said he'd better be
going."

"What did you say?"

The multitude outside roared enormously, and Jerry

turned and stared bleakly at the windows. Then the racket died away again. "I said I was glad he'd been able to come . . . and I hoped he'd had as memorable an evening as I had."

She gripped his hand suddenly. "You're a good friend to Killer, Jerry. Better, I suspect, than he deserves."

"No!" he said and was drowned out again. If demons made the same amount of noise as people, there must be thousands of them out there.

Then a sudden, heart-stopping silence, and Jerry spoke as though nothing had happened. "At times he's just a little SOB, Ariadne, but he's also the most faithful, trustworthy friend a man could have. Mera needs him; that's why I wondered about Thermopylae. A Greek's loyalty was always first to his city, his *polis* . . . Killer has transferred his loyalty from Thespiae to Mera."

Shout . . . shout . . . *shout* . . . SHOUT . . . What was that? It sounded like a word.

"Here it comes," Jerry muttered. "I mustn't say it, but you can probably make out the name. They're hailing the champion, the big banana himself."

Ast . . . something? Aster?

"Who?" she whispered.

"He has the Mera desk in hell," Jerry said grimly. Then the racket rose to a greater cheer than any they had heard yet, that went on and on . . . and stopped in a sudden, expectant hush. Jerry picked up one of the guns.

"But there's one disadvantage," he remarked, continuing the conversation as though nothing had happened. "You can never be quite sure. I've always refused Killer's entreaties. I just can't swim in those waters and in Mera I don't have to. That night he had heard me accept—there have been other times, I'm sure. But he doesn't dare ask. He never knows which is me and which is the god Eros in my shape, and, if he asked, I might deny it all."

"But here . . ."

"But here," he finished the thought, "here Outside, it has to be Jerry. So tonight he asked. And I lied."

Then he muttered, "And tonight I gave him a promise. That's another first."

There had been no need for him to tell her that. And if what he had been saying was true, then there would be no need for him to honor that promise when he returned to Mera, except that of course Jerry Howard would always honor a promise. If he returned to Mera.

The stove crackled loudly, and she jumped, her nerves rapidly reaching breaking point again—she had thought they'd snapped long ago. The light patches marking the windows seemed to sway.

"What the hell now?" Jerry muttered, studying them.

A deep creaking echoed from the yard, then silence.

More creaking sounded, then louder.... The light moved on the window patches.

"Oh, this is bloody ridiculous," Jerry muttered. "It's all a big fake for our benefit. There aren't thousands of demons out there. Just one big evil."

"Maybe they have elections in hell?" she suggested. "And this is part of the pizzazz?" The creaking grew to a splintering screech and she half expected someone to call out, "Timberrrrrrrr!"

A thunderous crash and darkness beyond the drapes. Wild cheering...

"That light," she said weakly. "It was on a telephone pole. I saw it ... it was a foot thick! More than a foot."

And whatever was out there had just snapped the pole.

She picked up the other automatic weapon, her hands trembling so much that she was not sure she would be able to fire it.

Then something struck the corner of the cottage with a blow that shook the whole building.

"It's him," said Jerry in a very hoarse voice, as though his mouth were bone dry. "No doubt about it."

"*Who?*" she shouted.

He hesitated and then shrugged. "Asterios."

A bellow of triumph, a great, animal roaring rolled through the cottage like a tidal wave...

"What is it?" she whispered. "What does it look like?"

"Hard to tell...can be almost anything...to the

Greeks he was . . ." His voice was lost in another crash, halfway along the wall, and she heard planks splinter.

"He's kicking tires," she whispered.

A third blow came, heavier yet, and the cottage rocked, dishes rattled, and logs fell off the firewood pile and rolled on the floor . . . then silence.

"It's behind the cottage," she said, thinking of those back windows and Alan and Lacey.

"There's no use." His voice was barely audible. "If it's what I think, then it's bulletproof. We need that anti-tank gun I mentioned, and even that . . ."

"Can't you shoot its eyes out, or something?"

He shook his head sadly. "It would hunt by smell or just by demon senses."

"What about the wand?" she demanded, shocked at the way Jerry seemed to be deliquescing.

"The wand would burn it like a hot poker, but not really damage it. And if we take the wand, Killer dies."

"He'll die anyway," she said. Lacey? Alan?

"It wouldn't help," Jerry sighed. "With the wand and a fast horse, you might escape back to Mera. . . . It's been done. But it would have to be a very fast horse."

The building rocked. Wood squeaked and then splintered and shattered. Graham started screaming. Something was tearing its way in through the back wall. Again came that rending noise, as if half the wall had been ripped out, and the tinkling of glass.

"There must be something!" she moaned, staring at the closed door in front of her, dim in the glimmer of firelight. Jerry, beside her, was mumbling incoherently.

Graham's screaming grew louder and another voice, Carlo's, joined in.

Jerry stood up. "All I can think of—" he said. "I'll stand alongside the door and when it comes in this room I'll jam the gun hard against its chest. Just maybe the bullet will penetrate its hide, then."

Or just maybe it would grab him first.

Thump. There was a rocking and a creak of floorboards.

"I think it's in," she said. "Heavy as . . . as hell."

Jerry walked around the sofa and stood beside the door, waiting. She stayed where she was and trembled.

Then a great crunching sounded, which she thought might have been the dresser, and thuds from the distance, as though the intruder was throwing the furniture out of the cottage altogether.

Graham stopped screaming. . . . Carlo stopped screaming. . . . More thuds. . . . Silence. Jerry said nothing.

With creaks and a shuddering, the whole building trembled as the visitor walked, probably stepping carefully in case the floor collapsed.

Then the bedroom door was ripped from its hinges and hurled to the floor with a crash, and two eyes glowed in the darkness beyond . . . much too far apart, much too high in the air. . . .

The size of it!

She could hear breathing, very deep, very slow . . . a sort of big-animal snuffling noise . . . an animal smell— rank, putrid.

Jerry started to whimper. . . .

Then it bellowed again, a cataract of noise that filled the cottage and went on and on, full of triumph and gloating and fury. One huge hand gripped the lintel and ripped out that section of the wall, hurling it away and raising the opening to the ceiling; and suddenly she could see it as the light flickered vaguely on its vast bulk . . . a black muzzle as big as a laundry basket with horns almost to the roof and shoulders that touched both sides of the doorway, an impossible chest, and arms hanging down at its sides, and . . .

NOT THAT!

Her fear dissolved as she erupted hate and anger; she snapped the submachine gun to automatic and opened fire. . . .

And then all hell seemed to explode into the cabin.

❧ 9 ❧

JERRY HAD BEEN STANDING BY THE DOORWAY, LISTEN-
ing in the darkness to that thick breathing, nauseated
by the fetid stench, trying to stop his gun shaking so
much. He had just decided that Asterios knew he was
there and was waiting for him and he had lifted a leaden
foot on a rubber leg to step forward.

Then his gun was gone, and he was on the floor. He
never knew afterward whether he had been struck by the
monster or by the bursting door frame, or whether it was
merely the force of the sound itself. The momentary roar
of Ariadne's Uzi, the shattering of glass as bullets rico-
cheted, the smashing of wood—all vanished before a
bellow of pain from Asterios like a great pipe organ at
full volume, unbearable in that tiny space. Darkness and
the stench of carbide and noise—and impact. Head
down, the brute charged; table and chairs crumpled and
were rammed into the far wall. The cottage rocked like a
boat.

Jerry rolled into a ball and covered his ears to ease the
pain in his head. Rampaging in pain-maddened frenzy,
the monster wheeled sideways, hurling the icebox across
into the cupboards. Then it straightened and lunged, still
roaring, at Ariadne, and she gave it another burst of gun-

fire. Louder yet, the monster went right by her and cannoned into the piano, exploding it out through the wall.

The cottage settled back on its foundations.

There was sudden silence... until hearing returned, and the children were screaming.

Dazed, Jerry clambered to his feet. Through the remains of the far wall and the acrid smoke, he saw a very faint tinge of light; false dawn, perhaps, but good enough.

Had they escaped? Apparently! The demons were gone, and he had no idea how or why.

Coughing, he reeled over to the other bedroom and could just make out Maisie hugging Lacey and Ariadne holding Alan. For a few minutes he leaned against the jamb, feeling confused and somehow more ashamed than relieved. The children's screams died away to whimpers as the women comforted them.

"What happened?" Jerry demanded. "What in Hades did you *do*?"

Ariadne's face was a pale blur; she looked up momentarily from her child.

"I shot it in the nuts," she snapped. "There, there..."

Jerry choked and then shook his head to try to clear it. Why not? The bullets would not have penetrated the monster's hide, but that would not have mattered. He had never heard of that technique, yet it made sense.

Suddenly he started to laugh. "You have written a whole new chapter into the book on demonology, Ariadne! And it took a woman to think of it!"

"Long overdue," she said vaguely.

Huh? "What do you mean?" he demanded.

"Oh... nothing. I didn't... Forget that." She went back to comforting Alan.

Jerry turned to the front room. A cool, fresh breeze had taken away the smoke and told of the coming dawn. The piano had totally vanished, probably scattered all over the clearing by the force of impact; there would be no more Mozart ever played on that instrument. Almost the only undamaged area was the rug on which Killer still lay by the door, blissfully unaware of the epic chaos that had erupted all about him—and he would be

speechlessly furious at having missed it. His face looked
like variegated marble in the faint but gradually increasing light, a statue with stubble. The wand glowed no
more, but when he knelt down and put his ear to Killer's
chest, Jerry could still hear a slow and steady thumping.

That left the other bedroom, and now he realized that
he was floating around in a self-indulgent, witless daze
instead of behaving like a competent leader and sternly
counting his casualties.

He stepped over the fallen door and for a moment he
thought that there was nothing else in the room. As he
had expected, almost the whole of the rear wall and part
of one side had been ripped away; the roof drooped dangerously. Then he saw that there was a limp sprawl of a
body in one corner, went over to it, and discovered
Carlo, alive.

He ran back into the kitchen, picked up a dagger that
had fallen out of the twisted ruins of the icebox, and
returned to cut the youth's bonds. Carlo groaned and
opened one eye.

"You're alive," Jerry said. It sounded as stupid to him
as it probably did to Carlo. "The demons have gone, it's
all over."

Carlo groaned again, tried to move, and lapsed into
obscenities. After a moment he gathered strength and
the sounds became stronger, but repetitious. If he had
suffered any new injuries, Jerry could not see them. The
bloody and pulped face was unbearable for him to look
at; how could he have allowed his rage to turn him into
such an animal? He decided to let Carlo do his own
stocktaking and go in search of Gillis.

Now the grayness in the sky had chosen a direction to
be east and was growing stronger—he could see trees
outlined against it and make out enough of the terrain to
risk walking. He jumped down through the open wall and
looked around the debris of planks and spars which lit-
tered the ground. No body. He shivered and not merely
from the clamminess of dawn air on his bare chest—
Meran weather was more accommodating, except sometimes on Killer's hunting trips. Had Asterios somehow
dematerialized his victim? There was the bed, hurled an

incredible distance from the cabin, and there something which had once been a dresser, even farther. He inspected both, and there were no human remains underneath either. Perhaps there had been other demons waiting outside to catch Gillis and remove him.

The hedge and grasslands had not reappeared—he was standing in a clearing in a pine forest, still dark and mysterious. He strode over to the barn and walked around it, saw nothing amiss there, and poked his head inside to inspect the mare. She screamed and reared in terror—he was going to have fun getting her harnessed up—so he shut the door again and left her.

It was good to be alive. He pumped up some water from the well and doused his head, then went briefly to inspect the light pole which Asterios had snapped so impressively—at least a foot thick—and headed back to the cottage.

He jumped in through the wall, and Carlo was sitting up.

"Any bones broken?" asked Jerry, in a cheerful, hospital sort of voice.

"Just my face," Carlo muttered, barely moving his lips.

Nothing to say to that. "Anything you want, then?"

"Water."

By the time he returned from the pump with a bucket of water, the women and children had emerged, and he had to break the news of Graham's disappearance to Maisie. She teetered on the brink of renewed hysterics, and Ariadne hugged her and soothed her back to shaky self-control. Alan started to laugh at the demolished icebox, found an apple, and proceeded to eat it.

A jam sandwich was produced for Lacey, Jerry's cape returned to him, as the children were now back in their own clothes, and Ariadne made a pot of coffee. Fortunately Asterios had missed the range, or the cottage would have surely burned to the ground.

"Now what?" Ariadne asked. She was pale—they all were—but she had combed her hair and looked better than anyone else, her Meran cape and pants once more clean and unrumpled, the bloodstains gone. She had a glow of satisfaction which no one else could match, and which was probably a rare experience for her.

"If we can, we should get the mare between the traces and leave," he said, then saw Maisie's face and added quickly, "after we've had a proper look for Graham, of course."

"Killer get up soon?" Alan inquired, studying the inert form on the floor.

"He's a heavy sleeper, Alan," Jerry said. They could load Killer in the wagon on that rug. Then he forced himself to look at Carlo. "If you want... that face of yours would heal in a couple of days in Mera, three at the most—bones and all." Even his dandruff would vanish, but it was not necessary to mention that. "I don't know if temporary stays are allowed, but I feel guilty as hell at having done that to you and I'll plead your case to the Oracle. Do you want to come with us?"

"You still peddling that bunk?" Carlo asked. "Fairyland bull..." He hesitated and then shrugged. "I'll come down the road with you to the highway."

"You may never reach the highway if you travel with us," Jerry said. "I suppose the Oracle will send you back here, but it might magic you directly back home, so you have nothing to lose. Maisie?"

Maisie crossed herself. Maisie was a problem—he could not leave her here alone. Reluctantly she agreed to accompany them, like Carlo, to the highway. It was an obvious face-saving decision for both of them.

"Daddy want coffee now," Alan said.

He had been trotting around busily on his stumpy legs, exploring this interesting disaster area. They all looked at him in astonishment, like a grove of fir trees examining a rosebush.

"Where's Daddy, Al?" Maisie asked, kneeling.

He pointed his apple at the bedroom. "I ask Daddy if he want coffee, too. Daddy likes coffee."

There was a stampede into the shattered room—and then outside, through the wall. Gillis was sitting on the grass, his shirt soaked with blood from a broken nose, his once-splendid blue suit a filthy, bedraggled mess, his face wearing a blank, dazed expression which reminded

Jerry of survivors pulled from ruined houses in the London blitz. His hands were still bound but his feet were free. He must have ripped the bonds in his terror as Asterios entered, fallen out through the wall, and rolled under the cottage. Gillis was not a particularly personable person, thought Jerry, but he had seldom been more pleased to see anyone.

Leaving a weeping Maisie to attend to him, Jerry and Ariadne headed for the barn.

She stopped at the door and looked around the clearing at the fallen pole and the shattered cottage and she took a couple of deep breaths of the pine-scented air. The sky was turning blue, clear and cloudless. She sighed with contentment.

"How far to Mera, Jerry?" she said.

"Just beyond those trees," he said, smiling. "Mera is always just out of sight. Usually half an hour will do it. No doubts?"

She smiled back at him. "None at all. I believe, and it's wonderful." Then the smile died slowly. "And Alan and Lacey?"

There was the problem. "We can only ask the Oracle," he said. "If the answer is no, then you may reconsider. It can tell you the alternatives and, if you choose to return, it can probably send you somewhere where Graham will never find you." But he wanted her to stay.

"How old is the youngest person there?" she demanded, frowning.

"Hard to say." He thought of Clio, of Rab the stableboy, and of a few others—all of whom worshipped Killer, who shamelessly took advantage of their admiration. "About sixteen, I should think. Killer's wife was probably younger than that, but she was an exceptional case. Killer was sent to rescue some unknown Greek philosopher, who turned him down. He fancied the man's granddaughter and brought her back instead."

She giggled, in spite of her worry. "We always get back to Killer! Is that allowed?"

Jerry shrugged. "According to Killer, he had a dandy fight with the Oracle over it." He doubted that very much; no one argued with the Oracle, not even Killer.

"But obviously a field man must have discretion—I'm going to take Carlo. I feel horrible about what I did to him."

She put a hand on his arm. "Don't feel guilty, Jerry. He deserved it. And be careful—he was swearing revenge on you last night. He's dangerous."

He turned in dismay to look back at the cottage, feeling shivers of fear. He still had the automatic in his pocket, but, like a total idiot, he had left the other guns there. Killer would never have made that mistake. But if Killer had been conscious when Asterios came, he would have been holding the gun instead of Ariadne, and probably none of them would have survived. Yet he *had* been stupid. . . .

She read his expression correctly. "If Carlo believes that his injuries can be cured in Mera, then he won't do anything, at least not now. You can't be perfect, Jerry. You've done very well."

He shook his head. "You did it. Without you none of us would have been here this morning. I wish I knew how you thought of it."

Her face darkened. She said, "Come on, let's see to this horse of yours."

The mare was obviously enjoying a nervous breakdown and did not wish to be talked out of it. Ariadne again showed her ranchwoman's skills and eventually soothed the mare and got her between the shafts in a way Jerry could never have managed.

"She's cast a shoe," Ariadne said, examining feet. "I suppose we have to use her?"

He said that they did; they certainly could not move Killer without the wagon. She agreed reluctantly, and they drove over to the cottage.

Loading Killer was surprisingly easy with the rug as a sling. Carlo took one corner without argument, his face unreadable—if he had remorse for trying to kill this man, he did not say so. As unobtrusively as possible, Jerry collected all the ammunition clips and tucked them in the wagon, rendering the guns useless, and then breathed a silent sigh of relief. The rest of the equipment he decided to leave—the Oracle could send him back for it, or perhaps it would all just vanish when they had left.

Gillis was less dazed, although his face also had suffered during the night and he looked like a survivor of some major disaster.

"We are going to give Carlo a ride," Jerry said, "as far as the highway. It is possible that we shall arrive in Mera first, but he knows that. You and Maisie may come with us or leave later. Please yourself."

The big man glared at him. "You are taking my children?"

"I am."

Gillis rose. "Then I am coming with you."

Maisie whimpered.

Jerry shrugged. "Very well—we'll all go together, and you can argue with the Oracle." *Just try!*

Ariadne took the reins, with Alan and Lacey squirming excitedly on the bench beside her. Jerry sat behind them, keeping watch on the three adults at the back across Killer's inert form. The sun was up, the sky was blue, the air was perfumed by the trees, and what he could really use was a good breakfast. The wagon rolled off down the road at a gentle pace.

Soon the cottage and barn vanished around a curve in the road, a road which had been straight the previous evening.

"Darling, I'm worried," Maisie said. "A place where people don't grow old or die is not right. It is a device of the Devil."

"I suspect it is a device of a sick mind, honey," her husband said. "The first chance we get, we're going to turn this character in to the cops."

Jerry chuckled. "Can you describe to me what Killer is holding?" he asked. He reached down and lifted off the blanket which he had laid over Killer's blood-stained form. The blood had dried now, and the skin on Killer's face and chest was white. Maisie crossed herself once more.

"A white rod thing," Gillis said reluctantly.

Jerry smiled and replaced the blanket, leaving the top of the wand uncovered so that he could see its color.

Gillis was bluffing, or else merely lying to comfort his wife. He believed.

The road was a grassed-over trail through the pines, not even the modern gravel road it had been the previous day, but quite adequate for the wagon's leisurely, rumbling pace. It continued to curve gently to the left.

"Ariadne?" the big man shouted.

"Yes, Graham?" she twisted round briefly and sent him a smile, perhaps the first genuine smile she had given him in years. She had not even reached Mera, and yet already it was transforming her.

"Suppose this fairy city does exist," Gillis said. "You know what you're giving up? The whole world for one small place, a ragtag of people collected at random from all cultures and times. That's a fair description, is it not, Howard?"

"Very fair," Jerry said. "Except that you have a choice of all sorts of countryside around it, without limit. And they're a fine bunch of people. There are no locks on doors in Mera—I left my house open because people go in and borrow my books all the time. They always bring them back, too."

Gillis snorted disbelievingly. "But this Oracle you talk of is the ruler? No elections? The Oracle lives forever, also, I suppose, and whatever he says goes?"

"That's true," Jerry said. The two cars had apparently disappeared in the night. The road curved emptily out of sight behind the wagon and also in front. He wondered if the others had noticed. "But there are no orders to give, except when someone needs to go Outside. I never heard of anyone refusing, so I suppose the Oracle knows who to ask."

Gillis scowled suspiciously. "This Oracle—what is he? Or she? Is it human?"

"It looks human," Jerry assured him with a straight face.

"But no freedom? No rights?" He had a lawyer's skill at arguing. "All your present friends and family lost forever, and home and familiar things?"

"Not everyone agrees to stay."

"And how about boredom? Do you never get bored?"
He was no fool, this lawyer.

"No," Jerry said. "There are too many good things to
do and good people to meet. I have no idea how many
folk live in Mera, but you can't walk there very long
without seeing faces you've never seen before, which
means new friends to make. When I get tired of being a
bookworm I go off to the exercise fields and try my hand
at wrestling or tennis or fencing, or go swimming or
boating—or fishing or hunting. I talk abstractions with
learned friends and read a lot and enjoy music. I party
with the girls and riot with the boys. Boredom is no
problem. Ask me again in ten thousand years."

The big man scowled heavily and fell silent for a
while.

The knob at the top of the wand was still white. The
road continued to curve gently ahead and behind.

The cross-examination started again. "What language
do you speak there, then? Do all these Greeks and Chinese and so on all learn English?"

"Killer knows about six words of English," Jerry said
and laughed at the disbelieving faces. "I can't guess how
he even picked up those. Where do you suppose I'm
from?"

"You've got no accent," Gillis said thoughtfully. "I
mean you have none to my ear, so I suppose somewhere
near Colorado."

"Where are you from, Carlo?" Jerry asked.

"That's my business," Carlo said.

Gillis' head whipped around, and he stared.

"Had an accent yesterday, did he?" Jerry said. "And
he doesn't now. Right? I'm English—or I was, once."

He let them worry about it for a while, while he worried about the unchanging scenery. Then he explained,
"The wand is doing it. In Mera everyone speaks and understands the same language. I promised Ariadne she
could read Homer in the original—or Goethe or Chaucer
or de Montaigne. Or Confucius or Gilgamesh. I gave
Killer his nickname as a pun on Achilles—it rhymes in
English and it rhymed in Mera. It doesn't rhyme in
Greek, but Killer got the joke in Mera. Puns translate,

which is impossible anywhere else; rhymes translate. It's magic, faerie."

The wagon rumbled along for a while in silence while they all thought about that, Maisie's pretty young face twisted with worry at this further demonstration of the work of the Devil.

"The wand will do the same translation job Outside," Jerry said. "It has a range of about a quarter of a mile— usually. But very rarely the range drops down to feet, or even inches, which is tricky if you have ten guys speaking ten different languages. A few times Killer has taken me along just because I know a little Greek from my school days. We can talk to each other, and I can talk to Marcus and Jean-Louis, of course."

"Why sometimes and not others?" Gillis demanded, his methodical lawyer's mind obviously disturbed at the illogicality of faerie.

"I'm not sure," Jerry confessed. "I think that sometimes the wands reduce their power output very low, or probably so as to avoid attention and calling up demons. Or perhaps there are times and places where faerie won't work. But there are times when the Oracle has warned that language will be a problem, and one thing you absolutely can not do in Mera is learn a new language, obviously."

The sun was back in his eyes again, and so far no one else seemed to have noticed the problem. Partly he was talking to hide his steadily increasing uneasiness and his frantic efforts to think of an explanation and a solution. Then Ariadne pulled up; the wagon stopped, and there was silence on the grassy forest road.

"We're going in a circle, Jerry," she said. He glanced up and saw the dread and hopelessness that were creeping back into her face, the hope of early morning gone once more.

It had been too easy.

He had his hand on the pistol, ready, and he pulled it out, trying not to show his rising fear. Asterios had been in the cottage, in the same room as Carlo and Gillis, yet they had survived. Or had they?

"I'm afraid the hayride is over," he said. "Obviously we are not all supposed to go to Mera."

"So you're going to ditch us?" said Gillis, his bushy black eyebrows coming down dangerously.

Jerry wasn't sure what he expected—a werewolf transformation? A suicidal assault? But so far the two men were merely angry men. "Right. The three of you out, please. I expect the road will return to normal as soon as we have left. Just keep walking and you'll reach somewhere. Out!"

Carlo jumped down, then Gillis, and he helped Maisie. Both men were clearly furious, but Jerry still held the gun.

"You're stealing my children!"

"Daddy!" squealed Lacey. "Maisie?"

Alan started to cry. They did not want to be left with their mother, and that was not good news.

"Drive on!" Jerry said, keeping his eyes on the men. The wagon started to roll forward again. It did not move much faster than a man could walk, but the three stood in the road and watched it go. Soon the curve of the road had hidden them from sight. Jerry heaved a sigh of relief.

"What's going wrong, Jerry?" Ariadne said quietly. "Are you sure it was their fault?"

He stood up, lifted the children over the seat, and told them it was time to change places. He warned Lacey to tell him if she saw anything behind them, wishing now that he had brought the big guns—another error! Then he clambered over beside Ariadne.

"To be honest, Ariadne, I don't know. We should have been there by now."

"It could be..." she jerked her head to indicate the children behind. "Adults only?"

"Would you come to Mera without them?"

For an instant she hesitated, then said, "No. Graham is a crook. Oh, he never *breaks* the law, but he bends it like a pretzel. He's one of those lawyers who think their job is to find ways around the law instead of upholding it."

That was a judgment and a good topic for debate and

not something he could comment on without knowing the facts; her opinions of Gillis could hardly be unbiased.

"Maisie is not a bad kid," Ariadne admitted grudgingly, watching the road continuing in its gentle curve. "But she's far too young to be their mother. Lacey has a great gift for music, and Maisie doesn't know an orchestra from a bandbox."

"And Alan?" he asked.

She smiled ruefully. "Alan is a little devil—he's been unusually well behaved since we arrived. Maisie can't control him now, and I'm terrified of how he'll grow up under Graham's influence."

"Well, it may not be the children who are the problem," he said. "It could be Killer."

"Why?" she demanded, frowning.

"Too much power?" he suggested. "Perhaps it is taking too much faerie to keep him alive, so it can't move us all to Mera."

She bit her lip and was silent, concentrating on the horse; and even to Jerry's inexpert eye the mare was limping badly now.

If the children were the problem he had burned a bridge, for he could never abandon them in the forest as he had discarded the adults. They would be the first children he had ever seen in Mera, whereas Killer would not be the first living corpse brought back by a field team. Other wands had managed the transference while keeping a badly injured man alive, why not this one? He wished he knew more about the mechanics of the wands, knew whether they could run down like batteries.

He hoped that his first guess had been correct, that either Carlo or Gillis or both had been possessed and so forbidden to enter Mera.

The sun crept slowly around them as the road continued its turn. The clearing and the cottage had disappeared, obviously, for they had gone more than once round the loop and there had been no side roads—unless they were spiraling like a phonograph needle.

Still no change in the scenery. If a major demon could be defeated as easily as Ariadne had trashed Asterios, then why did the demonologists in Mera not know of that technique? Asterios had been inside the cottage. Could one tell if one had been possessed? Maybe they all were.

Ariadne had shrunk back into herself and become the cowering, frightened woman he had first met. Alan and Lacey were unhappily silent. The sun was almost behind the wagon again, which meant almost a complete circle since leaving Carlo and the Gillises.

He remembered the first time he had climbed to the high-diving board as a child and how that had felt. And flying into flak over Cologne. And bailing out and counting before pulling the ripcord. He knew what he was going to do next, and it felt worse than any of those.

"Look," Ariadne said.

There were three figures ahead, and they had heard the wagon and stopped to look back: a woman in a pink sweater and green pants, a man in a badly mauled blue suit, a slighter man in jeans and a leather jacket.

The wagon stopped.

"It isn't working." She looked at him with doubt and fear . . . and anger and betrayal.

"Turn the wagon," he barked.

"Would that help?" she asked with a brief glimmer of hope, and then even that had gone.

"Turn it!" he snapped. Gillis shouted and started to run, with Carlo behind him.

There was just room to turn the wagon between the trees which flanked the road.

"Now we get out," Jerry said. His mouth was dry and his heart pounding. "Down you get, kids!"

"No!" Ariadne screamed. "I won't leave them."

"Us too. Come on! Move!"

She studied him doubtfully for a moment, then Lacey had jumped down, and Ariadne scrambled down to lift Alan, not wanting to be separated from them. She certainly did not trust Jerry anymore.

He knotted the reins, released the brake, and jumped down also, stumbling in his haste. Gillis was coming puffing up to them with Carlo beside him.

Quickly, before his nerve failed him, Jerry took out the automatic and fired one shot into the air.

The children screamed, Ariadne gasped—and the

mare dropped her ears and bolted. The wagon bounced and rattled, and he felt a sudden terror that the wand might be shaken from Killer's grip—then suddenly there was no noise, just a bolting horse and wagon moving in silence, then neither had a shadow, and before they turned the bend out of sight, horse and wagon faded away into nothing, and the sun shone down on an empty road.

Killer had returned to Mera.

❧ 10 ❧

THE ROAD SEEMED TO SWAY, AND THE SUNLIGHT danced strangely. This was it, then? He sent a last smile towards Ariadne and closed his eyes and waited.

"What is going on?" Gillis roared.

Jerry opened his eyes and blinked. The roadway had steadied, and the light was all right. . . .

Then he was hit by a wildcat, his arm grabbed and twisted, and he went hurtling to the grass; Carlo had the gun. One of the women squealed.

Jerry sat up and rubbed his shoulder, flexed twisted fingers and looked around the ring of angry and frightened faces. He saw that he was level with Alan and gave him a smile. Alan quickly hid behind Maisie's leg.

He was alive.

The wand had gone, and he had not crumbled into dust. His hands looked fine, no old man's liver spots. If his hair had all fallen out and his face collapsed into wrinkles, he thought it likely that someone would be kind enough to mention it. He started to laugh—he was alive.

"I said, 'what is going on?'" Gillis repeated.

"I'm damned if I know," Jerry said. He also didn't care at the moment. He had done it, the big one: He had sincerely offered his life for a friend. That the offer had been refused, so that he was still whole, was hardly less welcome than the awareness that he had been able to make it. J. Howard was now one of the good guys. He laughed again at life and sunlight and green trees. Not the same trees. He looked around. This was a forest, but a deciduous forest, hardwoods. Was that a lime? So something had happened, and all the others were too shocked to notice. There were some small and fluffy white clouds in the sky which had not been there before, and the sun seemed higher...yes, the air was much warmer and sweet-scented. Birds were chirping.

Carlo kicked him, and he yelped with pain.

"Up!"

Damn, that felt like broken ribs; nothing like a hard kick to bring a man back to reality. Winded and wincing, Jerry scrambled to his feet, no longer the man with the gun. Gillis' bruised face was registering satisfaction, and Carlo's puffed mouth was twisted in a smile. Maisie was kneeling to hug the children; Ariadne was standing by herself again, withdrawn and pale.

"Now explain!" Gillis said. "Where is that wagon?"

"It went back to Mera," said Jerry. "Either there were too many of us, or the wand was refusing to take someone—possibly the children."

"Or me," Araidne said sadly.

"Or me?" Jerry shrugged. "The one I was most sure of was Killer, and I did not dare take the wand away from him anyway."

"And the rest of us, what happens?" demanded Carlo in an accent which Jerry could not place.

"Jolly good question," he said.

"Cut out the horse—"

"Wait!" Gillis said. "I don't think he's clowning. He's a limey, and that's his real voice."

Carlo glowered but did not argue. Probably he could hear a difference in Gillis also.

"It's another place," Jerry said. "The firs have gone, see?"

They looked around at a much more open woodland and a narrower, dusty roadway with a slope to it.

"Where are we, then?"

"Not the foggiest," Jerry confessed. "I don't know where and I don't know when. I don't even know how, because the wand has gone, so there must be something else going on. We'll just have to wait for Killer to come for us."

"Why should he?" Gillis snapped. "How can he find us? And even if he wants to, it may be months before he's well enough."

Jerry turned his back on the gun to prove to himself that he could do it and walked a few steps to a fallen tree. He sat down and tried to look confident. Suddenly that gun had made him feel very mortal.

"Once back in Mera, he'll heal in a few days," he said. "But even that doesn't matter—it wouldn't matter if it were a year. If the Oracle can find us, it can put Killer right back here at the right time." He hoped.

The others looked at one another and then at their surroundings.

"Then Mr. Howard, I think we do not need longer," Carlo said, raising the gun two-handed. "I have a score to settle."

"Now, wait!" Gillis shouted.

The swarthy youth did not take his eyes off Jerry. "No longer your business," he said. "He mashed my face, and now I kill him."

"No!" Ariadne shouted.

"Not in front of the children!" Maisie begged, pulling them to her.

Now there was a kind thought.

"Go, then!" Still holding the gun on Jerry, Carlo jerked his head. "You all go down the road. I will join you afterwards."

It would be a shame to be killed so soon after having expected it and escaped. Jerry took a deep breath and said, "You realize that Killer may need me to home in on?"

"Another good reason," said the gun holder, with obvious satisfaction. He would be in no hurry to meet with Killer, who would likewise have a score to settle. That had been an ill-advised remark, J. Howard.

"Graham!" Ariadne said. "You're not going to let this man shoot him in cold blood?"

Gillis' hand fingered his swollen face, where Killer had struck him, the nose broken when he fell from the cottage. "I don't think I can stop him. Come, Maisie." He scooped up Alan, put a hand behind Lacey to urge her on, and the four of them started along the road.

Jerry was back on the high board and this time he was going to be pushed—unless . . . He looked at Ariadne. "What time is it?" he asked.

She glanced at her wrist. "It's stopped," she said.

Ah! Jerry felt all his taut muscles relax in a rush. He turned on a confident smile and directed it toward Carlo, who seemed to be enjoying the anticipation and was apparently in no hurry.

"Go ahead," Jerry said. "I dispense with the blindfold and waive the cigarette."

"You think I snow you, Limey? Think I can't shoot you? Think I don't have the *cojones*?"

"I'm sure you do," Jerry said. "You're a very effective young man, and I've been underestimating you. Go ahead, though. Try it."

Carlo's eyes narrowed. Obviously he wanted to see his victim cringe. "I think in the gut, like your friend. That hurts most."

Jerry lifted his cape, pulled his belt down a fraction, and pointed at his navel. "There's the bulls-eye, then."

Click.

Click again.

Phew! Jerry stood up. "Strange!" he said. "It worked for me a moment ago. Would you like me to try? No?" He held out a hand to Ariadne. "Come on, let's stay with the others."

Carlo snarled oaths, expertly cracked open the weapon, checked the ammunition, then put it back together. He pointed it at Jerry once more and . . . *Click.*

Hold it, though. Jerry had overlooked something else back at the cottage and somehow he did not think Carlo would have missed it. Yes, he had underestimated this kid—he was incredibly fast and obviously not overly troubled by scruples. "Try your knife and see if that works."

Carlo grabbed inside his jacket and produced the switchblade—but the blade itself did not leap into sight. Now *that* was interesting! Carlo glared with one and a half eyes at his tormentor and looked about ready to use fists and feet—and Jerry no longer believed he could snap this deceptively weedy youth.

He held out a hand. "Truce?" he said.

He got more obscenities, and this time certainly in Arabic, familiar to Jerry from his tour in Transjordan. Carlo was a curiously proficient linguist.

Jerry shook his head. "You need me to tell you what's going on," he said. "I can't afford to have you edging around behind my back all the time. You have a score to settle. So has my friend Killer. I'll make a deal with you—I'll keep Killer off you if you'll stay off me."

"I see no Killer!" Carlo snapped.

"I told you," Jerry said, trying to be persuasive without being too humble, "you need me to tell you what's going on. I've had more experience with this...er... guff than you have. Now—until we're back to Mera or back to civilization, we're all in deep fertilizer, Carlo my friend, and we'd better work together."

Reluctantly Carlo nodded. "Truce, then." He tucked knife and gun inside his coat.

He did not shake hands.

The three of them set off after the Gillises, who had vanished around a bend.

Ariadne was giving him a wondering look. "How did you know that the gun wouldn't work?" she demanded.

"Because of your watch." But he had not been quite certain; firearms were earlier than whatever technology they were using in watches in her time. Fairly certain, but not quite.

"And why did you send Killer back that way?" she asked.

"It seemed like the best thing to do," Jerry said. "He needs Mera to recover and then he'll bring help. I've been lousing up everything."

"You could have gone with him."

"And go crawling back among my friends with my mission a shambles like this?" he said, avoiding her eye. She put her hand in his and said no more.

She had said she would not go without her children, and apparently it was the children who had been denied access to Mera. He could have returned and reported a refusal. He knew that. The Oracle would know that. He could visualize Killer raging and storming and the Oracle forbidding any attempt to recover such an idiot. What would Killer do then, go out on strike? He might threaten to do just that—no more rescues before Jerry —and the other field men would certainly support Killer. But this was no ordinary industrial dispute. Probably the Oracle could make them all forget that they had ever known Jerry Howard.

Time would tell—and very little time, too.

And what exactly was going on, anyway? He needed to prepare some sort of story for the others.

For a few minutes he thought that the others had vanished—which might have simplified things considerably —but around two bends and up a steep slope the party was re-united. The Gillises were drooped on a fallen tree, taking a rest. The temperature had risen dramatically, and discarded coats and sweaters lay in a heap beside the stump. Maisie was wearing a filmy blouse over a clearly visible bra, Graham had unbuttoned his shirt to show that he grew fur under it. The woodland was thinning out into parkland, but they seemed to be on a hill, with nothing but sky visible beyond a close horizon. The road ahead continued to climb.

The newcomers flopped down on the grass. Jerry asked the time; both Maisie and Graham confirmed that their watches had stopped. They seemed mildly surprised to see him still alive, but offered no congratulations. Now he remembered the calculating machine he had stolen from Gillis and brought that out, but it would not work for either of them.

"Carlo and I have a truce," Jerry said. "I suggest you join it. We need to work together."

Of course a lawyer had to set out specific terms, but eventually it was agreed that the parties of the first, second, and third parts would all stick together until further notice. Gillis was understandably worried and trying not to show it before his wife.

Now the job was to try and establish some sort of leadership.

"First hypothesis," Jerry said, stretching out and leaning on one arm, "would be that we're in Mera, because of the gun and the watches not working. Discard that because of my accent and Carlo's." And both Alan and Graham had black hair, not blue.

"Second hypothesis would be that we're in the real world, but we've gone back in time. If that's the case, then we've gone back a jolly long way, because even the spring in Carlo's switchblade doesn't work." Then he had to explain about technology not working downtime.

"So what's the third?" Gillis asked, guessing from Jerry's tone that there must be a third.

"Just to add to the second," Jerry said, looking around, "if we're in the real world, we've also moved in space, because this vegetation looks all wrong to me. I wish I knew what those trees were, and those bushes. The grass is not very long—I think it must be grazed."

"Let's have the third hypothesis."

Jerry sighed. "I think we're in some faerie state. It just doesn't feel quite real, somehow. That would explain the watches, too. Who put us here, I don't know; they may be well intentioned or otherwise. We have no weapons and no food. I don't know about you, but I could surely handle a large breakfast."

Carlo asked if that was all he could contribute, salting the question with his usual obscenities.

"That's about it," Jerry admitted. "Plus a smattering of Greek."

"Why Greek?" Gillis demanded suspiciously.

"Just a hunch." He shrugged. "I may be way off the mark, but doesn't this vegetation look sort of Mediterranean to you?"

Apparently none of them were conversant with Mediterranean flora and nobody had any helpful suggestions.

They could go ahead and look for breakfast, they agreed, or they could go back to where they had arrived, in the hope that the place was somehow important—but then they might starve to death.

"Pony!" squealed Alan.

Heads turned, then Jerry sat up, Ariadne rose to her knees, Lacey said, "Ooooo!"

Standing in the middle of the track they had been following, slightly uphill from them, was the largest horse Jerry had never seen—a truly magnificent snow-white stallion with tail and mane sweeping almost to the ground and shimmering like spun glass. Dappled by sunlight through the trees, carefully posed before a dark mass of bushes, he looked every inch aware of his beauty and strength, arrogant, defiant, and contemptuous of mere bipeds in his forest. He tossed his head and whinnied quietly and then gazed carefully in their direction, while the sun flashed on the three-foot horn protruding from his forehead.

"Oh, Lord!" Gillis groaned. "If any of my colleagues ever hear that I'm seeing unicorns, I'll be disbarred for life."

"Nineteen hands if he's an inch!" Ariadne whispered. "Superb!"

Maisie crossed herself automatically and reached for the rosary she had been wearing around her neck. Jerry said, "No, Maisie! Not demon work this time!"

"No?" she said.

He knew he was grinning like a maniac, and his words almost fell over themselves as he tried to explain. Of all the monsters in the bestiaries—the griffins and yales and sphinxes and others—only the unicorn had a truly good reputation. It was not a Greek legend, but a Christian one. That probably meant that they had broken out of the evil influence of Asterios—although he still would not mention that name, just in case—or else, perhaps, some other power was making itself felt. The Romans had known of unicorns, but theirs were different and had black horns, and the Greeks had gone in for flying horses.

"Pegasus!" said Lacey.

Now he knew that they were not in any part of the real world, the world of machines and lawyers, but in some realm of faerie. And if he was going to trust anyone or anything, a unicorn would rank near the top of his scale of faith.

"Christian?" Maisie repeated when she got a word in.

"Father Julius is quite insistent," Jerry said. "He considers the unicorn a symbol of the Savior."

Father Julius, with his medieval reasoning, was the most impossibly muddled thinker imaginable, an angels-on-pins man, a juggler of faulty premises and contorted deduction. An argument with Father Julius was a wrestling match with a team of giant squid, but his faith and good intentions were beyond question, and in this case his opinion impressed Maisie.

The unicorn whinnied quizzically and scratched the ground with a flashing silver hoof.

"Perhaps we're supposed to follow him." Ariadne suggested.

"Let's try then," Jerry said, rising cautiously. "I doubt if any of us is qualified to catch him. You don't happen to be a virgin, do you, Carlo?"

Carlo grabbed him by the cape and balled a fist; hastily Jerry explained that only virgins could catch unicorns.

The youth stared at him doubtfully and then released him, apparently deciding that the madman was trying to be friendly. "I lost that sort of virginity on the night of my thirteenth birthday," he said...proudly? "To an uncle. And the other soon after." Progress—it wasn't much, but it was his first real conversation.

Gathering up their bundle of coats, the castaways stepped back to the road, Alan clutching his father's hand, and Lacey now by her mother, shivering with excitement. They had only walked a few paces towards the stallion, however, when he dropped his head, waved his horn menacingly in small circles as though taking aim, and started pawing the ground with a great silver hoof.

Dead stop.

"Apparently that's not the program," Ariadne said. She smiled thoughtfully at Jerry. "Next helpful suggestion?"

Jerry was visualizing a charge by that enormous beast, with himself shish-kebabbed on the horn. Ouch.

"Well, let's try the other direction," he suggested, afraid that honor required him to stay in the rear.

They turned around, walked a few steps, and stopped.

A short distance downhill, two more unicorns blocked their path—mares and not quite so gigantic, but postioned foursquare, dazzlingly white in a spread of sunlight, side by side in the roadway.

"Everyone back to the tree bench," Jerry said unhappily. "Let me see if this is negotiable."

Wishing he had a wand or an Uzi with silver bullets, he advanced slowly toward the mares. The stallion whinnied warningly, and Jerry glanced back uneasily, then tried a few more steps forward. Both gleaming horns went down, silver hooves pawed. He turned and beat a quick retreat back to the others.

"On the other hand," Ariadne said, "this is really a very pleasant spot to spend an afternoon." Her show of courage amazed him. Perhaps it was for the children, but he hoped that a little of it might be for him. She certainly was smiling more in his direction.

A pleasant spot if it had boasted room service.

So they could proceed neither uphill nor downhill. On either side the scattered bushes and clumps of trees stretched off into a background of greenery, with hints of a skyline not far off. If the stallion wanted them to move laterally, then he could so indicate by moving around them, but he seemed to be content to stay where he was.

"I think we're waiting for something," Jerry said.

Then, like a magic show, quite silently and right where he happened to be looking, two more unicorns emerged from the undergrowth and stopped, another mare and a unicorn foal, gangly-legged and boasting the merest stub of a horn, a white button.

Lacey saw them and said, "Oooooo!" once more, turning to smile at her mother in great delight—apparently Ariadne ranked ahead of Maisie in horse matters. Alan squealed with excitement, although surely he was too young to appreciate the rarity value of horned horse-flesh.

Beginning to feel that being taken prisoner by horses was a demeaning experience, Jerry turned around, and, sure enough, another pair of mares, younger-looking, had closed off the fourth direction. The humans were surrounded; time had come to circle the wagons.

"I wonder if they'll throw us some hay before sunset?" he muttered.

"There's lots of grass to eat," Maisie said. "Stop complaining." Lacey and Ariadne laughed, and Jerry regarded her with some surprise.

Time began to drag. The stallion watched them intently, barely moving except for an occasional swish of that long snow-and-crystal tail. The mares started browsing, but their attention was obviously on the captives also, and the slightest movement would bring their heads up at once. They were waiting, obviously, but for whom, or what? Then the stallion suddenly whinnied like a trumpet fanfare, and a shriller, faint reply came floating through the forest.

"Visitors on the way," Ariadne said.

With a patter of tiny hooves, two more unicorns came cantering in from the downhill direction, past the two mares. They wheeled around between the trees for a moment and then came to a stop in a clearing by the roadway, puffing.

Shetland unicorns? They were white and they had short horns that looked as sharp as needles, but they were tiny, child size. Yet these could not be the younger versions, for there was an undoubted foal to compare. They must be another species, then, the dwarf unicorn. Very rare.

"Compact models?" someone muttered farther along the tree, but Jerry had gone back to pick up a thought—child size.

He waited to see if anyone else had seen the connection, but when no one spoke he said, "Ariadne, Graham? We do have a couple of virgins with us."

"No!" they snapped simultaneously. But Gillis studied the two newcomers carefully—they were twitching their tails and studying him in turn from a safe distance—and then looked at Jerry.

"Say what you're thinking," he said.

"I think it's a rescue," Jerry said. "It may be a trap, but unicorns do have a good reputation. And I think we have to try it."

"*No!*" Ariadne repeated.

Jerry waited, but no one else would speak. "It seems pretty evident that they can't go to Mera," he said. " I don't know why, but there must be some rule—even faerie has its rules. Perhaps this is a way to get them out, and then—perhaps—there will be an attempt to get us out. Heck, it's worth a try!"

Stubborn silence. He tried again. "Perhaps we have a long way to go, and this is transportation for us? That stallion doesn't look as though he would let himself be ridden across a street for all the oats in Texas, but there are five mares and five of us adults ... and two of the little ones."

"Little pony for me!" Alan said, starting forward. Maisie grabbed him, and he exploded into screams, kicking and punching.

"Stop that!" Gillis barked and took him from Maisie. Alan's bellows became incandescent, and he turned purple, thrashing madly. "Cut that *out!*" his father roared. "Oh! Little *bastard!*"

His hand was streaming blood; Alan had bitten his thumb. Then he had squirmed from his father's weakened grip and was running towards the unicorns.

Ariadne and Maisie went after him, and the stallion roared his warning, dropped his horn, and started to move.

"Ariadne!" Jerry yelled. He rose also, and the huge white bulk rolled forward menacingly. "Come back! The stallion!"

Maisie and Ariadne stopped, looked at the obvious menace, then at Alan, and reluctantly retraced their steps. The stallion stopped and tossed his head angrily.

Alan reached the miniature unicorns and threw his arms around the smaller. The other nuzzled him, and he screamed with laughter, enthusiastically thumping the smaller on the ribs, probably to indicate affection. The unicorn was putting up with it, although its ears were flickering. He tried to mount and could not. The stallion whinnied, and the little beast reluctantly knelt down—head first like a cow, not as a horse would—and Alan scrambled onto its back.

Then the unicorn rose gently and started to pace around, while Alan kicked its ribs wildly and giggled with joy. The adults watched in astonishment.

"He's a born horseman," Gillis said proudly, sucking his thumb.

The stallion whinnied again, impatiently.

"Now Lacey?" Gillis asked.

"No!" Ariadne said, clutching at Jerry's arm.

"May I?" Lacey whispered.

"Be very careful," her father said. "If they point their horns at you, come back. They're not just ponies and they may not like you going close. Go slowly."

So it was slowly Lacey rose and slowly she stepped forward. All the unicorns watched her cautiously, but made no threatening move. Jerry kept his eyes mostly on the stallion, who was obviously in charge of this operation, and the stallion seemed to be more interested in watching the adults, which was a good sign. Then he heard a sigh of relief from his companions and turned his head, to see that Lacey had reached the two Shetland unicorns and had an arm over the larger's neck and was being in turn sniffed and nuzzled. Love at first sight. Virginity—try it some time!

Having established friendship, Lacey expertly leaned over, swung one leg up and jumped with the other, and was on the creature's back, squeaking with joy and excitement. The stallion kept his head up, merely uttering a brief snort, either approval or sympathy for a unicorn being so degraded. Lacey kicked her heels gently and was treated to a small circular journey. Yet it seemed to Jerry that the animal was making the decisions, not Lacey.

"This is incredible!" Ariadne said, but she had released Jerry's arm and seemed to be relaxing.

"Let me see if the mares will accept us," Jerry suggested. He took two steps, and the stallion dropped his horn again.

Alan and Lacey were still being shown how to ride unicorns. The two animals were performing a dance, trotting lightly around in a complicated circle and figure-eight routine, their tiny hooves flashing like diamonds. Alan was red-faced with excitement, Lacey more nervous, beginning to cast longing looks towards her father and Maisie. The children were clearly passengers now, not riders, and the ponies were training them.

"Totally incredible," Ariadne said. "Compared to this, even last night was plausible."

Trumpets again—the stallion issued a long and imperious whinny and flashed into motion, flowing off through the trees toward the foal and mare, his speed incredible and the ground trembling with the beat of his hooves. The mare spun around to move before he reached her, the foal cavorting after in a flurry of legs. Jerry turned his head to see the mares behind him starting a canter.

"No!" Ariadne and Graham shouted together. The unicorns were all moving now, even the two miniatures, with Alan and Lacey uttering loud screams and clinging fiercely to the manes. The herd left the roadway and thundered away through the trees, led by the stallion, with the two pony unicorns at the rear and the five adult humans in very cold pursuit, Maisie shouting vainly for Alan and Lacey to come back.

Jerry was fastest and led the pack, but the unicorns were traveling at many times his speed, and even so it was probably the ponies who were setting the pace. He knew that it was a ridiculous chase, but he had to try, panting along after the sound of hooves as the white shapes became indistinct in the wood, leaping and bounding over tussocks and fallen branches. Then the hoofbeats became fewer and stopped altogether. He reached the edge of the trees and a long grassy slope falling away before him to an edge that could be a steepening hillside or even the top of a cliff—and saw the whole herd in flight. They had not followed the land as it dropped; they had spread enormous white feathered wings and gone straight forward, out into the sky.

Beyond the edge lay distant blue sea, and high above it, gradually gaining height with the great stallion in the lead, outward and upward went the string of white winged horses, closely followed by the two winged ponies. And Lacey. And Alan.

❧ 11 ❧

AND THEN THERE WERE FIVE. . . .
  And then there was also a stupendous row. Ariadne blamed Graham, Graham blamed Jerry, Maisie blamed all of them. Carlo sat down on the grass and waited, thin brown arms on knees, until they settled it all. Jerry said almost nothing. He just stood there, his unshaven face weary and drawn, arms folded under his cape. Finally it began to penetrate to Ariadne that rage would accomplish nothing. She had been up and down too often—weeks of planning and scheming and then the escape with the children, and lately too many hours of hopes being raised and hopes being dashed—good brainwashing technique. She didn't think she could take any more. So she fell silent, choked back a temptation to burst into tears, and waited until Graham and Maisie came to their senses also.

Then there were five—first Killer, and then Lacey and Alan. Who was next?

At last there was silence.

"Have you all finished?" Jerry asked in that strange English drawl he now had. He got no reply. "Good show! Right, then, I agree that winged horses are a pagan symbol, Maisie, I agree that the unicorns did not have wings and therefore we were tricked, I agree that the children

135

are not qualified to fly horses at ten thousand feet—who is?—and I will even admit that I was not surprised when they were taken from us. I point out only that there is nothing we can do about it now, and also that it was the innocents who were removed, and therefore I still think it was a rescue and not a demonic plot."

"So now what?" Carlo demanded.

Jerry studied him for a moment and then turned to look at Graham. "You two chaps don't even need a shave, do you?" he said, and rubbed the gilt stubble on his own face. "Are you hungry?"

"Not especially," Graham said. "I could eat if you put it in front of me, but no, not really." Carlo shook his head.

"I thought as much," Jerry said. He turned without a word and strode back up the slope into the trees.

The others followed, shouting questions, and he pushed ahead angrily, ignoring them for a while. Finally, without slowing down he said, "As to where I am going —I am going back to the road in the hope that I may find Killer waiting there—if I can find the spot. As far as the shaving and hunger thing is concerned—well, never mind, it's only a guess, and my guesses aren't working too well."

Nevertheless, they all knew now that he had a better grasp on what was likely to happen in this looking-glass world than any of them did, and they were going to stick to him like paint.

Maisie in particular was having trouble with her footwear, with the sweater, and the children's discarded coats that she was clutching; they were constantly getting entangled in branches. Graham still had his suit coat over his arm and looked hot and angry, as did Carlo. Ariadne was discovering that her Meran outfit had astonishing versatility—it never snagged on thorns or attracted burrs, it showed no trace of the blood which had been splattered on it, and the soft felt boots seemed to be not only waterproof but also tough enough for any terrain.

In a small space among cypress trees, Jerry came to a stop and let the others catch up with him. He looked them over thoughtfully, and she decided he had just administered a small lesson—they were all out of breath and more docile.

"The road has gone," he said. "You noticed?"

"Perhaps we've been going in circles?" Maisie said and he shook his head.

"I've been keeping an eye on the sun. The vegetation is changing, too—drier and fewer trees. That frondy gray-green thing is an olive, I think." He pointed. "Mountains? They're new." Sure enough, rocky peaks glimmered far away and blue in the heat haze.

"So where do we go now?" Graham asked.

"Downhill. You may be all right, but I need food and water. People tend to live in valleys, not on hilltops."

He turned to go, and Ariadne put a hand on his arm. "Jerry," she pleaded, "explain this hunger thing. I'm not hungry either and I know I should be."

He looked very weary—the way they all should, after so long without food or drink since their solitary cup of coffee for breakfast. "I think you four have been put on hold," he said. "The men don't need a shave, and their bruises still look fresh and new—they aren't changing color."

"I don't understand," she said. It was all true, and she had not noticed until he mentioned it.

He was obviously worried and not saying everything he was thinking. "Neither do I, but I suspect you four are in a different category from me. It's as though judgment has been suspended: you could be put back in the real world at the time and place you left it and you wouldn't have changed." He pointed at Graham's pants. "Those bags of yours—they're frightfully filthy, but you haven't torn them at all. That's curious."

The others looked at one another, and there were no arguments except that Carlo said, "The hell I haven't changed," and put a hand to his face.

Jerry frowned and looked as guilty as Al caught with his hand in the cookie jar. Ariadne didn't think he need feel guilty—Carlo had deserved it.

"You and Graham were in the front seat, weren't you?" he asked. "Maisie, you were in the back?"

"What has that got to do with anything?" Graham demanded.

Jerry shrugged. "I told you, it's only a theory. But somewhere back in reality you have a car, probably wrapped around a fir tree. Front seat passengers often get facial damage, don't they?"

Graham snorted with derision. "You mean we wake up with mild concussion, and this is all a dream, like a fairy tale?"

Jerry flushed angrily. "I wouldn't count on it if I were you, but it might be one alternative. Have you another explanation for that chin of yours?"

He turned and set off down the hill without waiting for a reply.

Soon they were plodding down a rough little valley, its sides bearing a few oaks and what Ariadne thought might be chestnut trees. There was very little else except grass and a few animal droppings. There was no shade to shelter them from the cruel and scorching sun. The enchanted unicorn forest had been free of insects, but now hordes of flies had appeared, although they weren't bothering her much. If Jerry had been hoping to find a stream, he was being unlucky. They stumbled along and sweated, with Graham periodically shouting to Jerry to slow down for Maisie's sake, although the problem lay less with Maisie herself than with her impractical shoes; her legs were a good deal longer than Ariadne's—probably one of her qualifications for matrimony, she decided cattily. Far overhead floated a solitary hawk, or possibly a kite or a vulture.

Tiring of the others' grumpy silence, she moved forward beside Jerry and said, "Sorry."

"For what?" he asked.

"For being such a quarrelsome and ungrateful idiot," she replied. Then he had to apologize to her, and they had a conversation going. She learned how he had arrived in Mera, bailing out of a crippled bomber in a fog bank, low over the North Sea, drifting down through it and emerging in sunlight below... "not quite what I expected"... and settling gently on the grass outside the North Gate, where his now good friend Gervasse was waiting for him, asking what had happened to his balloon.

He pointed then to black dots on a patch of hillside visible over the valley wall. "Goats!" he said. "Notice how they're overgrazing everywhere? They're going to have a serious erosion problem here soon."

Then he edged her gently into her history, and she told him of music, scholarships, auditions, and then pregnancy and marriage; of motherhood and then another attempt at music; of her terminally ill marriage, of another pregnancy, of gin and divorce and gin and legal battles and gin. . . . "And, yes," she admitted, "everything Graham said last night was true. I got so I would do anything for the stuff. Fortunately I don't remember the worst bits."

The valley, now almost a gorge, took a sudden bend. He laid a hand on her arm to stop her and they waited for the others to catch up. She had not noticed, but he had been watching.

"There's a building ahead. I'll go on and scout, if you like, while you wait here."

She felt very uneasy at the thought of being separated from him; he seemed so much more competent than any of the rest of them. The others were feeling the same, frowning, and shaking their heads.

"Let's all stick together," she suggested, and everyone agreed. Jerry shrugged and then smiled.

"Reconnaissance in force, then," he said. "We'll all hang together."

Nevertheless, he went much more slowly. She felt—and probably they all did—horribly conspicuous in that bare valley below the empty blue sky. Finally they reached the building and could see that it was apparently deserted.

It stood at the base of a very steep slope, a small, flat-topped structure with a modern-artish sort of sculpture set on top of it and a walled enclosure in front, all built of massive gray stone blocks, the lower portions green and wet and slimy. In the center of the front wall a trickle of water ran from an algae-draped overflow into a trough where the turf had all been trampled away. From there a dry stream bed of pebbles trailed off down the valley. Without hesitation, Jerry leaned across the stinking trough and took a long drink.

"Ah!" he said, wiping his face with satisfaction. "The very best champagne! Next?"

Graham pulled his face and shook his head. "It smells like the runoff from a feed lot . . . not for me, thank you!" The others all seemed to agree, and Ariadne was certain that she did not want to taste that foul brew.

"There you are," Jerry said. "You're different; I needed that."

"Lord knows what you're going to catch from it, though," she said.

He smiled. "If I get back to Mera it won't matter—and I suspect that if I don't, it won't matter either." Champagne? It seemed to have put new life in him—his worried expression had turned to a half grin. He nodded up at the walls. "Let's explore," he said.

Steps halfway along the downstream side led up to a bronze gate and into a courtyard, most of which was occupied by a rectangular pool, the walkways around it being narrow and surrounded by low walls. The water was coated with patches of green slime and stank horribly.

"I wonder if the Department of Health inspects this?" Graham said. "You going to swim, too, Jerry?" Graham's attempts at humor were invariably forced and ponderous, but the truce was in effect.

Jerry grinned and said, "Not today, thank you. Any of you know what that is?"

He pointed to the main structure, at the hillside end. A low doorway led into darkness, a flight of stone steps in one corner led up to the roof, and on top of that was the free-form sculpture, one massive block of stone carved into two horns.

Silence.

"It's an altar," he said. "To the god of the spring—no, it would be a goddess, I think. They're called horns of consecration. Stay here, Ariadne."

He walked around the end of the court and paused momentarily to peer into the darkness of the doorway, pulled back and made a nose-pinching gesture to show that it stank, ran up the steps at the side to take a quick look at the altar, came down, and went around to stand on the opposite side of the pool from them. "Look at my reflection," he called. "What am I wearing?"

Magic again! There was Jerry in his wide green trousers and cape, with the silly cap on his head, standing on the side of the pool, while at his feet was his image—a darker-brown man with black hair hanging in ringlets and wearing only...

"A loin cloth and sandals," she said, while the men muttered curses and Maisie a prayer.

Jerry nodded, as though he had expected as much. "Can you see yourself, Ariadne?"

She peered over the edge and...Good God!

Jerry laughed, and she supposed she was blushing. "You want to come around here and show the others? Well, I'll describe it. A long red skirt, sort of conical, with a tight waist—that looks uncomfortable—and hoops of yellow on it. And a red bodice...tastefully supporting, but not concealing, the bosom."

She backed away from the revealing mirror quickly.

He walked over to the downstream end, where the overflow ran out, and sat down on the wall to study the view. The others joined him. Alongside the dry stream an obvious path led on down the valley, the road to the shrine from...from where?

"You look charming in it," he told her, smiling, and she stuck her tongue out at him.

He stared out at the winding, grassy valley and the path. "I'm starving!" he said. "There were some charred scraps of something nasty on that altar, but I'm not quite that hungry, yet. The building is to pen the livestock before sacrifice, I think—or else it's the slaughterhouse. It certainly smells bad enough for anything."

"Just a minute," Graham said, giving him a suspicious look. "You recognize that costume?"

Jerry nodded and said nothing until they pestered him further.

"All right, then," he said. "You know by now that these clothes are a faerie disguise—Ariadne and I look like natives in them, no matter where we are. None of us here can see that, because we all believe in Mera, but our reflections show what others would see. And yes, I think I know who wore those bare-breasted dresses. It fits."

"Then where are we?" she asked.

"Well, obviously we're not in the real world," he said. "Not with flying horses around. This whole adventure has had a Greek flavor to it. Perhaps that was Killer's influence, because Killer dominates anything he touches, so it may have been he who brought the demon in that particular shape last night; or it may have been you, Ariadne."

Of course she should have thought of that. "My name, you mean?" she asked, and he nodded. Why was he so cheerful again?

"Whichever of you it was, we haven't escaped from that myth influence, obviously."

Winged horses were a Greek legend, also.

"So this is Greece?" asked Graham.

Jerry shook his head. "It isn't any real place—if we'd had dragons last night, instead of what we got, then we would be in the equivalent of King Arthur's Britain, I think, or the Black Forest of dwarfs and elves, or the Sweden of Beowulf and Grendel. But on those terms . . . no, it isn't Greece, it's Crete."

"Why Crete?"

"Because that's where the Minotaur lived."

They sat on the wall in silence for a moment.

"What's that?" Maisie asked nervously.

"What came last night," Jerry said. "A bull's head and a man's body. Greek legend. It lived in the Labyrinth at Knossos, in Crete, and it ate human flesh."

"But didn't some Greek kill the Minotaur?" Graham demanded.

"Certainly," Ariadne said. "Theseus. He had help from the daughter of King Minos; she gave him a ball of gold thread to find his way out of the Labyrinth. I know that story."

Maisie and Carlo looked bewildered.

"Her name was Ariadne," Jerry said, chuckling. "So

maybe it was Ariadne who brought the Minotaur shape, or Killer fancies himself as Theseus, or else the senior demon who handles Meran affairs is most comfortable as the Minotaur. He takes other forms. He probably has a million names, but Asterios is one of them and Asterios was the name of the Minotaur. We didn't escape last night. Ariadne sent him away mad, but we're still in his power. Just be very glad that Alan and Lacey were rescued, right?"

"But if the Minotaur was killed by Theseus..." Graham argued.

"And St. George slew the dragon. But it was the Minotaur who came last night."

"Then what the hell do we do now?" Carlo demanded.

"You..." Ariadne said, staring at him, then at Jerry. "You two have lost your accents!"

Jerry grinned. "You've noticed? And someone has sacrificed a ham sandwich on the altar."

Men! Kids' games! A range of a quarter of a mile, he has said—she glanced around the empty landscape and then looked hard at the oblong building. Jumping up from the wall, she marched along the side of the pool to the doorway.

"Come out of there, Killer!" she said.

He came stooping through the low door and then straightened, blinking in the sunlight and grinning at the same time. Strangely, he was not wearing a Meran outfit, only a short beige loin cloth with a white wand hanging swordlike at one side of his belt and a dagger at the other. The next thing she noticed was his deep tan, replacing the hideous marble pallor of his coma. Then his face—the crushed nose had healed and, as Jerry had said, it was not a bad nose at all, high-bridged and straight. Her father's nose had looked somewhat like that, and Alan had it, a Greek nose.

"Well, are you a sight for sore eyes!" she said.

He beamed at her. "Old friends should greet with a kiss," he replied, advancing with his hands out.

Damn! She had forgotten that side of Killer. Instinctively she backed away, but she had also forgotten the pool behind her. Air under her foot... her arms flailed

... in a flash Killer's hand shot out and clutched the front of her cape, and then held her, sloped helplessly backwards over that filthy water.

His eyes gleamed with delight. "Now certainly it is worth a kiss!" he said.

He wouldn't! Yes, he would ... she could see it in that devilish grin. If she refused he would open those fingers, and down she would go; he would not hesitate at all.

She grabbed his wrist, and he tilted her further backwards; one push would do it.

"A small one, then," she agreed.

Effortlessly he pulled her upright, gripped her with an arm like the clutch of a backhoe—then another arm like another backhoe—and deliberately crushed all the air out of her lungs before pushing his mouth down on hers. There was no such thing as a small kiss to Killer, obviously, or a short one.

"Cut that out, Killer!" Jerry roared somewhere nearby.

But Killer had his eyes shut and was too busy to listen; he was clearly not going to stop until she responded, so she responded. His teeth were all healed, she discovered.

Finally he released her, and she staggered, bewildered, half-suffocated, and aware that she had just been kissed by an expert. He guided her away from the pool edge, appraising her reaction with obvious satisfaction before turning to Jerry, who returned the hug, turning his face away. Then they thumped each other on the back enthusiastically and finally stepped back for a careful study.

"Very careless, friend, not to search more carefully," Killer said, teasing.

Jerry was smiling ear to ear. "I knew from the smell that you were in there," he said. Killer was back, and all was right with the world again.

Killer swung round to the others. "The very beautiful Maisie—do you also greet old friends with a kiss?"

"No, she doesn't!" Graham snapped.

"Citizen Gillis!" Killer said and stared him down without another word. "And Citizen Carlo? You have had an accident, I see. Could that perhaps have been my friend Jerry losing his temper?"

He flashed a questioning grin at Jerry, which grew wider as he saw the shamed reaction. True, he was the much-desired rescue, but he was dominating them all by sheer impudence. He turned back to Carlo, who was standing, hands on hips, seeming relaxed, but also ready to leap if necessary, his swollen face guarded. He dangled his leather jacket by one finger and in his sleeveless shirt he was a sapling by Killer's massive oak tree.

And why was Killer wearing local costume instead of a Meran outfit? Because he thought he looked good in a loin cloth?

"I have a score to settle with Citizen Carlo," Killer murmured.

"Hold it, Killer !" Jerry said. "We have a truce just now—I promised you would settle no scores yet."

"Oh, you did?" Killer found that amusing.

"Yes, I did."

"Ah, well, perhaps this is not the time. When we get to Mera, then. It will be something for us both to look forward to, no?"

Carlo made an offensive gesture.

Killer's eyebrows went up. "Oh? You wish to be friends?"

"I don't think that's what he meant, Killer," Jerry said.

Killer was studying Carlo thoughtfully, and Carlo was holding his stare. "Who knows what he meant? Well, we shall see."

He glanced around them all once more, and his amusement died away. He put his head on one side and looked up at Jerry. "You sent me back, friend. I am very grateful. But the Oracle is not pleased with you."

Jerry flushed under his stubble. "I didn't think it would be. You have come to take us back, though?"

"No," Killer said sadly. "You have made a terrible screw up, Jerry friend. I can not."

Ariadne's heart fell through the ground, and she saw the shock ripple around the other faces.

"Come!" Killer said. "It is a long story. Let us sit

down." He walked past Carlo to the stairs and went up two steps before sitting down. That put him higher than anyone else could be, and she wondered how conscious that action was, if it was merely a reflex from centuries of manipulating people. But Graham could play those games, also, and he eased Maisie over to the wall and sat there—that was the second best spot. Carlo slouched a few steps and dropped cross-legged in front of the stairs; Jerry was about to join him, but Ariadne slipped a hand on his arm and said, "Here is fine." So the two of them sat down where they were, well to the side of the steps.

Killer innocently leaned back on his elbows, parted his knees, and glanced around to see who was interested. She had half expected that—now she was getting to know Killer, and he was a shameless exhibitionist. Jerry noticed and gave her a glance that was half disgust and half thanks.

"Now," Killer said, enjoying the attention. "We must exchange stories—the Oracle did not tell me everything. The first thing I knew was when I was being carried into the hospital by Sven and Ethelfird." He looked meaningfully at Carlo. "There was much pain for a couple of days."

Carlo shrugged and said nothing.

"By the end of the second day," Killer said, "my friend Jerry had not come to see me, so I went to see the Oracle. I was doubled over like Sisyphus, Jerry—you would have laughed to see me." He did not look as though he found it funny.

"But the Oracle would not see me—there was no one there. So I went back the next day, and still there was no one."

Jerry nodded but did not speak.

Killer waved away flies—the place was thick with them. "The next morning I felt much better and when Clio came to see me I took her into bed and found that I was fit for duty again. So I went to see the Oracle once more. It said that you have loused up, Jerry." He shook his head in exasperation. "You invited the demon in!"

"No!" Jerry barked. "Oh, damn! Yes, I did." He looked in dismay at Ariadne. "I told you its name!"

Killer shook his head. "You had two children with you."

Jerry looked indignant. "I didn't know that made any difference!"

"Neither did I," Killer said. "Your friend Gervasse did not either and he got very excited when I told him. All the philosophers are twittering like starlings over it."

"Where are my children?" shouted Graham, before Ariadne could ask the same question.

Killer shrugged. "I do not know. The Oracle said that they made a difference—they could not go to Mera, but Asterios could not have them either. It seems they are sacrosanct, like Delphi."

Graham looked at Maisie, who smiled and nodded. Then he glanced over to Ariadne, and they smiled at each other. It was a long time since that had happened.

"But the Oracle would say no more about them," Killer said. "I do not see them. . . . Where are they?"

Jerry explained, and Killer was impressed. "Then they must be safe," he said. "I told little Lacey that dreams came true, and she got her flying pony!" He waved at the bugs again; they all were being pestered except Jerry and Ariadne, whose Meran clothes were apparently insect-repellent.

"So if I hadn't been such a bloody idiot as to say Asterios' name during a siege, then we should have been safe?" Jerry demanded.

Killer shrugged. "The Oracle did not exactly say that, but it implied it. And it did not tell me what else happened."

"You tell us what is going to happen next, then we'll bring you up to date," Jerry said angrily.

"If you wish." Killer gave Jerry a rueful smile. "I can't take you back. The Oracle did not even wish me to come and see you. You know I like fights, friend, but not with the Oracle. But I argued! You see, you have issued an invitation. If you go back to Mera, then Asterios can come also."

Jerry hung his head and muttered curses. Ariadne put an arm around him.

"What about the rest of us?" Graham asked.

"Damn flies!" Killer said. "The rest of you don't matter. I mean, you don't count in this battle. It is between Asterios and Jerry, now—or between Asterios and Mera. I asked the Oracle about you; it said, 'Their fate will be decided also.'"

Jerry was staring at Killer with horror and, beneath his tan and his stubble, he was pale. She could feel him shiver. "You mean I have to fight the Minotaur?"

Killer hesitated and then smiled, lording it over them from his perch, smiling a perfect set of teeth in a nearly handsome boyish face, spoiled only by that one red scar. "Well . . . you know where you are?" he asked.

"Near Knossos?"

Killer nodded, but that had surprised him. "I was told not to let you go any closer than this until you make your decision. You have a choice, friend Jerry—two ways to go. But both ways lead to the Labyrinth." He seemed genuinely sympathetic.

Jerry gulped. "I am to be Theseus and kill the Minotaur? That doesn't sound very likely, does it? It was still around for him to kill, and we can't both kill it."

Ariadne hoped that if he had to be Theseus, she did not have to be the Ariadne of the legend.

"Perhaps you both can kill it," Killer said. "This is not the real Crete, and probably Theseus' was not either, right? It is a fake, like the cottage, a false Knossos made by Asterios-the-demon for another Asterios-the-Minotaur. Let me tell you what the Oracle said about the Labyrinth. It is an amphitheater. The people can watch. The Minotaur lives in a sort of shed in the middle, and there are walls around it."

"A maze."

"Right. So they put the sacrificial victims down in the maze, and the Minotaur comes out of its shed and hunts them around the maze until it catches them."

"Good God!" Graham said, and they all exchanged horrified glances. "Public spectacle? And then it eats them?"

"It depends how hungry it is," Killer said. Even he looked disgusted, and Ariadne thought it would take a lot to disgust Killer. "Sometimes it plays with them first, the Oracle says."

She thought of the horror in the cottage. "You mean it rapes the women, I suppose?"

"I don't know," Killer said. "Perhaps it rapes both women and men. Perhaps it likes to bite pieces off and then let them run some more. Maybe it tosses them on its horns. The Oracle just said that it likes to play with its victims. The people—the priests and Minos, the king—prefer to put in more than one sacrifice at a time; it is more fun, watching them all run around and laying bets on what the Minotaur will do. It takes three days to eat up a body."

She felt so nauseated that she thought she might be physically ill. The others looked no better.

Jerry licked his lips and made an obvious effort to stay calm. "Who are these victims?" he asked.

"Anyone they can get," Killer said. "The Oracle said that if you were captured, as strangers, then you would be sent to the Labyrinth." He smiled faintly. "You have two choices. One is to kill the monster, but there is another. You issued an invitation, but if you can get into the Minotaur's house, then you cancel out the invitation."

"Oh, bull!" Graham said angrily. "Silly games!"

"Faerie has its own logic," Jerry said. "And that's more logical than some things. You mean this shed in the middle of the Labyrinth?"

Killer nodded. "Your door to Mera is in the Minotaur's lair. All of you."

"All of us?" echoed two or three voices, and he nodded once more.

"Either way, you all go to the Labyrinth. You are trapped in Asterios' web and you will be drawn in, sooner or later. I am sorry, my friends!" He looked it, too. "I did not make these rules and I talked very hard to get the Oracle to agree even to this meeting."

"If silver bullets from an automatic rifle won't penetrate the Minotaur's hide," she asked, "then what will?"

He shrugged. "That was the demon. This Minotaur may be only a monster."

Ariadne wished she knew Killer a little better—his eyes seemed restless; she thought he was beginning to lie, or at least was not telling everything. Jerry was so downcast, staring at the paving stones in front of his crossed legs, that he did not seem to be paying much attention.

"Technology doesn't work," Jerry growled. "So it would have to be a sword."

"Not even steel," Killer said. "This is Bronze Age; I brought a silver sword, which might do a little better. Old Venker made it specially, but it took him three weeks. Three weeks!"

For a moment Jerry managed a smile. "You're in better shape than I've seen you in years. No fighting for three whole weeks?"

"Nor wrestling, nor boxing..." Killer scowled. "The girls seem to like it." Ariadne wondered what the boys thought—a Killer deprived of his usual brawling would likely have been the butt of much banter.

Jerry had gone back into his depression. "I wish I were a better man with a sword.... So we go into the Labyrinth, and then I either fight the monster or try to get past it in the maze and into its den?"

"Not that simple," Killer said. "This wand will send you there—all of you—if you wish. But the Minotaur will smell the faerie at once, and the demon part will come and it will know what you are trying to do. It will stay in its house until night. It can hunt by smell, you know, or the demon will sense where you are. It will not let you past."

Jerry muttered oaths and glanced despairingly at Ariadne. She hoped her smile of encouragement did not look too false.

"The other way," Killer said, "is just to stay here. There is a procession on its way to the shrine for a ceremony and there are soldiers with the priests. They will be here in an hour or so. Then you will be put in the Labyrinth, and the Minotaur will not suspect—it will think you are an ordinary banquet, so you will be dealing only with the beast, not the demon, or so the Oracle says. But if I give you a sword, you will be disarmed, of course."

Jerry scrambled to his feet and walked away to the far side of the pool.

"Let ourselves be captured?" Graham said. "How do we know that we'll all be put in the Labyrinth and not turned into galley slaves and concubines?"

Killer waited for Jerry to come wandering back, then said, "The Oracle told me, 'They will not be badly treated, because sacrifices are holy, and they will all go in together. It is rare sport to have five captives at once.' If the Oracle says so, then it is so."

Jerry folded his arms under his cloak and stared bleakly at Killer. "Did it say whether we can succeed?"

Again that faint shadow of deceit crossed Killer's face. . . .

"It said that you are probably not a good enough swordsman. And it said that the other way at least some of you should be able to get past and reach the center of the maze. Should, not will."

Then he twisted round to face Ariadne—and give her a chance to peer up his loin cloth if she wanted. She was so annoyed that she almost missed what he was saying. "The Oracle said that you could help."

"Me?" she said blankly.

"Yes. Like the other Ariadne, Theseus' Ariadne. It said that if Jerry wants to go by daylight, then Ariadne will help." He shrugged.

"A ball of thread? Why would that help if all we want to do is get to the middle? Theseus used the thread to come back out."

He shook his head apologetically. "It wouldn't say more. I brought a ball of twine for you, but I don't understand either."

Jerry looked around the others. "What do the rest of you think? Do we go with fire, and sword, and faerie to fight the demon or do we try to sneak by the monster as innocent sacrifices?"

No one wanted to speak first, but then Carlo looked up and said, "I like to see what I'm doing. I don't like the dead-of-night scat." A mean look came into his face, and

he added, "Why fight when you can get what you want
by other means?"

Graham put on the pompous expression that meant he
was going to lecture someone on responsibilities. He
said. "How can you hesitate? Obviously you take a
sword and fight it like a man. The other way you will be
surrendering to whatever the local authorities choose to
do with you—that's crazy." Maisie nodded in loyal
agreement.

Jerry looked at Ariadne. She was thinking of the
monster in the doorway—the gloating, the triumph, the
strength, and the grotesquely exaggerated maleness.
Would it not be better to try to outwit a monster than
fight a demon? And anything was preferable in daylight.

"I think I agree with Carlo," she said.

He nodded and turned to Killer. "No silver swords,
then. Christians to the lions."

At least lions did not rape their victims first—or was
that during?

Killer looked pleased—why? "My friend," he said. "I
would come with you if I could, but the Oracle made me
promise." He might be worried that Jerry would doubt
his courage. He hesitated as though about to say something more, and then did not.

"I'd rather you didn't," Jerry said gruffly. "I have
enough on my conscience."

Killer nodded sadly, then put a hand on the step and
vaulted sideways, landing almost at the doorway. "I have
local clothes for you," he said and vanished inside.

Jerry slouched over the wall and leaned on it, gazing
glumly at the green-brown hillside. Ariadne joined him.

"Jerry?" she asked quietly. "Are you quite sure that
you can trust Killer?"

He looked at her sideways, bleakly. "We must trust
him."

"It's just that I thought he looked shifty, there at the
end."

Jerry shook his head and turned away. Then he said,
"No. Trust is a funny thing, Ariadne. He would steal his
best friend's wife or help himself to anything he fancies
and he likes dangerous practical jokes, like bricks on top

of doors, but those are Meran things—they don't matter there. But he wouldn't betray me. Not Outside. Never."

She was not satisfied. "He wasn't lying at the end?"

"No," Jerry said, and sighed. "He was lying all the way through. Almost nothing he said was the truth. That's why we have to trust him."

❧ 12 ❧

T*HE CROWD ROARED* ...
     Ariadne stood on the platform, a bronze rail in front of her, facing an amphitheater under a blistering furnace of a sun, wearing nothing.

It couldn't possibly be happening to her.

But it was.

Fortunately, she was drunk.

Three days in a dungeon had been bad enough. Three days in a dungeon with Maisie ... no, that wasn't fair. She'd been very, very glad of Maisie's company, and each had consoled the other. It would have been much worse alone, and there could have been worse people to share a dungeon with. Not really a bad kid, Maisie, short on brains, but well-meaning. She'd been cursed with an incredible body in what was still—this was twentieth century reality she was thinking of now, not this legendary Bronze Age fantasy—still a man's world and had managed to handle that problem well enough to be still a virgin when she got Graham to the altar, which was certainly more than she, Ariadne, had managed. Not a bad kid, just not good enough or old enough to be mother to Lacey and Alan; she was certainly welcome to Graham.

The primping and preening ... after three days in that dungeon, they'd been dragged out before dawn, taken to a sort of bathhouse, and there been groomed by a team of giggling female slaves—deloused, bathed, then dried and rubbed until they glowed, and massaged with warm oil so scented with poppy that it had made her head swim, but had felt great. Their hair had been curled with hot bronze tools, the blond locks being treated as one of the wonders of the world, although their shortness was obviously regarded as scandalous. Their eyes, lashes, and brows had been painted with black stuff, their toenails and fingernails varnished, and their nipples rouged. That should have warned her about the dress requirements. Then wreaths of flowers had been braided into their hair. She had expected the fancy garments to appear then.

They had put a coat of blue paint on her breasts and green paint on Maisie's—much more paint—and a matching stripe on their backs, and that had been it. She had a vague idea why they were different colors and she did not want to think about it.

Drunk, but not her fault. Just drunk enough to keep her from fainting from terror.

The amphitheater was as big as some football stadiums she'd seen, made all of stone. Squinting against the sunlight, she ignored the center itself and looked at the stands. The place was not full, but there were several thousand people there. Curiously, there were no seats; each level seemed to be flanked by a low wall, which would stop people falling into the row in front, of course, but it seemed a strange way to watch a show. Many spectators were sitting on those dividers, but that meant they had to twist around to see what was going on down in the arena itself.

After the bath and beauty treatment, Maisie and she had been taken to another room and offered a meal of four or five dishes that they had hardly touched. The platters themselves had been incredible, solid gold plate so embossed with intricate designs that she had been tempted to throw the contents on the floor just to be able to admire the artwork. But the food had not appealed— salt fish, something that was probably sliced octopus, and a sort of grain mash like the stuff she fed to chickens. After a few sample mouthfuls she had decided that they were all spiced to heaven and heavily salted, and their purpose, therefore, must be to make them drink, so she had pushed them all away and warned Maisie.

That had provoked vast consternation and whispered discussion among all the slaves and the fancily dressed women who were probably priestesses. There had been long harangues, then, in the gibberish language, and even threats, and gestures that they must drink and eat, especially drink. When they still refused, several butch-type female slaves had been brought in, and a large funnel produced. The threat had been obvious, and so both had yielded and drunk as required—two drafts apiece from enormous gold goblets almost too heavy to lift.

So she was off the wagon, and the world had a familiar, enjoyable vagueness to it again. Lousy wine. And the volume! She needed to go again already, but perhaps that was nerves.

The crowd roared.... She half turned in time to see Maisie being brought out and marched up to stand beside her at the rail, facing the amphitheater, blinking in the sunlight, and bombed to the earlobes.

Ariadne gave Maisie a grin to cheer her up. "Wave to the nice people," she said, "and see what happens." She hadn't dared—she was too crushed by her nakedness before this huge throng.

Maisie stuck out her dainty chin. "And why not?" she said. She was drunk and in the past she had won beauty contests wearing little more than this; so she threw up her arms in a salute. That sort of gesture made Maisie bounce spectacularly. *The crowd roared....*

They hadn't been badly treated by the standards of the Bronze Age; not by the standards of the squalid little farms and the dingy, filthy streets she'd seen, or the monstrous half-built megalithic walls of the palace which meant massive public works being done at the wrong ends of whips. They'd been arrested by soldiers with shields and bronze swords and helmets shaped like colanders. These brown young men in leather kilts had been fascinated by the sight of blond women and unable to resist looking to see if that sort of hair was present elsewhere, but had behaved themselves reasonably well otherwise under the watchful eye of a five-star general in gold armor who wore a helmet made of boars' tusks. Jerry had become absurdly excited over that helmet—indeed, over the whole procedure—and either he was incredibly brave, or had tremendous faith in the Oracle, or he was just plain crazy.

She could use a shot of gin to take away the taste of the wine. Why the wine, anyway?

Why had the Oracle said that she could help? The ball of twine that Killer had given her had gone with all their other possessions—with rings and rosary and earrings—and, anyway, twine would only be useful for coming back out, which they were supposed not to need to do, if you believed what Killer said the Oracle said.

Maisie hiccuped and giggled and waved to the crowd again.

Ariadne forced her eyes down to look at the Labyrinth and saw the small stone roof in the center, the Minotaur's pen—one flat slab in the middle of a great expanse of rectangular walls. There was a very low doorway on this side of it, facing towards the royal box, the top of the doorway just visible to her over the top of the first wall in front of it. Even as she first looked, something crawled out of that door and stood up.

The crowd roared . . . the Minotaur! A wave of dread and nausea swept over her, and she gripped the bronze railing tightly and fought down a throbbing blackness that threatened to wash her away in that wave. Was that what the wine had been for then, to keep the victims from fainting with terror? A mercy?

She had looked away and now she forced her eyes back to it—just what she had seen in the cottage, except that if it was truly as large as that, then this place was even more huge than she had thought. It was yawning and stretching like a man waking from sleep, except no human being had ever had arms like that, perhaps no gorilla ever had. It was not unlike a gorilla, either, with the thick black hair over the front of its body, its arms and shoulders and chest far out of proportion to the legs.

But it would need those shoulders to support the gigantic bull's head, that bestial black muzzle with the black horns curving upwards and outwards.

Asterios the Minotaur had heard the crowd noise and was emerging to see what was for breakfast.

But where were the men?

They'd been separated that first night in the village and transported in separate carts to the city, thrown into separate dungeons. Ariadne had not seen or spoken to Jerry, Carlo, or Graham for three days. Perhaps they had gone earlier? No, Killer had said three days to eat a body.

She saw bones. The roadways between the innumerable walls were black dirt, and there were bones protruding from it in places. Directly below her—about twenty feet down, maybe—she could see a shattered skull, half-buried in dark slime.

She swung around, turned her back on the Minotaur, and looked at the rows of spectators behind her and the front of the royal box directly above. She could not see the occupants, or if King Minos was present, but she could catch a glimpse of a guard at each front corner, in those strange helmets, like pineapples made of boars' teeth. A type of helmet described in Homer, Jerry had said, and dug up at some site in Greece—so what? Below the box was the door from the players' dressing rooms, and there was Jerry, naked as a newborn, with flowers in his hair and two soldiers prodding him on with spears.

He had an all-over tan, she noticed, and his breasts . . . sorry, sir, pectorals . . . had been painted yellow to match his hair.

It was foolish to be embarrassed at a time like this, but Ariadne turned around to face the arena again as he emerged from the tunnel, and *the crowd roared*. Third victim, ladies and gentlemen, in today's gala presentation. 5—count them—5!

It was good to see him again, though. Maisie was all right, but now she wanted male support. Three days with Maisie, trying to make conversation in the semidarkness of a tiny stone cellar, sparsely furnished with straw that was itself well furnished with lice, staring at a rank bucket and the inevitable bowl of beans and jug of water which was all they had been fed—they were fortunate that neither of them had felt any real desire to eat or drink. They had talked of the children and the things they had said or done. Ariadne had rambled on about Lacey's great future in music, and Maisie had nodded and not truly understood. They had even talked of Graham, and it seemed his sex life was much the same as before, just as insatiable and inconsiderate as ever. But if Maisie enjoyed being a trampoline, that was her business...and perhaps she, herself, had found it flattering or something when she was that age.

Brown-tanned, yellow-breasted, Jerry staggered up and put an arm around her shoulders, then lumbered into the rail, and came to a stop. He looked freshly shaven, oiled, and smelled of poppy as she did, and his yellow hair had been curled. What would Killer say if he could see him now?

"Shgood shee yuh," he said, with difficulty. Oh no! He was almost too drunk to stand.

"They got you too, did they?" she said angrily.

He tried to focus on her, without much success. "Coarsh! Woodnt tushit. Foarshd ush." His mouth and throat were bruised, so there had been a struggle.

She turned to Maisie in dismay. She had not expected that the men would have been liquored up, also. She herself was happy and slightly dizzy, but the soberest of the three of them. It took a lot more than two goblets of that watery wine to get *her* sloshed. Jerry was having trouble standing upright. Drunk as a lord; they must have poured gallons into him—why? Just to slow him down? Killer had said it was a sort of national sport, the Minotaur stakes. Why slow the runners?

The Oracle had said that Ariadne could help. Well, she was an alcoholic, and the others were not. She would not be capable of driving a car, but perhaps only she would be capable of doing anything at all. She thought she could probably carry Maisie, or perhaps drag a staggering Jerry, but certainly the others must fend for themselves.

Why this enforced drunkenness? Was it only a kindness or was there some other purpose? Were sober victims a threat to the Minotaur?

The crowd roared. She turned to look at the tunnel, but there was no sign of the other two. She looked into the Labyrinth and saw the cause of the excitement—the Minotaur was taking a pee. Big deal.

Then came a louder roar, and she turned once more to see Graham reeling out of the tunnel ahead of the guards. The applause was halfhearted; evidently the spectators disapproved of big ones—slow runners? Much to her surprise, she felt sorry for him. His second marriage was doing him no good—he was developing a paunch. He was huge and hairy and the top of his chest was painted black, about the only color they could have used on him. He looked pathetic and rather hideous. He hit the rail beyond Maisie and doubled over. For an instant she thought he was going to topple straight down into the Labyrinth, but he was merely throwing up. That might help, if it got rid of some of the wine.

Poor Graham—the end of a promising career in crooked law. He had at first refused to come on this crazy surrender mission, arguing that it would be better to flee off to the hills, or perhaps to the other side of the island to build a boat. He had declined to remove his twentieth-century clothes until Killer had drawn his dagger; and he had finally come with the rest, bringing the obedient Maisie, only because he had known that the two of them could not survive in the wilds and were better off clutching at the thin straw Killer offered than drowning without it.

They had been a strange company, trekking down the valley in their simple wraps and loin cloths towards arrest and captivity. Jerry had looked all right—not bad at all, actually—and probably she and Maisie had been passable. Carlo's extreme skinniness had seemed unhealthy, although he was a wholesome brown color; but Graham in a loin cloth had been only marginally less ridiculous than Graham now in a wreath of flowers, his tan ending at his neck and elbows, hairy, out of shape, and flabby. Fortunately their strange on-hold suspension had also made them immune to sunburn, or they

would all, except Carlo, have been broiled that day.
Jerry's tan had proved adequate, although he had become badly dehydrated.

The crowd roared.... The Minotaur was moving. It
strolled away along the side of its pen and vanished behind it.

Coming to inspect the goods! Her knees wavered, and
her hands started to shake horribly. If it got here before
they were thrown in, then it would be waiting down
there for them....

Then the roar grew even greater and Carlo came reeling out, his chest smeared with white. Tremendous ova-
tion! She wondered if that was because he looked more
like a runner than the rest of them? Or because he was so
skinny that the Asterios would leave him till last? He
blundered into the rail beyond Jerry and shook his head
a few times.

Asterios had appeared again, coming towards her, one
wall away from its pen now, and the crowd was beginning to get excited. Up in the royal box, someone was
singing a hymn.

How far did Asterios have to walk?

Did the monster know the correct way? Did it have
the intelligence of a man or of a bull or of something in
between, she wondered, and decided even a bull could
probably learn the route in time, or follow it by scent.

Carlo belched and sagged to the ground. Two soldiers
came forward and hoisted him to his feet again, leaned
him against the rail. "F'off," he muttered and closed his
eyes.

"Get a grip on yourself!" she whispered urgently.
"We've got to do some running soon."

Eyes still closed, he spoke out of the corner of his
mouth, forming the words carefully. "I'm not as pissed
as I look."

That was bad. Anyone who thought that was usually a
lot drunker.

The Minotaur had turned a corner and was moving,
presumably, across her line of sight; she could not see it
when it was going that way. There was movement in the
crowd, and suddenly she understood why there were no

seats in this amphitheater—the spectators would move around to keep watch on the players! Those Labyrinth walls were about ten feet high, pointed on top, and even the huge Minotaur was only visible to someone looking along the length of whatever walkway it was in.

"Ariadne," said Maisie, who had been trying to hold a conversation with Graham without success, "why are we all color coded?"

"I don't know, dear," she lied. Obviously it was for gambling—ten talents on the white to be last to die; four talents that he rapes the blue before the green. . . .

Then the Minotaur appeared briefly, coming through a gap in a wall and then continuing on in the same direction as before.

Oh my God! That was how she could help—that was why they had all been doped! She could figure out this infernal Labyrinth! Without that information they would be running blind with a fifty-fifty chance of error at every branching, while the Minotaur probably knew every stone in the walls. And the men had been drugged more heavily because she and Maisie were only women and therefore too stupid to worry about. From here she could see the whole thing. The monster had come out and turned right and then it must have turned left and then . . .

She shook her head to try to clear it. That wouldn't work! She would never be able to remember the sequence and then reverse it so that they could know the order they would need; and she hadn't watched to see if it had bypassed any turns. . . .

The monster's pen faced towards her, and she could see that there was a wall all the way around it, with a gap in the far side . . . but the walkway didn't go all the way around. If the monster had turned left from its door it would have met a blocking cross wall.

"Wash th'ell shappening?" demanded Jerry, swaying and looking as though he might be going to throw up also.

"Shut up, I'm thinking!" she snapped. Then . . . "You feel like puking?"

He nodded miserably.

"Then do it! Stick a finger down your throat."

She went back to studying the Labyrinth, catching a glimpse of the Minotaur heading away from her in the distance, its horns just visible over a wall.

Concentric boxes . . . the pen in the middle and a group of concentric boxes, each one having a single gateway through it, none of them opposite another, so far as she could see. Nine boxes? Count again. Ten. No! Nine it was. The opening to the first one was at the far side, so to get to the middle, if you started from just below her, you went . . . right—the left way led to a dead end just around the far corner. The next gateway you went . . . remember you're coming this way, so reverse hands . . . left? No, right again.

The hymn had ended, the crowd was beginning to shout for blood in one continuous roar. And there was the Minotaur, three walls away from its pen now, standing looking towards her, studying the situation—counting its breakfast, if it could count to five—seeing how the ceremony was coming on. Then it started to move again, faster now, striding along like a man out walking a dog.

A troop of guards holding short swords came running out of the tunnel into the prisoners' enclosure, and the din increased once more.

Right, right, left . . .

Right . . .

She would never remember a list of nine of them, or would it be ten? Did nine walls make ten walkways? No, nine gates were what mattered.

Jerry threw up disgustingly over the rail, and she ignored him. Graham had sunk to the ground and passed out. Maisie was weeping.

She needed a pencil and paper. . . .

The soldiers had raised a bronze plate from the floor, exposing a shaft.

She needed a notebook. She had nothing except a wreath of flowers. Pull petals? He loves me, he loves me not. She had fingernails—could she scratch the initials into her arm?

Better than that—she had this Bronze-Age fingernail

polish! It wasn't very hard, probably just a wax since it had been hot when they put it on her. It would rub off on the rail easily—scratch for right, no scratch for left.

Start with the right pinkie, scratch. Next finger, scratch again. Right, right . . .

She found the third wall, found the gap in it, traced it around—walking on the inside, remember—left that time. Fourth finger, fourth wall . . .

The guards dragged Graham over to the shaft and dropped him in, keeping a screaming Maisie back with their swords, while the crowd booed and booed: too much wine. Graham came shooting out in the Labyrinth below Ariadne, right where Jerry had just vomited— tough. Fifth wall . . .

Maisie shrieked horribly, was drowned out by the crowd, and vanished into the shaft, thumping into Graham's prostrate form below. Left thumb.

She was next!

She ducked quickly past Jerry and Carlo. Where was she? Left thumb . . .

Jerry went quietly, not staggering too much, but she hardly noticed until she heard him below her, pulling Graham out of the way.

Seventh wall . . .

Carlo was next. He paused at the top of the shaft, waved to the crowd, and got an ear-hurting roar, while the soldiers stood back and grinned. Then he made a grab for one of them, but they were too quick for him, or else his reflexes were slowed by the wine. But the crowd cheered once more as he was tossed roughly and head-first into the shaft. So he truly was more sober than he had pretended—sneaky!

Eighth wall . . . and she had no more time. The soldiers did not drive her with their swords—hands were more fun. For a moment she almost squirmed loose, oily and slick with the sweat of fear, but then she, too, was dropped into blackness. She shot down a long, greasy, bronze slide and out into the corridor below, with its stench and unspeakable filth. The hatch cover clanged shut above her.

A loud buzzing next to her ears . . . ugh! Obviously no

one ever came into the Labyrinth to clean; the floor was thick with excrement and rotted flesh and offal, crawling with insects. Her stomach heaved, and she scrambled hastily to her feet, coated with the disgusting ooze and standing ankle-deep in it, brushing off nasty crunchy bugs, her head swimming with the foul air. There was the skull she had noticed, tooth marks obvious on it at this distance.

She looked at her companions. Jerry and Carlo were trying to get Graham to his feet. Maisie was leaning against the wall with her eyes closed and her lips moving, praying again.

Start by going right. "This way!" she shouted, grabbing Maisie's arm. The other two had pulled Graham up and had his arms over their shoulders—they almost filled the width of the corridor and they swayed horribly. "Run, damn it!" she shouted, and they started reeling along ahead of her.

Speed! They must move! They had to get into the Labyrinth proper before the monster reached this outermost passage, or it could simply drive them back into a dead end. "Faster!"

Maisie fell. Ariadne dragged her up again and slapped her face, hard. She opened her eyes very wide, white in a filth-coated mask of a face, and the two of them hurried on after the three men. Graham's feet were starting to move. It was horrible stuff to run in, slippery, soft goo with hard lumps in it—probably bones because some snapped, some rolled, and some were sharp. They careened round the second corner and the first gateway coming up on their left. Now she had to make a decision —did they keep on towards the center and the approaching monster, or did they duck up the blind alley and wait for it to go by? Always assuming that it would work its way to the outside first and not play the same game and just wait for them?

There was the gate—check the first finger. "Right!" she said.

The triple-header stopped, and Jerry disentangled himself, leaning Graham against the wall. "How d'you know?" he demanded blearily. He was recovering—the exercise and fear were cutting through the wine.

"I know! Trust me!" she begged him. "I've got more capacity for liquor than any of you. *Move*!"

They moved, and now Graham could manage better, although he kept falling and having to climb up again. They raced along that endless corridor, and, while it was unspeakably foul, at least it was cool and damp, not like the heat-baked platform had been. The two stone walls stretched out ahead to the corner, and beyond that rose the much higher wall that led up to the stands—and above that a narrow wedge of the stands, with spectators running in from both sides to watch their progress.

They rounded the corner—another empty and endless passage ahead.

They were making too much noise... but surely the din of the crowd would drown it out?

Another corner, and this time she grabbed at shoulders and stopped everyone, then crept ahead and took a quick peek around. Empty. "Come on, then...."

Here was another question—how far had the Minotaur come? Was it still advancing, or was it standing in the right-of-way, waiting for them, or had it gone down a blind alley to let them pass so it could drive them to the center? They wanted to get past it—perhaps it wanted the same thing. Most of its victims were only interested in hiding for as long as possible and would not want to reach the middle of the Labyrinth, as she and her companions did; the magic door to Mera was for them only.

Then they reached the gateway, and again she called a halt and crept forward alone to reconnoiter, to poke her head through for a quick glance left and another quick glance right. No monster.

Which way? Right was right if they were going to the center. She led them left and heard the crowd boom with excitement.

They reached the corner, turned it, and stopped at the sight of a dead end.

"Wrong!" Jerry said. "Come on!"

"No!" she said, and managed to stop them—they were all wide-eyed and too tensed up or drunk to think

straight. Graham had his eyes open, but could barely
stand without support. Jerry and Carlo were better, but
still confused.

She made them stay where they were and went back
to the corner they had just turned. She lay down in the
filth. She dug out a small hole for her head and looked
back with one eye showing, her innards heaving and
roiling at the stench and the creepiness of the bugs. The
surface was very uneven—she hoped that the Minotaur's eyesight would not be good enough to notice half a
head at ground level.

She played the waiting game . . . waiting . . . waiting. . . .

Then she noticed the crowd noise, rising and then falling again. The sacrificial victims were not moving, so the
spectators were reacting to whatever the Minotaur was
doing.

And there it was! It had come around the corner at the
far end of the corridor she was watching and was advancing towards her, all its obscene ugliness revealed by
the stark sunlight. Lord! It was huge, seven feet tall,
maybe eight, broad and hairy and with that enormous
head and deadly horns. . . .

It plodded up to the gateway she had come through
and stopped. The crowd grew silent. It stepped into the
gateway and looked to its right, then to its left. It backed
up again and rolled those great animal eyes in her direction. It took a step. *The crowd roared.*

Bastards! Bloody bastards! Asterios could get clues
from the crowd!

The Minotaur stopped, and the crowd fell silent. Then
the monster turned towards the center of the Labyrinth
and reached up with those impossible arms, gripped the
top of the wall, and pulled itself up, walking its human
feet up the stones. It peered over into the corridor it had
left behind. Then it dropped back down again, splatter-
ing filth, and once more paused to look in her direction.

It knew they were there.

It had guessed from the crowd reaction, perhaps
could even see her watching it.

Then the monster turned, walked back to the gateway, and went through it, out of sight. Now it was she

who could listen to the crowd noise—low...lower...
rising again. So the Minotaur was still playing its hesitation game outside the gate, pretending to be making up
its mind whether to go left or right.

It likes to play with its victims.

Lying there in the cool, foul sludge, with sharp bones
sticking in her, she waited. It wasn't fair! The Minotaur
could look over the walls; she had not thought of that
before.

What else had the Oracle told Killer—that Minos
liked to put in many victims at one time? Surely the
crowd would not get so excited if this spectacle happened every three days. What was special about five
victims, apart from the opportunities for gambling?

The Minotaur's head appeared in the gateway again,
checking once more. So it was still there, playing with
them, and the crowd was loving it.

She waited until it was facing in the opposite direction, then wriggled back and stood up. She put a finger
over her lips to warn the others and she pointed at the
corner of the dead end.

Graham was still by far the most heavily drugged, but
he was persuaded to stand by Jerry in the corner, making
a ladder of their hands and shoulders. Maisie was over
first, then Ariadne followed, wriggling and cursing on
that nastily pointed top. For a moment she could look
over the whole expanse of the Labyrinth, see the tiny
square roof in the center that was life—if Killer was telling the truth—see the clumps of people in the stands,
yelling their filthy heads off at this new development.
Then she was down beside Maisie in the third box.

There was an interminable pause; she should not have
left those three drunkards by themselves. Then Graham
came next, landed heavily, and took his time getting up
and back against the wall so that Jerry had something to
stand on when he pulled Carlo over. Then they were all
in the third box, past the Minotaur.

"Which way?" Jerry demanded, rubbing a scraped
and bleeding chest.

"Same again," she said, pointing at the wall.

So they went over the next wall—and the crowd

boomed once more—but a flat wall was harder to manage than a corner. Graham slipped to the ground as she climbed on his shoulders, and they fell in a heap. Jerry slapped Graham's face as she had slapped Maisie's, and at the next try they made it.

Then the next wall, and as she went over that one, catching a brief glimpse of the whole Labyrinth once more, the Minotaur's head appeared in the distance, and the two of them stared at each other across a wide expanse. Then she dropped down, and probably the Minotaur did, too, for then it bellowed—that same dreadful, earth-shaking noise she had heard in the cottage, and loud enough to drown out even the insane yelling of the crowd.

If it could look over a wall so easily, it could probably climb over one, also.

They tackled another wall, but now they were getting more skillful, and the men were certainly sobering. All five of them were filthy and slick with muck, scraped and bleeding from the stones, but they were starting to perform together like a team of acrobats. How many walls was that? Why was the crowd quiet? Why was the crowd yelling? Where in hell was the monster? Was it racing around the passageways towards them, or was it also scrambling over the barriers?

Jerry was suffering the most, because he always had the job of pulling Carlo up, which meant being doubled over the wall with Graham holding his feet. Ariadne suddenly saw that the effort of climbing was probably no longer worth it—the inside boxes were small. "Let's run!" she said.

But her fingers were too filthy, the nails too scratched, for her notes to be any use now, and they started the wrong way, came to a dead end, reversed, and retraced.

The running was even harder now, hard on bare feet, for there was less filth and more bones—long piles of ribs, shattered skulls, and limb bones along the sides of the passages, with only a narrow track down the middle for running. Evidently both the Minotaur and its victims had preferred to do their defecating away from the center of the maze—and surely they must be almost at the center now?

Then it saw them. They had just turned a corner when the Minotaur's head loomed over a wall ahead—not the one which ended the passage, but the next beyond. It bellowed and started to scramble over. Maisie stopped in horror, and the others cannoned into her.

"Keep going!" Ariadne shouted.

"Damn right!" Carlo yelled and gave her a shove, so they all ran forward once more. They had just reached the corner when the great hairy hands appeared on the ridge of the wall above their heads. Jerry stopped and selected a couple of skulls as missiles.

"You go on!" he said. "I'll see what I can do."

As the other three raced away, Ariadne picked up a largish thigh bone and smiled at Jerry. "Lift me?"

He was almost sober now, and he turned his filthy face to her and grinned "Give him hell!" he said. He backed up to the wall and cupped his hands. She clambered up onto his shoulders just in time—the monstrous bull head rose on the other side of the wall, the huge bovine eyes looked into hers. There was a pause, for the monster's hands were gripping the coping stone, and it could not grab for her; then she swung the thigh bone as hard as she could at the leathery black nose. Bulls' noses were particularly sensitive, weren't they?

Evidently this one was; a roar of pain boomed out, both head and hands vanished. There was an audible crash of smashing bones as the Minotaur fell backwards, and then the noise of the crowd drowned out anything more. She almost toppled also, was steadied by Jerry's hands against her legs, scrambled and slithered back down, and found herself standing with his arms around her.

"I would kiss you if you weren't so disgustingly filthy," he said.

"I bet you tell all the girls that."

He laughed and said, "Come on!" and they ran off along the passage toward yet another gateway.

She did not know which way to turn, but as she hesitated the other three came running in from her left. So they all went right, and two more corners brought them to the front of the Minotaur's pen.

There was a very low and nasty-looking black entrance. For a moment no one seemed to want to go first, and then they heard the crowd noise rising to frenzy— the moment of truth was fast approaching, Asterios closing in—and with a scramble they all dived for that doorway, to find out how much of what Killer had said was true. . . .

❧ 13 ❧

I T WAS A DARK AND NOISOME HOLE, BLACKNESS WITH A small patch of light by the door, and they were all so filthy that they were invisible; but they huddled together for the comfort of human contact and watched the light, waiting for the shadow of a horned head to block it out, and listening to the distant murmur of...of running water?

Then Jerry realized that the doorway was not in the center of a wall, but in one corner.

"We made it!" he yelled, and suddenly started to shake. He thought he might be going to throw up, but he tottered over to the door and then outside, and was momentarily blinded by the sun glaring off the pool—and someone out there on watch gave a great howl of welcome.

He took two steps and threw himself into the water.

It had been foul, slimy and repellent three days ago. Now it was the most blissful experience he could remember. He dunked and thrashed and finally stood up, waist deep, to watch as four other people, black with the horrible ooze of the Labyrinth, came tumbling out the doorway and followed him in with monstrous splashes. And there was Sven...and in through the gate poured Tig and Marcus and Jean-Louis....

* * *

The rescue team had been waiting two days. They had cleaned out the building and the spring itself inside it, so that there was a flow of clean water coming down the rockface, and each of the arrivals in turn could go in and rinse off in sweet fresh water and then emerge into the sunlight once more, swathed in great towels and grinning insanely.

There were hugs and kisses. There was Ariadne being introduced to Clio, small and childlike and shy, and to the vociferous blond bulk of Helga. There were bone-creaking embraces and rib-breaking thumps from Sven and Tig. There were Meran clothes for all of them in blues and reds and grays. And outside, later, beside a huge wagon and three tents, a picnic was spread on the grass under blue sky and a gentle breeze of warm and fragrant fresh air.

Jerry sat beside Ariadne. "That's twice you have defeated the Minotaur," he said. "I was sent to rescue you, you know—it's humiliating to have you constantly saving me like this."

She smiled and said softly, "I promise never to do it again."

Then she started to shiver. He took her hand. "All right?"

She nodded bravely. "As long as you don't wave a gin bottle near me . . . yes, I think so."

"They brought no wine or beer," he assured her. "I asked Helga. The Oracle foresaw this. Spring water for everyone."

She looked relieved, but he was worried by her trembling and paleness. Nor was he happy about Tig and the others. They had been boisterous in their greetings, but not boisterous enough. Their eyes wandered while they spoke; they knew something he did not.

They nibbled cold chicken and crusty bread and quaffed spring water. When they had finished, Jerry took Ariadne's hand in his, and they looked at each other with doubtful smiles. Her decision was coming—the way to Mera was open, and the children could not go, wherever the children now were. She would come to Mera, obviously. He would take her to the house of the Oracle. What then? She would refuse to stay without the children. He did not even know if he could go with her, back to the real world, did not know if that was permitted— did not know if he could bear to give up Mera. Surely there could be no greater sacrifice than that, and surely it would take a terrible love to need it.

Three enormous Percherons were hobbled nearby, and the picnic was just ending when a distant cannonade announced the return of Killer on a fourth, cantering back up the valley. He threw himself off, narrowly missing the food, and there were more hugs and more kisses —and an instant feeling that now things were about to happen.

"Have you spoken again to the Oracle?" Jerry asked and saw an invisible visor drop over Killer's face.

"Briefly," he said.

"And?"

Killer glanced around, and everyone was listening. "We can pack up and prepare to go," he suggested, and his tone hinted that there were other possibilities.

"How close are they?" demanded Tig, whose great square beard and shoulder-length ringlets were strangely black in this Outside sunlight, not blue as Jerry usually saw them.

"About thirty minutes," Killer said, "just around the next bend. Twelve of them."

"Twelve of who?" Jerry asked, noting the gleams in the men's eyes.

"Soldiers," Killer said. "Your friends. We strangers at the shrine have been reported, so they are coming to collect more Minotaur fodder." His teeth gleamed as he returned grins from Tig, Sven, Jean-Louis, and Marcus.

Jerry looked apologetically at Ariadne.

"Not more fighting?" she said in dismay.

"What do you mean 'more'?" Killer snapped. "We haven't had a decent brawl in ages. Right?"

Right, said everyone else.

"There are only twelve of them," he continued, "and there are . . . six of us?"

Jerry sighed. "Six of us," he agreed.

Killer chuckled and thumped his shoulder and headed for the wagon to unload swords. Jerry turned to Ariadne. "I have no choice," he said quietly. "Killer has the wand. They will fight whether I go or not. I can't let five friends go against twelve, now, can I?"

She shook her head and said she supposed not.

Killer came around then, handing out scabbards with huge and heavy bronze swords. He paused to give Carlo a contemptuous stare. "I still have to settle with you. It will have to wait until after this, though...unless you would care to join us?"

"Just a minute, friend Killer," Jerry said firmly. "I made a truce with Carlo, and we're not back to Mera yet."

Killer glared at him, threw down the swords, spread green wings as he put fists on hips. "I was not a party to any truce," he said truculently.

Jerry knew he must not lose his temper; with Killer that was always a mistake, and the others were all listening. "I had the wand at that time," Jerry said.

Killer frowned and gave a very small and very reluctant nod. Then the familiar devilish glint came into his eye. "If I give you my promise not to settle with this Carlo maggot, then will you keep the promise you gave me?"

Jerry had to think back to that night at the cottage—his promise to Killer had been for when Ariadne and the children reached Mera safely, so it was not valid and would never be. He glanced around at the ring of puzzled faces and down at Carlo, casually stretched out on the grass, his brown face distorted by those hideous swellings where Jerry had clubbed him, still looking as though they had been caused only a few minutes before. This was one way to make reparation.

"Whatever you want," he said, and Killer's teeth flashed in triumph. He glanced down at the kid. "You are forgiven, then, maggot," he said and turned away.

"You have a spare sword?" Carlo asked, and Killer stopped and turned around slowly. "Yes. Ever used one?"

"No," Carlo said, climbing to his feet. "What about armor?"

"Just shields. We don't need armor against bronze, the clothes'll do." Killer's eyes were shining—a new recruit?

Carlo studied him for a moment. "Can I try one against you, just so I'm sure?"

Killer was rarely at a loss for words, but for a moment the challenge silenced even him. He looked at Jerry out of the corner of his eye. "Can I trust him?"

"No."

Then Jerry wished he had not said that, for it only made matters worse. True, the Meran costume was safer and certainly lighter and more comfortable than any armor ever made in the Bronze Age, but injuries were possible, and to stand still for a free sword stroke from a potential enemy would be the act of a maniac. Slowly Killer stooped, picked up a sword, pulled it from the scabbard, and handed it hilt-first to Carlo. He folded his arms under his cape and braced his shoulders. "Anywhere but the eyes," he said and waited.

Carlo tried a couple of trial swings, scowling at the weight. "Head all right?" he asked in a matter-of-fact tone.

Ariadne took Jerry's hand, and the circle of onlookers grew even more tense.

Get on with it!

"Fine," Killer said.

Carlo shifted his grip and tried again. "Is it all right to use two hands on this thing?" he demanded.

"Yes," Killer said. His forehead was getting shiny.

The swordsman glanced around. "Stand back and give me room?"

The onlookers backed away, all frowning angrily . . . and with no warning at all Carlo swung the sword one-handed, in a sunbeam flash aimed at knocking off Killer's cap. The sword bounced, Carlo staggered, and Killer dropped to his knees with a grunt, the cap still on his head. Then Killer was up, rubbing his neck and looking dazed; Carlo was flexing his fingers and frowning.

"It's seven then?" Killer asked.

The boy shrugged. "Bug off," he said, threw down the sword, and walked away.

And Killer's face went bright red as the onlookers first gasped and then burst into roars of laughter.

Jerry was puzzled. He had still not worked out what Carlo was or what happened in his head, not even after three days in a dungeon with him. And that had been no beginner's first attempt with a sword.

"Carlo?" he said, and Carlo stopped and looked around.

"Please?" Jerry said. "We'd like to have you with us."

The boy stared at him for a moment, looking puzzled. Then he shrugged and nodded to Killer. "Okay—seven," he said.

Killer forced a smile and held out a hand. Carlo ignored it, stepping by him to pick up the sword and buckle on a scabbard.

"Awful weapon," he remarked to Jerry. "I'm better with a machete."

Jerry lay in the bottom of the wagon with the five others, while Killer drove it down the track to meet the Cretan militia as they came slouching around the bend. The whole affair seemed a quite unnecessary and very stupid piece of bravado, as Graham Gillis had pointed out vehemently when offered a part. He had stayed with the women and ignored Killer's sneers, which probably showed that he had more real courage than Jerry did.

Then the wagon reached the soldiers; as the leader shouted for it to halt, Killer cracked his whip over the team. The wagon lurched forward, the soldiers scattered, and then the Merans leaped down from their wooden horse, the Greeks among the Trojans.

It was short and relatively bloodless, as Jerry had known it would be; the Cretans were not fighting for faith, farm, or family and had no yearning for glory. The nine survivors fled off down the valley, strewing armor and shields behind them. Two others were handed a towel and told to make bandages out of it, being within translation range of the wand, then left where they were while the Merans loaded their booty in the wagon and prepared to head back to the encampment. The Cretans, Jerry recalled, had been a peace-loving people. One of them was dead, killed by Carlo.

Jerry climbed to the driver's bench beside Killer, who had produced Venker's silver sword, taken on the Cretan leader, and accepted an almost instantaneous surrender. The wagon lumbered up the hill at a slow pace.

"Right, friend Achilles," Jerry said. "What was all that for?"

Grinning, Killer leaned down and produced the Cretan leader's boar-tooth helmet. "For your collection, friend Jeremy."

Jerry took it and thanked him solemnly; a Meriones helmet would be the pearl of any helmet collection, and he knew he would be greatly excited to own it when he had time to reflect. In the back of the wagon, Sven and Tiglath were gloating over matched sets of six swords and six shields apiece.

"What else?" Jerry demanded. "You weren't by any chance getting practice with that silver sword, were you?"

Or just testing himself after a long idleness?

Killer kept his eyes on the horses and said nothing.

"You have not told me the whole truth!" Jerry insisted.

Killer put an arm around him. "You never tell lies to your friends, Jerry?"

"Of course not!"

Killer grinned sideways at him, disbelieving. "I will not hold you to your promise, Jerry. That Carlo maggot is not worth a promise—you saw that he killed one? Bastard! I know that you love me as a friend and show that love as best you can. So you can forget your promise, and I shall pray to Eros for you."

Sven and Tig were now discussing possible trades to make a single matched set of twelve. Jean-Louis and Marcus were comparing helmets and greaves. Killer had no use for booty, or his house would be full of it. Killer collected bodies. Live bodies.

"That was a promise," Jerry said. "But now it is a

deal. I hold you to it; tomorrow at dusk, at your house. *Now tell me the rest of the story!"*

Killer still did not look straight at him, but his arm tightened. "Thanks," he said. "That will be very nice."

"Then tell me why you are trembling."

"Anticipation!" Killer snapped; but he took his arm away.

Jerry had moved to sit near the back of the wagon with Ariadne, who was pale and shivering. The rest of the company sprawled along the sides, flanking a jingling, clinking jumble of tents and armor heaped in the middle. Killer had called Marcus to sit up on the driver's bench with him, and they were deep in talk. It was strange that Killer had brought Clio and Helga along, probably an order from the Oracle, but perhaps it was only the presence of women that was subduing the raucous male buffoonery Jerry would have expected. The four great horses leaned against the yokes, and the wagon rumbled off downhill, one direction being as good as another for a trip to Mera.

Directly across from Jerry was Maisie, looking very cute in a gray Meran costume, her cap perched jauntily on her golden hair, and managing a few weak smiles when she caught his eye. She no longer seemed to be worrying that a visit to Mera would imperil her soul, not after meeting Asterios. Beside her Gillis looked absurd in his old Outside clothes, the long-suffering blue suit he had insisted on retrieving. He scowled continuously.

Carlo, beside him, still wore his customary sulky expression, bony arms protruding from his cape and crossed on uplifted knees. He had not joined in the joviality that had followed the battle, the loud release of tension. Once Jerry offered him a smile and got a hint of a one-finger gesture. The truce, if not over, was wearing very thin.

"Tell me about that red-headed man," demanded Ariadne quietly.

"Sven?" said Jerry, and told what he could remember —Denmark about tenth century. Sven had never gone a-viking, being an oldest son, and had missed most of the land battles of his day; he had been rescued when he was in his sixties, although now his beard was as red again as ever, and he seemed no more than thirty at the most. He reveled in combat, making up for his wasted, peaceful youth—just a big, rowdy boy at heart, Jerry said. Helga was Norwegian, he thought, a couple of centuries later, but they were a finely matched set, those two.

Tiglath, from Nineveh, was a more interesting character, but his story would have to wait, because he was sitting next to Jerry.

The wagon rocked its way around the bend where the great battle had been fought, and the valley opened out into flatter and lusher land that had not been there before. The sun seemed to be losing its skin-removing virulence, and he thought the air was taking on a gentler, Meran flavor, an odor of nearby sea and richer grass.

Tig and Sven and the others were avoiding his eye again. Killer's hair had turned midnight blue, and Tig's beard. Jerry was just about to comment. . . .

Then there it was.

"Look!" he said, feeling a lump in his throat as the wagon rolled out onto a green plain, and the hill city came into view on their right, gleaming rose-red behind its circling wall.

"It's beautiful!" Ariadne said. "Just as lovely as you said—no, better. Oh, Jerry!" She seemed to have lost her craving; the paleness and quivering had vanished as fast as the Cretan landscape.

"The top of the hill is the house of the Oracle," he said, raising his voice like a tour guide. "Do you see it, Maisie?"

She smiled in astonishment. "It's a church," she said. "The one with the red spire, you mean?"

Gillis gave Jerry a suspicious glare. "Is this another magic trick?" he asked.

Jerry laughed. "'Fraid so. I see something that looks like Stonehenge, a circle of big slabs on end with others laid across them. I was stationed near Stonehenge in the war, and it impressed me. Killer, I know, sees a Greek temple, with Doric pillars. So Maisie sees a church, what do you see?"

The big man snorted. "It looks like a jail to me."

"Ariadne?"

"More like Killer's view, I think," she said hesitantly. "A circle of columns with an entablature?"

He wasn't at all sure what that was. "Killer's is rectangular. Yours sounds more like my Stonehenge with a bit of culture added to it."

Carlo angrily refused to give his opinion and looked worried.

"There's the gate," Jerry said, feeling absurdly excited. "North Gate, of course . . ."

The gate was closed.

He had never seen that before, and, even as the shock registered, the wagon rumbled to a halt. The men were glancing at one another, looking sick. Even Helga . . . only Clio caught Jerry's eye and she was as puzzled as he, and worried. *What the hell was going on?*

Then Killer rose and turned, glanced over the passengers, and said, "Jerry?" and tossed him the wand.

Jerry caught it and stood up also. "Will you please . . ." he said, and then Tig had risen as well, enormous Tig, and placed a blue-furred hand on his shoulder.

"We all had to promise, Jerry," Tig murmured in his deep voice. "And we had to promise to keep you out also." What could be seen of his face was grave and worried.

Cold shivers crawled deep inside. "Out of what?" Jerry demanded.

Tig quietly pushed, and Jerry crumpled back to his seat.

Killer jumped down from the bench and walked out over the grass, carrying a sword which flashed brilliantly silver white in the sunlight. He stopped and looked back, hesitated. Then he laid the sword down and stripped off his clothes.

"Jerry?" Ariadne said. "I know he's a show off, but what is this?"

He knew now, but he wasn't going to say. Which of them?

Killer picked up the sword again, swung it a couple of

times. Then he put his hands on his hips and looked at the wagon.

"Asterios!" he roared.

"Jerry?" Ariadne demanded again, gripping his arm tightly.

"Wait and see," Jerry said. His lips were dry, and his heart was pounding.

"Asterios!" Killer repeated. *"I know you for what you are. Come forth!"*

Gillis stood up.

Maisie looked up, reached up—and recoiled, staring. She jumped to her feet, threw her arms around him, and somehow forced him back to his seat.

"ASTERIOS COME FORTH!" Killer yelled once more.

Gillis tried to rise, and Maisie held him down, whimpering. Ariadne was clinging almost as tightly to Jerry, staring across at her former husband and shivering.

Again Killer made his call.

Carlo lurched to his feet and jumped over the side of the wagon to land on the balls of his feet, crouched like a wrestler.

Maisie screamed and then burst into tears.

Carlo put his head back and roared. His head was growing. . . .

Ariadne clutched Jerry even more fiercely and buried her face against him. He struggled to free himself and tried to stand up; Tig held him down with one hand.

"We all promised, Jerry!" he repeated. "We must not help him."

"But why?" Jerry squealed. Carlo was no longer visible—it was Asterios now, still swelling and growing, ripping the remains of its clothes from the inhumanly hairy, inhumanly bulky body, the animal head directed toward Killer.

"It is the only way Killer can return," Tig said grimly. "He was in the cottage when you issued the invitation."

"But Killer went back!" Jerry noticed that his own voice was almost a scream. "I sent him back!"

Sven turned around from studying the Asterios transformation to look at Jerry. "Killer has not been back in

Mera. He was allowed about this close. Clio and Helga
came out and nursed him back to health."

Oh no! This was a long way from the center of
faerie.... "How long did that take?"

"About a year," Sven said. "North Gate has been
closed all that time."

"He said he's talked to the Oracle!"

The red-gold head was shaken gently. "He lived in a
tent out here. He hasn't been into the city. He hurt bad
for months, Jerry."

God...Jerry buried his face in his hands. Then he
looked up, smelling the hateful stench, seeing the enormous bulk of Asterios looming at the side of the wagon.

Tig said, "Once he started to get better, you'd be astonished how many people came out to visit him. They
had to be lowered down the wall in a basket, hundreds."

"Clio..." said Jerry, trying to imagine this strange
un-Meran situation. "Girls, I suppose?"

Tig smiled grimly. "Clio understands. All sorts of people, just for friendship—hundreds. Mera showed how
much it appreciates him, Jerry."

"But what happens now?"

"We watch," Tig said. "Your friend Gervasse has
talked to the Oracle many times. They worked this out.
This is a better place to fight than the Labyrinth."

"Watch?" Jerry wailed. "Is that all we can do?"

Sven nodded. "It must be Killer, and no man may
help him."

The change was complete. Asterios threw its head
back and bellowed, the terrible roar that had echoed
around the cottage and through the Labyrinth and which
now came rolling faintly back from the walls of Mera.

Asterios charged. Killer crouched, waiting, watching
the horns approach—then leaped aside, swinging the
sword. Both seemed to have missed, and Asterios came
to a stop, swung around, and bellowed thunderously
again.

"I made no bleeding promise!" Jerry squirmed against
that clamp on his shoulder and was forced down again.

"You stay there, or I'll wrap that wand around your
neck!" Tig said, sounding as though he meant it.

Asterios charged again across the turf. This time Killer ran also, and they rushed headlong at each other —and Killer jumped, swinging the sword beneath him, and the monster threw itself flat. Then it was up again before Killer could recover his balance, incredibly fast, whirling around and grabbing for him with its great gorilla arms. Killer's sword flashed, and the two jumped apart simultaneously, blood streaming from the Minotaur's side. The watchers cheered, but Killer did not take his eyes off his enemy.

Asterios started to back away, seeking to gain ground for another charge, and Killer paced after. Even with the length of the sword, the short man's reach was hardly greater than those arms and if Asterios ever got its hands on him . . .

Carlo . . . why Carlo? Jerry had expected Gillis.

Asterios lunged, reaching out his arms and then whipping them back to safety before the flash of Killer's sword, while the deadly horns scythed at human flesh. Killer was fast, superbly fast, but he did not have the brute reflexes of the monster.

Or the reflexes of a demon. A demon in daylight was not at its best, but it was still a demon.

Again they paced, the Minotaur seeking ground, Killer denying it. Another lunge, another escape. Now the Minotaur advanced, head down, and Killer retreated.

Asterios rushed, the sword flashed and thudded against the massive bony head, while the arms below reached out. Killer jumped back, stumbled, struck again. That massive skull was impenetrable, it was both shield and weapon; the arms below were vulnerable, but also certain death if they ever connected with the man. There was no science for fighting Minotaurs—Killer was inventing it as he went along. Round and round, to and fro . . . he wiped his forehead with his free arm. The monster was bleeding from the gash on its side, and several cuts on its head were streaming blood also, but in a battle of endurance it would be Killer whose mortal flesh would fail first.

Helpless, Jerry squirmed, and the others cursed and

ground their teeth beside him. Gods were being invoked: Thor, Hercules, Mars, Jesus, and Medinet Habu.

"What happens if he loses?" Jerry demanded. "Then it comes for the rest of us?"

Even under the blue thatch, Tiglath's face looked sick. "No. It is Killer it wants. If we stay in the wagon we are safe."

Somehow that made it worse.

Then the Minotaur bellowed and charged, thrusting with its horns—right, left, right—and Killer backed frantically, thrashing at the head with his sword, seeking an eye, severing an ear, fighting now for space, and being steadily pushed back across the blood-spattered grass. One horn caught the sword, twisting it sideways, momentarily out of play. The arms reached for Killer, and he squirmed out of reach, teetered off balance, and was caught by the horns.

The massive head swung up with a roar of triumph; Killer went spinning through the air like a ball in one direction, and his sword went flashing away in the other.

❧ 14 ❧

KILLER HIT THE TURF AND LAY STILL, DEAD OR BRO-
ken or unconscious. Asterios stared over toward
him for a moment and then turned to survey the wagon-
load of onlookers. It raised its head in another bellow of
triumph, mocking the onlookers' impotent fury. Then,
still breathing hard from its exertions, the monster
turned its back on them once more and paced in leisurely
fashion over to its victim.

Jerry wailed. "If we all go? All of us?"

"*NO!*" Sven thundered. "There is a deal. The Oracle
said we must not, and we promised."

Ariadne had been tempered in a thousand battles with
a lawyer. "*What* did the Oracle say?" she demanded. "Its
exact words?"

It was little Jean-Louis who answered. "It said, 'Asterios wants Killer more than it wants Howard. It has
agreed that he may have a sword and the rest of you will
be safe in the wagon; the legions will stay away. I have
agreed that no man will help Achilles.'"

The Minotaur still had its back to them, standing and
staring down at Killer, idly kicking his head from side to
side.

"Right!" she said. Grabbing the wand from Jerry's
limp hand, she vaulted over the side of the wagon and

186

was running before she reached the ground. She heard the roars of outrage behind her being choked back.

The fight had moved a long way from the wagon.

She knew she must look absurd, a powder blue midget racing into a battle against a giant. She wasn't sure what she was going to do or why she was doing it. She didn't like Killer; he was a dirty-minded, obnoxious little punk, but she wasn't going to let that hateful monster kill the boy if she could help it.

Killer was starting to twitch. The Minotaur was behind his head, and he must have opened his eyes and looked up and seen it staring down at him, for he tried to rise—and Asterios put one foot on his face and pushed him down again.

It likes to play with its victims.

And Ariadne was still running, silent on the grass.

Then Asterios uttered a quieter, rumbling whinny that might have been a laugh, clasped its hands behind its back, and bent over, twisting its head. She thought for a moment that it was merely peering into Killer's eyes, but then she saw the horn, directly over the boy's heart . . . and Asterios continued to bend.

Killer reached up and grasped the horn, and the cavernous chuckling noise came again. Blood was visibly trickling from the monster's cuts down onto its victim, and Killer was now obviously taking the strain, trying to hold that icily descending horn away from his chest. He squirmed, doubling himself to bring his legs up, pressing his feet against the massive head . . . and Asterios rumbled mockingly again, remorselessly increasing the pressure. It must outweigh Killer three to one—he could never resist its weight. The horn moved steadily lower, gently folding his limbs ahead of it, touching his chest. . . .

Still it had not seen Ariadne. Still she ran. Perhaps she could ram that wand down its horrible throat; Jerry had said wands could burn the demon.

Asterios was bent almost double now, its legs apart, its back toward her, its rear vulnerable. It had not heard her, or it would be moving faster to destroy one victim and then turn on another.

And then it either heard or saw her. Roaring, it jerked loose from Killer, unclasping its hands, raising its head —too late. Without slowing down, swinging the heavy wand two-handed like a golf club, she struck upward as hard as she could between the Minotaur's widespread legs; flame and smoke spurted from its crotch as faerie wand met demon flesh.

With a deafening scream, Asterios collapsed in a heap on top of Killer. Ariadne fell over both of them and then was thrown clear by the monster's wild convulsions.

She struggled to her feet and staggered, dazed. Killer and the still-bellowing monster seemed to be writhing together in some horrible embrace. Then Killer had rolled free and was scrambling to his feet, so splattered with blood that it was impossible to tell whether or not he had been wounded—but he *was* mobile. The distant onlookers broke into hysterical yells of joy. Ariadne started to run for the silver sword shining in the grass. That was a long way, too. She grabbed it and headed back again, reeling and breathless and miserably aware that she was badly out of shape. The wand and sword were slowing her down.

She came to a gasping stop and held out the sword.

"Put it back!" Killer screamed. "You must not interfere!"

Asterios, still roaring, clutching its genitals, had risen to its knees.

"No *man* may interfere!" She tried to yell and could hardly get the words out at all.

But Killer's face was inflamed and furious beneath the blood stains. He had one hand pressed against a slash across his chest and he was swaying on his feet.

"Put it back where it was, you stupid bitch," he snarled at her. "And get back in the wagon where you belong."

Behind him, Asterios made an attempt to rise and sagged again, bellowing.

She was almost too furious to think. This was a clash of cultures, like Jerry's story of Thermopylae—Killer would not accept help from a woman. A ball of twine would be all right, but she was not supposed to interfere in a hero's actual battles.

Asterios lurched to one knee, then to its feet, bent double still.

The *Iliad*? Hadn't there been goddesses involved in the battles between Greeks and Trojans? It was his bible, Jerry had said.

She took a deep breath, suppressed her panting, drew herself up as straight as she could, and said, "Don't you know who I am, Achilles?"

"Ari..." he said, then the rage faded, and his eyes opened wide. "Athena?" he whispered.

Asterios half straightened and started to shuffle forwards, one hand reaching for Killer's neck.

"Quickly, mortal!" Ariadne said. "Kill the Minotaur!"

Killer nodded, grabbed the sword, and jumped clear of the monster's grip, just in time. Ariadne raised the wand threateningly in case it came for her, but Killer swung the silver sword in a blazing wide arc at Asterios' throat.

The Minotaur toppled backward to the turf, and Killer raised the sword, two-handed, and thrust it down, burying it in the monster's chest.

The wagon exploded in cheers, erupting people as a volcano throws rocks.

Killer turned to stare at Ariadne, and she held out the wand. "You have done well," she said.

He was panting, naked, splattered with blood, and for a moment she thought he would kneel to her. Then his eyes narrowed suspiciously. She also was gasping and sweating, too much for a goddess. Realization flickered in his eyes. Then he grinned and lifted his hands invitingly.

She threw herself into his arms.

It was the kiss at the shrine all over again, and this time she did not even try to resist. She could not breathe in his grasp, could not think, was conscious only of the pounding of their two hearts and his naked form against her and of a great joy that this Killer had survived. She dug her fingers into his back and returned his kiss wholeheartedly.

He was an obnoxious little punk, maybe, but now she knew she would not be able to resist him. Whenever he called, she would come.

Jerry led the pack at first, then slowed, and he was the last to arrive at the celebration, the group that was standing around Killer and Ariadne, waiting for them to break loose from their embrace.

He wandered over to inspect the prone form of the Minotaur, the silver sword still protruding from its rib-cage. Killer would certainly break his rule against booty and have that head mounted. Jerry pulled out the sword and wiped it on the grass. Then he heard much laughter behind him: Killer was accepting congratulations from the others now. Even the Gillises were in there.

Ariadne broke free and came towards Jerry and then stopped.

He held out a hand. "Well done!" he said.

She shook his hand, lowered her eyes. "Thank you."

"Doesn't this carcass look smaller than you expected?" Jerry asked.

"Jerry . . . I don't know why I did that."

He forced a smile and hoped that it looked genuine. "Did what? Displayed that incredible courage of yours yet again? You're the bravest person I've ever met, Ariadne—man or woman. Don't be sorry for that. Or do you mean kissing Killer?"

"Both."

He shrugged. "Quite understandable. He's had four hundred years of practice. I'm the only one, almost, who has ever been able to refuse him—and even I'm lined up now." He was sounding bitter and childish; she was hurt.

"Damn!" he said. "I'm not jealous of Killer, Ariadne, truly. Every husband in Mera—Oh, hell! I mean I don't own you."

She studied the Minotaur. "Yes, it is smaller. . . . Jerry! It's shrinking!"

So it was; bloodstains fading, pelt disappearing. Already the monstrous head was barely more than human.

One by one, the men came over and shook Ariadne's hand. Their awkward discomfiture amused her.

Then Jerry was grabbed roughly from behind and whirled around by Killer, still wearing nothing but smears of blood and a huge grin. He had a gash on his chest, and his lips were bruised, but the bruises could easily have been done during the congratulations. "You're the only one who hasn't..." he shouted, and stopped when he saw where Jerry was pointing.

· Now everyone noticed the transformation—there were screams and shouts. Carlo had his eyes open, looking dazed and confused, but unwounded and unbloody. The onlookers fell into an uneasy silence.

"Helga?" Jerry said. "You have some spare clothes? Clio? See if you can find some water." He knelt down beside Carlo. "Relax," he said. "You'll be okay in a minute."

"The gate is open!" Tig exclaimed, pointing.

Not only was North Gate open, but a stream of citizens was pouring out of it, too far off to recognize, but obviously preparing to welcome the hero.

Killer was scowling down at Carlo. "Hades!" he muttered. "I can't have him skinned now, can I?" He glanced around and spoke loudly to regain his friends' attention. "Who shall ride beside me when we make our entry? Jerry! You shall have the honor!"

Jerry rose and shook his head. "I'm in disgrace. Ariadne, obviously."

Killer frowned like a thunderstorm.

"Not me, thanks," Ariadne said. She looked over at the growing crowd. "No, Killer, let Clio ride beside you."

He was astonished. "Clio?" he said scornfully. "What's she done? Why Clio?"

"Because she's your wife," Ariadne shouted, "and no decent man would think twice!"

Nobody spoke to Killer like that.

"She has a point!" Jerry said hastily, moving to put himself between her and the deadly raised wand, the clenched fist. The fiery glare swung on him, and he braced himself for the shattering impacts, knowing he could never be fast enough to block them. Then, astonishingly, Killer spun on his heel and stalked away—

hopefully to get dressed. The onlookers relaxed with an audible sigh like the sound of wind in straw.

Jerry knelt by Carlo again to hide his trembling.

Ariadne crouched down beside him. "Jerry . . . thanks! But he wouldn't have . . . would he?"

"Why don't you ask Clio?" he muttered, and helped Carlo sit up.

More surprise—Killer did order Clio up to the driver's bench beside him, and her youthful face glowed with the joy of summer dawns.

A double line of citizens cheered them to the gate, with Killer standing up, holding reins in one hand and the wand in the other, accepting the applause with juvenile glee, and taking his time.

Even inside the city, the jubilation continued. There were, usually, only two real wagon roads in Mera—Wall Road, which ran around the perimeter, and Main Street, which spiraled up the hill to the house of the Oracle. It was this way they followed, rumbling along slowly while citizens came running alongside to cheer. Jerry had returned to his former seat at the back, with Ariadne close beside him, and he was astonished at the number of people who wanted to welcome him back also, trotting by the wagon and reaching up to shake his hand, standing on their doorsteps or in their storefronts to lift their caps in greeting and call his name. He was kept busy, for at the same time he was trying to keep up a commentary for Ariadne, aware that he was babbling with excitement, taking as much pride as if he had created Mera all by himself, and also seeing a little of it freshly through her eyes.

"Notice how old it is?" he said. "Ancient, in some parts, a terrible jumble really, and yet it all seems so bright and new, as though it had just been put together by a planning commission."

"Not a committee!" she answered, smiling. "By a great artist, perhaps. It's beautiful. Who cleans the streets?"

"They clean themselves, I think, like the clothes," he said. "But if I think Fishermen's Walk needs a polish, I go out with a broom, and others do the same. There's the Concert Plaza—we don't go in for halls in Mera, because of the weather—recitals and ballet and plays. I had a part in a Sophocles Festival that Clio organized, and Shakespeare is much better here, where you can get all the shades of meaning. . . ."

He pointed out the art stores, most of them run by the artists, the cafes run by the good chefs, and some of his closer friends. "Look, Maisie, there's Father Julius that I told you about." He commented on some of the houses and the people who lived in them, noticing for the first time in decades that among the crowds of all races, the old, the middle-aged, and the young—there were no children. Then . . .

"There! There, in the sidewalk cafe!" He lifted his cap in greeting, and the man rose and responded with a smile. "I told you you would recognize him."

She went pale, nodded, and whispered, "Mozart!"

"We don't have many celebrities," he said. "I think you'll get on well with him—he doesn't suffer fools. There's old N'bana, my favorite witch doctor; Ali Al'iza —he used to be a slaver—and that woman was a priestess of the sun . . ."

They passed Jewelers' Lane, Farmers' Market, and Poets' Corner, and at last the crowds thinned out. They came to Hospital Court, where the road ended, and they all climbed down from the wagon, laughing and thanking Killer for the ride. Here they stood high above the city, on an open area flanked by great cypresses and the final little rocky crest of the hill, and he pointed out the low, airy building of the Hospital to her.

"It's not needed, of course," Jerry said, "except for people like Killer, who more or less has his own bed there; but healing is fastest up here, close to the Oracle and the center of faerie. No doctors, but a wonderful old couple look after the patients. . . ."

Ariadne took a deep breath of the fragrant air, the gentle breeze stirring her honey-colored hair and making it gleam in the sunshine. "And now we go to the Oracle?"

"Yes," he said, ". . . in a little while."

Sven took the reins and turned the wagon. The other Merans wished them good luck and wandered back down the hill, following the jingling, creaking wagon, leaving Jerry and Killer and their four rescued mortals. Killer stood clutching his wand, putting on the brave front of a returning hero without being very convincing; Jerry was holding his boars' tusk helmet.

Gillis seemed strangely good-humored, although looking absurdly out of place in his battered suit with his tie knotted loosely and his coat over his arm. Maisie clutched her husband with one arm and a shapeless bundle of pants and sweaters under the other and was obviously upset and worried. Carlo was slouching even more than usual and had apparently not bothered to recover his Outside garments.

"Let's go see this Oracle of yours, then!" Gillis said. "I think I am owed some explantions and apologies and I am obviously not going to get them from you."

Jerry led the way to the steps. Ariadne held his arm and peered at him curiously as they went.

"You're not looking forward to this, are you?" she asked.

Be honest. "No. A visit to the Oracle can be a very trying experience anytime," he said. "And I did screw up badly."

They wandered up the gentle stairs until they reached the wide, flat expanse at the very top of Mera. Over in the center was a raised platform, supporting a high circle of huge rectangular slabs of pink granite, topped by a circle of similar slabs—Stonehenge. The pavement inside was empty. Ariadne, he supposed, was seeing polished columns, Maisie a red chapel. . . .

"Let me show you the view first," he suggested. "People come up here often, to sit and look and gossip, and if the Oracle wants to send a message, it calls one of them in."

There were indeed about a dozen people scattered around, some of them standing and leaning on the stone balustrade which ran all the way around, others sitting on the raised benches. They nodded politely and did not interfere—they could tell that these newcomers had come on business, and one thing which never failed in Mera was good manners. Except in a few people like Killer, of course.

The whole city lay spread out below them, and the country beyond. "There's North Gate, where we came in." The meadow outside was where Killer had fought the Minotaur, but they knew that, and beyond that lay a low range of grassy hills, blocking any further view. The sky to the north was dark and stormy, and that was normal.

He pointed out the Concert Plaza again and a few of the streets, leading them gradually around to the west and a view of wooded hills with sunlight spiking off silver streams. "Do you like fishing?" he asked Ariadne. "Or canoeing? I used to be a good man with a punt at college."

She smiled, squeezed his arm, and said nothing.

They carried on around the balustrade until they were looking south, and the landscape that day was all spring-like: orchards pink with blossom and dark loam fields being plowed by teams of oxen.

"So you have peasants?" Gillis said. "They feed their masters in the city?"

"We have peasants," Jerry said, "because they want to be peasants. They work or not as they feel like, as does everyone in Mera. They live in the countryside because they prefer it to the town. Most people have a job of some sort because they enjoy doing it and it gives them satisfaction and a sense of identity. Craftsmen like to make things, cooks like to cook, the farmers like to grow things. There's no nine-to-five in Mera, no serfs, no wage slaves."

Then he pointed out the Dance Floor and the start of Fishermen's Walk, and they had come round to the east, where the blue sea sparkled away endlessly. They gazed down to the little harbor and its pink granite quay and tiny specks of men unloading their catch from the fishing boats. A bark under full sail was coming in very slowly in the gentle wind, and a dhow was already unloading cargo, its gowned crew indistinguishable from the Merans helping them.

"So there are four ways out of the city," Gillis said. "Didn't you say?"

Jerry nodded. "Three gates and the harbor. North to duty and danger, west to fun and adventure, south to the fields. East is the harbor."

"And where does that lead?"

He tightened his hold on Ariadne. "That leads away for ever. If you are going to return to the real world, Graham, you and Maisie, then you will leave by ship—and you can never return. That much I do know."

"I admit that it is a beautiful place, Mr. Howard," Maisie said, plucking up courage as she did when she was talking of her faith, "but I do not wish to stay. I fear the Devil's works."

Jerry leaned on the rail and nodded sadly. "That is what Father Julius says, that you lose your immortal soul if you stay in Mera. He has been here for centuries, busily trying to persuade us all that it is our duty to leave, go back, and repent."

She flushed angrily. "You did not tell me that before. And what of his own soul?"

Jerry smiled. "He says his duty is to spread the message—I think he expects to be the last one out. He is a kind and charming old man, and we are very fond of him, but his thinking is as muddled as a creel of eels."

"We shall not stay, Graham!" Maisie said firmly.

He shook his head. "Never! You are lotus eaters here, Howard. You do not grow or develop, you produce nothing except for your own satisfaction—contribute nothing to humanity, achieve nothing. Is that not so? You are basically the same person you were forty years ago, fossilized forever in a happy stupor of self-gratification."

Jerry thought about that, watching the harbor far below him. "Yes," he said at last. "What you say is quite true. This is the land of the lotus eaters, but perhaps there are those whose digestion will not stand a harsher diet? And also there are those who owe no debt to the world because of what the world has done to them. You may be different. You will not be forced to remain."

The big man snorted and turned to look at the house

of the Oracle. Killer was watching him with some amusement and being astonishingly quiet for Killer.

"This Oracle?" Gillis demanded. "You said it is human, yet you always talk of it as neuter—as 'It'. Tell me what to expect."

"Expect the truth," Jerry said. "And the truth is not often palatable. It is not like other oracles, where you ask questions and they return ambiguous answers. This one asks the questions, and you tell it the answers—and you cannot lie to it." He heard Ariadne draw in her breath, and her grip on his arm tightened.

"That's why we have no police—and no lawyers," he added, and Gillis scowled angrily.

Then Killer straightened suddenly. "I am called," he muttered, and walked off across the courtyard toward the house of the Oracle, tapping the wand against his leg.

"I heard nothing," Ariadne whispered.

"No, you wouldn't," Jerry said.

He must be showing his apprehension plainly now, for the other four were frowning at him.

"I should perhaps have found better clothes," Gillis said uneasily, "if we are to have an audience with the ruler of the city."

Jerry laughed and got glared at, so he explained. "Clothes are the least of your worries. You will meet the naked truth in there, Gillis—and you will be naked before the truth."

The big man flushed angrily. "What does this Oracle look like, then?"

Jerry glanced at Ariadne, at the wary Carlo, the disapproving Maisie. "Can't you guess?" he asked. "What you will find in there is a mirror."

⹈ 15 ⹊

KILLER TROTTED UP THE STEPS, WALKED INTO THE circle of pillars—and vanished. Ariadne gasped with surprise and looked at Jerry, who nodded.

"He will come out soon," he said. "It takes longer when you are in there than when you are waiting." He was paler than usual, and his strange nervousness was increasing. "There is one rule—no, not a rule, just a kindness. Do not speak to him afterward until he is ready. The frivolous refer to this area as the recovery room."

As though to emphasize the magic, a pair of white gulls sailed down on the wind and flew through the circle of columns, turned momentarily blue as they crossed the center of faerie and then floated away toward the harbor.

Jerry put his arm around her again and led her away from the others; they leaned together on the rail.

"Ariadne," he said. "I love you. I never say that lightly—you and maybe two others in my long life. I want you to stay. I want you to marry me. Here we can truly live happily ever after."

She had been afraid of this. She took a long time to find the words. "You have been showing me the kingdoms of the world, haven't you, Jerry Howard? Maisie would say, 'Get thee behind me, Satan.' Oh, Jerry, no

198

woman has ever been offered more, and yes, I could love you dearly . . . but you know what you are asking me to give up!"

He nodded miserably.

"Graham as a father?" she said. "A kid like Maisie for a mother? I am not worthy either, Jerry, but I had licked the drink thing, I really had." Was that true? She had thought that before. "I could be a better mother than Maisie, but Graham and his lawyer friends had tied me up in knots so I had to make an appointment and then sit there in his living room and drink tea and eat cookies and ask how school was going—like an unpopular aunt, not a mother. . . . I am sorry, Jerry, truly sorry. I love your faerie city and I think I love you and I could even learn to put up with your strange friends, like Killer, but I have a duty. . . ."

Killer came slowly down the steps, his walk mechanical, his face wooden. He was pale under his tan, staring fixedly in her direction. Suddenly she saw him for the first time not as an over-sexed, muscle-bound juvenile, but as a man with experience beyond her imagining. She wondered what the Oracle had said to him to upset him so, and what dark shadow of guilt he carried from Thermopylae. Then he seemed to change his mind and headed towards the Gillises and Carlo, hesitated again and abruptly changed his destination once more. He walked to an empty stretch of the rail, leaned on it, and gazed out across the sea in silence.

Carlo jerked around, looked at Graham and Maisie, then went sauntering over to the house of the Oracle, slouching as usual. And he, too, vanished as he passed within the columns.

It reminded her of school, of waiting to be called into the principal's office. Yet there could be no more beautiful place in the world to wait, here on the hilltop in this crystal-pure air with this incredible view. She could wait here happily forever. *Forever!*

"Why?" she asked suddenly. "Why should Killer be scolded? Surely he is the conquering hero and the Oracle should be giving him praise? Is it always disapproving, never pleased?"

Jerry smiled wanly. "It would be interesting to listen to a conversation between those two...but one always goes alone to the Oracle."

Carlo came rushing down the steps. "Hello!" Jerry muttered in surprise.

Carlo raced across to the rail, bent over it and threw up, then hung there, limp as a wet sock. Ariadne was horribly reminded of the prisoners' gallery in the Labyrinth. But why? Jerry's eyebrows had shot up into his yellow thatch.

"What's happening?" she asked.

"I've heard of that," Jerry said, "but never seen it. Apparently the truth may sometimes be not merely unpalatable, but even intolerable. Our friend must have a remarkable past, for one so young."

Carlo straightened and looked around to see who was watching, then turned away again. His face had healed.

Maisie had obviously been called next. She kissed Graham and strode across the court, holding her head up bravely.

Ariadne said, "When I am called, Jerry, I want you to come with me."

He shook his head and stammered.

"It would not be decent," he protested. "I told you—you will have no clothes on."

"I had none this morning in the Labyrinth, and neither had you," she said, amused at his prudishness. "You want to marry me, you said. A little nudity usually helps a marriage."

He wiped his brow. "One always goes alone. When you have been there, you will understand."

So that was it. "Your past can be no worse than mine."

"Yes it is." He turned away, and there was a long silence.

Maisie came briskly down and smiled happily at Graham as he in turn headed for the steps.

"Ariadne," Jerry said. "I am a coward and a murderer."

"Jerry?" she said, but he did not look at her. "Jerry, we have been through hell together these last few days

—literally. I know what sort of man you are. I won't judge you on your past."

"People don't change in Mera," he muttered.

More silence.

"Ariadne?" said a soft voice—her *own* voice, coming from the house of the Oracle. Her heart jumped, and she started to move . . . just as Jerry did, also.

"I was called," she said.

He blanched. "So was I."

"Then we do go together," she said firmly, and he nodded unhappily.

They walked hand in hand toward the steps. Graham came slowly down, ignoring them, and headed for an empty stretch of rail, ignoring Maisie also. That would have been another interesting to conversation to listen to—Graham Gillis speaking the truth about himself? Most potent magic!

The columns were as polished as glass, pink and black crystals shining in the sun, and the space within was much, much larger than it had seemed from outside. They walked hand in hand across the floor, the granite slabs as shiny as the columns and warm beneath her bare feet. She had not even noticed her clothes vanish. Jerry's palm was damp, and his grip uncomfortably tight.

As Jerry had said, their destination was a mirror—a very large, rectangular mirror, stark and free-standing in a gold frame. Before it stood a long, low table, like a coffee table. No black and white in Mera, but the table was shiny black and the wands lying across it—several dozen of them—were gleaming white. Here, then, was truth, untarnished gold, black and white. The glass of the mirror seemed very thick, and walking forward in it, alone, was her naked self. Two visitors and one reflection—an awesome demonstration of magic. As she and the reflection drew close, though, she saw that it was not accurate: no sag in the breasts, no stretch marks, a youthfully flat tummy. So that was how she would look if she stayed in Mera? She was being bribed—by whom or what? She felt suddenly angry and suspicious.

Then Jerry and she had reached the table and stopped.

Jerry, she noticed, was staring at a point above the reflection's eyes, so he was seeing himself, not her. For a moment the two people and the one reflection stared without speaking; then her reflection suddenly folded its arms, and she jumped with surprise.

"Ariadne," the reflection said, "I am Mera. Anything I ask, you will be compelled to answer. Anything spoken aloud here—by me or by you—is true. But if you are unable to speak a thought, that does not mean that it is necessarily false, for there are some truths which you are not allowed to know. Do you understand?"

She nodded.

It looked at Jerry. "Gillis told you of her failures, but you will not tell her yours. Yet you just asked her to marry you. Is that fair?"

Jerry's lips moved in silence, and then he said, "No."

His hand was trembling.

She tried to say that it was not important—and she could not.

The reflection seemed to know; it glanced at her with amusement and then stared up at Jerry again, apparently quite unashamed by its nudity.

"So shall I tell her?" the reflection asked.

Jerry shuddered and nodded. Ariadne tried to say she did not want to hear. Again, the words would not come, so she did want to know.

Another shape whirled in the mirror beside the woman and then took form as a young man of middle height, dark-haired and sporting a very bushy moustache. He was wearing a World War II flying suit, goggles pushed up on his helmet. Jerry was staring down at the table of wands.

"Introduce me, old boy," the newcomer said mockingly.

Jerry glanced up briefly, as though to confirm his fears, winced, and dropped his eyes again. "Lieutenant Smythe-Williams," he muttered. "First name, Kevin."

"Pleased to see you," the airman said, running his gaze appraisingly up and down Ariadne. She felt herself blush, but her reflection did not. "And who was I, Jerry? Finish the story."

"You were my tail gunner," Jerry said, keeping his eyes on the floor.

"Oh come on, old chap!" Kevin said. "I know we have all the time in the world, but the lady is going to get frightfully tired standing there for years while you mess around. Out with it, laddie!"

"Don't!" Ariadne said.

"He shall," said her reflection.

"We were badly flakked," Jerry said without looking up. "It didn't look as though we'd get back across the Channel. I could barely hold her in the air...I told the others to bail out. K...Kevin had been hit, wounded. He was pinned in there, with a spar through his leg. He had to stay. I tried to fly the plane home, but it got so that I could barely hold trim, we were getting low and ...I bailed out and left him."

The airman laughed. "So I rode the barrel over the falls, stapled to my seat, while he floated down into Mera and decided it was really quite a nice spot for a gentleman to live. Nicer than fighting a beastly war, nicer than going back to face the others when they came out of POW camp."

"Could he have landed that plane?" Ariadne demanded angrily.

"Answer the pretty lady, Jerry," said Kevin Smythe-Williams.

"I was flying it," Jerry said. "Perhaps I could have flown it all the way across. I don't know. *I don't know!*"

His hand had gone quite limp, and she squeezed it. "Then you made a judgement. You tried your best—"

"It wasn't my best," he said. "I was still flying it."

"And there you have it!" The ghost in the mirror smiled and stroked his moustache. "You left the controls and you hit the silk and left me. Not nice, Jerry! And you didn't tell the lady my other name. The chaps didn't call me Kevin, did they? Nor Smythe-Williams. They had another name for me—one that you gave me. A little jealous of my successes in those days, weren't you, Jerry? What nickname did you hang on me, Jerry, old chap?"

"We called you Ladykiller," Jerry whispered.

"And for short?"

"Killer."

The ghost nodded, satisfied. "That should do, then, shouldn't it?" he said. "Except maybe for my famous last words?"

"No!" Jerry cried, looking up in horror. The apparition chuckled and started to fade from sight, but its voice came faintly, as though from a distance and distorted by a crude intercom, sprinkled with static, "Jerry? Don't leave me! You still there, Jerry? I'm trapped, old man.... For God's sake, Jerry..."

The despicable whining seemed to go on for a hellishly long time, and then there was only herself standing there in the mirror. Jerry had fallen to his knees, doubled over and weeping like a child. She started to kneel down beside him and then decided it might be kinder not to remind him that she was there. A very cruel business, she thought, and wondered what its purpose was.

"Oh, get up, you blubbering ninny!" snapped her reflection, and he climbed slowly to his feet again, wiping his face angrily and visibly shaking.

"Now!" the reflection said. "The mission I sent you on—why did you send Achilles back with the wand?"

Jerry gulped and moved his lips. "I thought I would save Killer and this time I would stay..."

"You thought you would redeem yourself, then? Make up for the first Killer, whom you deserted?"

"Yes. Yes!"

The reflection shook its head. "You said you thought that. But that wasn't the reason, was it?"

This was incredibly cruel. Jerry had somehow managed to go even paler. Again he couldn't find words.

"Oh, get on with it!" the reflection snapped, sounding faintly like the vanished ghost. "You had been told to take clothes for one; there are no children in Mera. Obviously you were supposed to bring back the woman and no one else. Why did you send Killer back and not come with him?"

Jerry stuttered and mouthed; it took him a long time to find the truth. "She would not have come. I wanted her."

"Go on," the reflection said.

"I was sorry for her."

"And more than that?"

Jerry blushed scarlet, right down to his shoulders. "Sex! I wanted to take her to bed. I was crazy—I wanted her insanely—more than any woman I had ever met."

The reflection looked amused. "And you still do! Well, that's the truth but not the whole truth."

Jerry looked surprised. He tried to speak, hesitated, and then blurted, "I have come to admire her personality. I am in love with her." He sighed and smiled briefly, shyly at Ariadne. "Thank you," he said to the mirror.

"Don't mention it," her reflection snapped. "You thought Killer would insist on bringing you back. You were trying to blackmail me through Killer!"

Jerry gulped once more and said, "Yes, I was."

The reflection nodded angrily. "And why did you pistol-whip Carlo? Because he had stabbed Killer?"

Jerry hesitated and then said, "Revenge! Because he had nearly let the demons get me."

The reflection nodded again, looking satisfied. "Have you ever been intimate with a man?"

"No! I was taught... brought up... I can't..." He fell silent, staring down at the table again.

"But you have promised Killer. Will you keep your promise—and how do you feel about it?"

Jerry pulled a face. "I plan to. I hope I don't throw up."

The reflection laughed, her laugh. "You very well may. You'd better let me handle it for you. It won't be the first time, as you well know. Tomorrow night at dusk, you told him."

Jerry blushed scarlet, looking down at his toes and wriggling them. "But..."

"Your gratitude does you credit," the Oracle said, obviously amused, "but I can give Killer a much better time than you could."

Jerry suddenly laughed. "Thank you," he said, sounding relieved.

Then the joking was over. The Oracle turned to stare at Ariadne, and she cringed, waiting for the horrors.

"Why did you steal Lacey from Graham and Maisie?" the reflection asked innocently.

Well, that was an easy one—because she loved her and wanted her. She opened her mouth, and nothing came out.

Nothing at all? That was the truth, wasn't it? Lacey was her child. She loved Lacey—but she could not even say that. The silence was dragging on and on, and Jerry must be waiting, but she could not even look at the mirror, let alone him. And she could not speak. There must be a knack to this, a way to learn how to find the truth, because she wanted to say something, and nothing seemed to have words any more.

Her reflection sighed. "Well, we can come back to it. Are you an alcoholic?"

"Yes."

"Still?"

No.

"Yes."

Why had she said that?

"Are you a good mother?"

"Not when I'm drunk." She couldn't add to that. . . .

"Look at me!" the reflection snapped, and it began to change. It had a blue dress on. She knew that dress—two years ago. And it was swelling, growing enormous, bigger than the Minotaur—ten feet tall. It glared down at her terrifyingly.

HOW OFTEN HAVE I TOLD YOU NOT TO INTERRUPT MOMMY WHEN SHE'S PRACTICING?

Oh, God! Was that how she had seemed to Lacey?

Then it was her small naked self again—and she fought back. "Lots of parents snap at their children. I don't think that was fair."

"Was it fair?"

"Yes."

"See?" the reflection said. "A little effort, and we get the truth. Tell Jerry what you saw when the Minotaur came to the cottage."

Lord! But she managed that—the story of Graham at

that other cottage, Graham drunk and very horny and wearing a cowboy hat. Jerry took her hand sympathetically, but she did not look at him.

"So the Minotaur reminded you of your former husband?" the reflection asked waspishly. "Why did you fire at its genitals?"

"They're the most tender spot on a man, a male animal," she said. "Even if silver bullets couldn't penetrate the skin, they could hurt it there. It worked, damn it!"

The reflection smiled. "You were a good wife for a lawyer. You have made true statements, but you have not quite answered the question. Try this then, describe Maisie Gillis."

She did, and it was not hard. Those days in the dungeon had helped her appreciate Maisie as a good kid, not bright, but well meaning.

"She loves children?" the reflection demanded.

"Yes!" Ariadne said quickly. "And Lacey loves her, I admit it."

"Here you have no choice but to admit it," her inquisitor replied. "So who is the more suitable mother, the good kid who is loved and has a husband to help, or the solitary alcoholic?"

She had a choice of two names, and hers would not come out. "Maisie. But . . ."

"Yes?"

"But I don't think that Graham is a good father!"

"Ah!" the reflection said triumphantly. "Back to the first question. Why did you steal Lacey from him?"

She was furious to discover that she was weeping as Jerry had wept. She wiped her eyes and took a few long, deep breaths. "So that he could not have her."

So now she knew.

"And why did you attack the Minotaur in the way you did?"

"Because it reminded me of him!" she shouted. "Because of that night he attacked me! Because I wanted to hurt him, to hit him there. I hate him!" There was more she could have said, but that was suddenly very clearly the truth and it would do. She was not repentant.

Jerry put an arm around her shoulder.

"Ariadne," her image said. "You may stay here in Mera if you wish. Here you will never age, die, or be sick. As you have already discovered, the alcohol craving has no power over you here. If you do not stay, you will be returned to your car at the moment when you took the turnoff to Hope, North Dakota, and none of this will have happened."

So here it was. "And I have told truly that there I am still an alcoholic," she said sadly. "What will become of me?"

The reflection did not speak, and Jerry muttered, "It will not answer that."

"What of Graham and the others?" she asked.

The reflection seemed to hesitate and then said, "Your decision will determine your reality stream. What they decide does not. Your decision does not affect them."

Ariadne tried to say that she wanted to go home... and was silent.

She tried to say that she wanted to stay, with no more success. Obviously she did not know what she wanted. She looked up at Jerry in despair. "How long can I take to think?" she asked.

It was again her reflection which spoke. "As long as you want, but you can not leave here until you do. I have seen people stand there for two days."

"Can I stay and then change my mind later?"

"Yes," said her own voice from the mirror. "But after that you can never return to Mera, and, after Mera, nowhere else is fit to live, so you can never be happy again —and the demons will surely get you."

She swung back to face the mirror. "Is that some sort of a hint?" she demanded—and got no answer. She tried the experimenting that Jerry had obviously been using, trying to make a statement to see if it was true. "Piano was my demon." *True!* "I was hoping..." No, apparently she had not been hoping to resume her concert career. "It is too late for me to succeed in the career I might have had." *True* again! An alcoholic, then, with no chance for fame, for standing ovations, for the international circuit of Paris, Moscow, London.

She was weeping again. Too late! The piano demon had ruined her for motherhood, and she had wooed the alcohol demon, and that had ruined everything.

But Lacey . . . Lacey had as great a gift, hadn't she?

No, she didn't. The words would not come.

Lacey had a small talent only.

She had been fooling herself, then, hoping to relive in Lacey the career she had missed for herself. Oh, God! What damage would she do to Lacey trying to force her?

Jerry had been biting his lip in silence at her side. Now he said, "I have said truly that I love you, Ariadne. Do you love me?"

"I . . . I don't know. It is too soon to tell. I am very attracted to you. I . . . admire your personality. Is that the right expression?"

It sounded so feeble compared to what he had said! She smiled encouragingly, realizing suddenly how much people depended on lies, how painful was this undiluted truthfulness.

"Jerry," she said, "it's not because of that Smythe-Williams."

"Not?"

"You're not a coward, Jerry."

"I'm not?" He looked astonished.

"Silly man!" she said. "You wouldn't have ordered the others out over enemy territory if you'd thought that plane was going to stay in the air. How long did you fly it after that?"

"A couple of hours," he mumbled. "Longer."

"You are *not* a coward," she repeated. "You calculate odds. You would have gone to Killer's assistance today if Tiglath had allowed it, wouldn't you?"

"Yes!" he said—and was obviously astonished and happy that he could say it, here in the house of the Oracle.

"So you are not a coward, and that isn't it."

His delight flamed in his face and then vanished. "Do you love Killer?"

She cringed away from him. "I . . ."

"Well?"

"I don't know how I feel about Killer." Well, at least that came out.

"He has a lot more to offer than I do," Jerry said miserably.

She lost her temper. "If that means what I think it does, then you're just being disgusting!" she shouted. "That does not impress me—if anything, the reverse! He would be worse than Graham. I'm not turned on by his muscles, either! Physically, I'm no more attracted to Killer than you are, Jerry Howard!"

There was silence, then, as they stared at each other in astonishment, and the reflection smiled mockingly from the mirror.

True?

"Oh!" Jerry said, puzzled.

"But . . ." She did not understand either. "He needs a damned good spanking," she said. "Yet he seems to hypnotize me. He has the same charisma—charm—that Graham had. If he calls me to his bed, I'll go. . . ." *True!* Oh, hell! What had she said?

Jerry took her hand and smiled sympathetically. "I know. Maybe when he's finished with both of us, we'll have each other?"

"Maybe!" Always Killer! She still did not know whether she wanted to stay.

She did want to stay.

But her duty as a mother . . .

"Pilots who desert their crews . . ." she said. "What about mothers who desert their children?"

Jerry started to stammer and finally managed to blurt out, "If you go back, Carlo will kill you."

True?

"What?" she said.

Jerry looked triumphant. He turned to her reflection. "She saved Killer! Doesn't Mera owe her something? Tell her!"

The reflection sighed and nodded. "Very well. I'll bend my rules for a special case.

"Carlo is better known as Hassan Aref," it said. "He is a terrorist, highly trained and gruesomely successful, an expert on remote detonating devices. He is not usually for hire, but two of his companions are in jail. Gillis has agreed to defend them if your car returns safely from your trip—and you do not."

She gasped. Graham! Jerry swore under his breath.

"It is cheaper than alimony," the reflection remarked acidly. "You are a nuisance and an embarrassment to him. You stopped twice on your journey to eat; they could have had you arrested on a kidnapping charge, right? They did not. The presence of two men at the cottage was a surprise, but they were going to take the others, the possible witnesses, to a motel. Then Carlo would have returned. . . .

"Three bodies in a burned-out cabin in North Dakota would not have readily been related to the solitary Mrs. Gillis who had disappeared in Colorado. It would have been an even better solution than the unmarked grave which he was planning earlier."

"See?" Jerry shouted. "If you go back you will not know this. You will stop somewhere for the night, and they will get you! It's obvious!"

True!

The Oracle interrupted. "It is also obvious, Jerry Howard, that his future may be even more despicable than his past. Had he returned later, he would have been mistaken for a demon by Killer, who was armed with a submachine gun. The world would have been rid of Hassan Aref, or Carlo Vespucci—and that was the main purpose of your mission!"

Jerry gaped and blushed. "And instead Killer and I took him in. . . . That was how the demons rallied so quickly?"

"Is he a demon?" Ariadne asked.

"He carried a big one," the Oracle replied. "And Gillis' was reaching a fair size. That was why they survived Asterios' arrival in the cabin—they were his already. But it took a great deal of daemon to materialize the Minotaur today, and Asterios had to suck the daemon out of all of you to do it. Of course, if they return Outside, they may get reinfected."

"If?" she echoed.

"Do not concern yourself with their decision. It does not affect you."

She still could not decide.

"Advise me, then, if you are so clever!" she snapped at the mirror. She wondered if the Oracle could lose its temper.

Her reflection smiled, but with less mockery and a trace more sympathy than it had been showing. "Do you know the story of the Judgment of Solomon?" it asked.

"Of course." Two women had fought over a baby, and Solomon had threatened to divide the child; the real mother had withdrawn her claim. Why was that relevant?

"I am wiser than Solomon," The Oracle said, "and I can execute his Judgment. What does the story tell you of the nature of love? What is love, Ariadne?"

She wiped her eyes and forced a laugh which sounded as false as a brick bell. "I fear we shall stand here for years, if I must answer that..... If the happiness of the loved one is more important than one's own... would that be love?"

The woman nodded, smiling. "That's not bad! Does it help?"

Yes, it did. If she believed the Oracle, then she had no reason at all to go back, for Carlo would kill her that night. But she was not quite certain she did believe the Oracle.

But love... She thought of Lacey struggling with piano lessons. She thought of Lacey hugging Maisie. Even of Lacey and Peggy. She looked at Jerry's anxious face and knew that she wanted him to be happy.

"I love you," she said.

True.

She turned back to the mirror.

"I shall stay in Mera."

True again.

❧ 16 ❧

"**A**RIADNE GILLIS, WILL YOU MARRY ME?"
"No."

Oracle, mirror, table—all had gone now, and the two of them stood within the small circle of columns, decently dressed once more.

His shock was painful. "No?"

"Ask me in a year," she said. "If I am to swear fidelity for ever, then I must be sure."

"Oh!" he said, downcast.

And she must somehow settle with Killer. Perhaps, as Jerry had hinted, all Killer wanted was to carve another notch. But perhaps not, and she would not commit herself to Jerry if she was doomed to be Killer's mistress, ever available upon demand. The thought made her shiver with physical revulsion, but she could also see that Killer was in some ways astonishingly reminiscent of Graham, certainly another man who knew what he wanted, another man who liked his women malleable. Even that hypnotic charm—Graham had possessed that in his youth, and she had found it as potent as gin. Until the Killer threat was exorcised, she would make no promises to Jerry.

When they reached the top of the steps, she stopped and stood for a minute, looking at the rose-red city below and North Gate and the stormy sky of Outside glooming over the sunny hills. Forever—it would take a long time to adjust to that idea. Those storms could touch her no more, she was safe in Mera. By her side was a fine and honest man whose love for her had been authenticated by the Oracle—and if she was settling in for eternity, there could be no more trustworthy or truer man than this. She looked up at the worried expression on that gaunt face . . . a man strangely slow to find himself, the sort of man who comes late to love, then falls hopelessly and irrevocable for one woman, and never cares for another.

"You could stay with Helga," he suggested tactfully.

She shook her head. "I would rather we went to your house and admired each other's personalities," she said.

He nodded. "I shall sleep in the bathtub, of course."

She laughed. "Don't you dare!" she said. "You may think you don't have much to offer, but you looked very interesting this morning, and as often as you care to offer it, Jerry Howard, I shall be quite eager to accept."

He grinned and took her in his arms, and they kissed —tentatively, gently, then with growing joy and meaning. She had forgotten how long a kiss could last, how maddeningly sweet it could be, how intoxicating. Killer's kiss had been deliberate technique; this was mutual discovery, and perhaps the rejuvenating magic of Mera was working through her already, for when they finally separated she felt like a giddy adolescent on her first date. But Jerry looked every bit as delirious and scarlet and starry-eyed as she felt.

"My darling!" he said. "I have waited forty years for you."

She knew her eyes were flooding. "And I could jump up on that balustrade and run all the way around it shouting 'He wants me!' No one has wanted me in years, Jerry."

"Mera will be sweeter still with you," he said.

"I would not have taken it without you."

Then they joined hands again and walked down the steps, and she saw that probably they had not been gone very long, hardly longer, perhaps, than that kiss had taken.

And yet . . .

And yet there was something missing, something worrying. A dripping tap at the back of her mind. Something overlooked, or someone . . .

"Killer!" Jerry said firmly. "Let's deal with him first!"

Killer, at least, was recovered, leaning against the stone balustrade, watching them with a little-boy grin. It was to him they went first.

"So the pretty lady is staying?" he said. "And my friend Jerry is in love at last! I am a very good best man, and the best good man, too."

"Just make sure you leave it at that, then!" Jerry said.

Killer eyed Ariadne thoughtfully. "I love my friend Jerry, and this sweet lady of his shall have my love also."

"Keep it Platonic!" Jerry snapped, flushing, but there was a curious twinkle in Killer's eye.

"He doesn't trust me!" Killer mourned, and he took her hand and kissed it tenderly. She thought that a true courtier would have removed the green cap from the cobalt curls before trying such a gesture.

"Now," Jerry said, firmly changing the subject, "I was told to guide the Gillises to the harbor. Carlo is remaining."

"The maggot?" Killer snarled and turned to look. "Then I have an excellent job for him." He marched over towards Carlo, who was leaning against the rail by himself, watching them; Jerry and Ariadne went in pursuit.

"I hear you are staying in Mera?" Killer said.

Carlo waited a moment, looking him up and down, and then said, "So?"

"When I left here, with Jerry," Killer said, "we were planning a game. It has had to wait a long time, but now it will go ahead. It is called mayhem. Would you care to join my team—or Sven's, if you prefer? I am sure he would welcome you."

"I don't play games," Carlo answered.

Killer tried to look disappointed. "Pity. I admit it is

rowdy; the teams are as big as possible, and there are very few rules. Perhaps, it would be too rough for you?"

"Sounds very childish." Carlo was not to be baited, obviously.

Killer started to turn away, then stopped as though he had just thought of something. "Wait! We shall need a referee, and you are a stranger. Would you consent to be referee?"

Carlo's eye flickered to Jerry and back to Killer like a snake's tongue. "Possibly. I'll think about it."

"Great!" Killer said with enthusiasm and offered a hand.

It was ignored. "I have a question, Mr. Howard," Carlo said, keeping his eyes on Killer. "This party swaggers around a lot. Is there any law against cutting him down to size?"

Killer went very still.

"There are no laws in Mera," Jerry said cautiously. "But Killer is not an easy man to cut down."

"Watch me!" Carlo said, very softly. He eased himself off the rail and stepped forward. Killer's shoulders drooped slightly as he edged into a crouch.

Carlo spat.

Killer sprang.

Carlo rolled over on his back, one leg straight, lifting Killer, who struck the balustrade and vanished out into space. Ariadne screamed, rushed to the rail with Jerry, and looked down. Killer was sprawled on a rocky bank about fifteen feet below them, apparently unconscious.

Carlo was back on his feet, half-crouched, ready for Jerry . . . Jerry started to laugh. He roared, howled, and bellowed with laughter, leaned on Ariadne to recover himself, and had to wipe tears away before he could speak. She did not think it funny at all—more pain for Killer, who had suffered so much? She bit back an angry comment.

Jerry held out a hand to Carlo, who obviously suspected a trick.

Jerry said, "Straight up! I want to shake your hand. That was marvelous! It's about time somebody did that to Killer." He finally convinced the puzzled lad that he was serious and shook his hand.

"I thought you were his friend?" Carlo said.

Jerry almost broke down into laughter again. "Oh, I am! But he needed that. And don't worry about him— he'll be crawling around you on his knees, begging for lessons."

"What's this mayhem thing, then?" Carlo asked. "Why did he want me to referee?"

"It's a game, so-called," Jerry explained, avoiding Ariadne's eye. "No holds barred. The winning team is the one that scores the last goal. That means that the whole of the other team has fled or been crippled."

Ariadne shuddered.

Jerry grinned. "One rule they don't tell you until the game is about to start is that the first goal is scored with the referee, not with the ball."

Carlo stared unbelievingly, looked at Ariadne, and then said, "Bull!"

"True!" Jerry said. "A referee would be useless anyway in mayhem, and that's more fun than tossing a coin for kick off. I was referee once—two broken legs, a dislocated shoulder, and a crushed kidney. I was lucky."

"Craziest thing I ever heard of," Carlo said.

Killer crawled to his feet without looking up and went limping off down the slope toward the hospital. He staggered a lot and was clutching a bleeding ear.

Jerry hesitated, smiled apologetically at Ariadne, and asked Carlo, "Do you need a bed for the night, until you find somewhere? I've got a couch in the library that would fit you."

Carlo shook his head, but he actually smiled. "The Oracle said someone would come and fetch me and put me up for a day or two. Some mouthful of a name beginning with 'Itti.'"

Jerry whistled and rolled his eyes. "She's a little Hittite girl. Very nice!" He grinned at Ariadne. "One of Killer's favorites. Could be very enjoyable hospitality, Citizen Carlo!"

Carlo said, "No foolin'?" and looked impressed. Then

he glanced around to see where the others were and turned to Ariadne.

"Ma'am?" He paused and looked at his feet.

"The Oracle told me," she said quickly. "But it didn't happen, and I'd rather not hear any more about it."

Startled, he studied her eyes for a moment and then nodded. "That Oracle sorted my cards for me." He scowled. "I've been very dumb."

"We all have, Carlo," she said. "It sorted my cards, too."

Carlo had probably had little choice but to stay in Mera—where else could a penitent terrorist be safe?

"I suppose I need to find a trade now," he said. "That'll feel funny."

Jerry shook his head. "Not necessarily. Killer has none, but unofficially he's commander-in-chief of the Meran army. He has no authority except his own personality, but you could join his group. He's always on the lookout for good men."

"So I've noticed," Carlo said.

Jerry turned pink again, in that shy way of his. "You don't have to . . . I mean, that isn't necessary."

Carlo shrugged. "So I have something he wants—I can set a price, can't I?"

"No, you can't!" Jerry snapped. "That won't work with Killer, any more than your fancy judo would work on demons." He glanced uneasily at Ariadne and then said, "Listen! The last time I played mayhem, I was on the other team. I got to Killer, and he had a broken wrist, so that helped the odds, and there were about eight guys on top of us. I gouged one of his eyes out—just before he broke my neck."

She was horrified. "No! Jerry! Wanton brutality!"

But Carlo nodded. "He was testing?"

"All the time!" Jerry said. "Can you take it, can you dish it out? The games, the hunting trips, the fights, the mayhem—they're not just senseless rowdyism. He learns, trains, teaches, and tries things—and *tests*. It's how he has survived so long and rescued so many, many people! Hell, there are dozens of men in Mera that would give their large and small bowels to be invited out on a rescue by Killer, but he doesn't think they have the guts to start with and he won't trust his back to them."

"Gotcha," Carlo said thoughtfully "A challenge, Mr. Howard?"

It was a new view of Killer, and Ariadne recalled the cheering welcome in the streets.

Jerry had embarrassed himself with his own vehemence, but was saved by an interruption. He smiled over Ariadne's shoulder. "Here comes your landlady. You come and see us tomorrow."

He introduced Carlo to a very pretty girl, who blushed and stammered; but in a couple of minutes Carlo had her giggling, and his arm was around her as they walked away.

"See that?" Jerry demanded, astonished. "Give that kid ten years, and things will get very interesting! I wonder if Killer has finally met his match?"

Or his successor—but Ariadne did not say so.

That left Graham and Maisie. They were sitting on one of the benches, gazing into each other's eyes. Maisie looked ready to melt, quite sickening. Jerry scooped up the Cretan helmet from the bench where he had left it and led the way over.

"I hate to interrupt," he said, "but I was instructed to lead you to the harbor."

Graham looked at him, then Ariadne, and then smiled. "Congratulations," he said.

Was it so obvious? Did it matter?

"Thank you, Graham," she said.

He blushed—he actually blushed! "Ariadne . . . I think I'm now what they call 'born-again'. Jerry, we need that Oracle of yours in the States; we could dispense with a lot of psychiatrists and policemen and . . . yes, and lawyers and priests, too. Ariadne, I owe you an apology, more than I can . . ."

It should really have been very funny. Five days ago she would have probably gone into hysterics. Now she felt more sorry for him than anything else. It was embarrassing, for Graham penitent was as hard to shut up as Graham rampant, and suddenly damnable likeable again.

As the four of them started off down the steps towards
the Hospital, she managed to edge next to Maisie and
leave Jerry to handle the enthusiastic breast-beating of
the born-again Graham.

Maisie was not much better. Her session with the Oracle seemed to have been very short and quite sweet,
although she was very insistent that she must see her
confessor as soon as she got back. But in the next breath
she said that the Oracle had told her she would remember nothing of Mera when she returned—that the
whole affair would be wiped from her life. How one
could confess what hadn't happened was beyond Ariadne's comprehension.

They strolled down Hillside Path. She would have to
learn all these names. And then a long staircase . . .

How did one get back to Colorado on a ship, Ariadne
asked. That sounded like quite a feat, even for the Oracle. Maisie turned pink and said that they would have a
cabin and could sail on as long as they liked and she had
always wanted a cruise in a sailing ship. And the third
time they made love, the Oracle had told her, they would
wake up in their own bed at the ranch, on the day before
Ariadne had achieved the kidnapping—which now
would not happen.

It sounded very sugary, especially designed for Maisie.

Musn't be catty! Maisie had been through a lot and
had certainly earned a reward. Perhaps the Oracle had
decided wisely, but the way Maisie and Graham had
been clinging to each other, it might be a short voyage.

Woodworkers' Wynd . . . Brewers' Mews . . . she tried
to take note of the quaint little stores, the delicious-
smelling cafes and bake shops, the flower-encrusted
open spaces for sitting, the jewellike miniature parks,
but Jerry was continually introducing her to people as
proudly as though he had invented her.

Maisie bubbled like a hot pool about the transformation in Graham, of the promises he had just made her,
of how very fond they both were of Lacey, and how
well they would raise her—until suddenly she realized

that Ariadne would not be seeing Lacey again. Then she sobbed the rest of the way to Fishermen's Walk.

"This is it," Jerry said, stopping suddenly at a big ivory door and holding out the boars' tooth helmet. He had noticed her weariness or her impatience with Maisie. "Why don't you make yourself at home, and I'll be right back?"

Ariadne nodded. "I am very tired. You won't mind if I say good-bye here?"

Graham puffed himself up like a toasted marshmallow. "Then we should tell her our good news, shouldn't we, darling?" he said, and Maisie turned from pink to scarlet.

"Wonderful!" Ariadne said in the most sincere tone she could manage.

Maisie simpered. "I wasn't sure—but the Oracle never lies, you say. It says a boy. It even told me the day."

Handshakes and hugs.

"So I shall have a son!" Graham said, with the faintest hint that his second wife was more competent than his first.

More hugs and kisses were exchanged, and Ariadne walked up the steps with the Cretan helmet under her arm, blew a last kiss to Maisie, and entered Jerry's house.

The big room amused her; it was so exactly what she would have expected from Jerry, precise and restrained by good taste just on the right side of being ostentatious. Thousands of books, he had said, and certainly there were thousands. Still, she had lots of time . . . happily ever after? It would take forty years even to get used to that idea.

She felt drained—hardly surprising after a day which had started in a mythical Cretan prison and ended in Fairyland, with mortal combat and marriage proposals thrown in. A good little wife would perhaps fix supper for her man, but she was not going to play that role. Mostly he ate out anyway, he had said. She would just sit and wait for him.

Yet the quiet did not soothe her; she was too jangled. Her head was spinning. Imagine binding all those books, the work involved!

Poor Jerry . . . how did he sleep? In the dark of night did he listen to Smythe-Williams' craven whimpers crackling over the intercom—was that the explanation for his endless round of play and work, the frantic seeking after happiness?

And what of Killer, who had somehow failed his own standards at Thermopylae? Killer with his hyperactive brawling and lusting—was he seeking only distraction and exhaustion, burying by day the corpses that crawled from their graves by night?

And she, who had just abandoned her child to a crook and a dumb kid—she, who had given up piano for motherhood and then screwed that up and lost both—perhaps the ghosts of might-have-been would come to her also in the silent hours.

This Mera which she had so irrevocably chosen, was it eternal happiness, or eternal regret?

Maybe Maisie was right.

Oh, Lacey!

And Graham, damn him! That last remark of his, "So I shall have a son." That bothered her. That niggled.

Judgment of Solomon. What had the Oracle meant by that? Not, surely, that Ariadne would be divided between Jerry and Killer?

Restless, unable to settle in spite of her fatigue, she rose and started to explore. The big double doors led only to a cluttered and smelly workshop, and that would be for the other Jerry, the informal Jerry who hid behind the shyness. Another door led to a hallway with two doors and a spectacular staircase. This was a much bigger house inside than it looked from the outside—more faerie, perhaps. She found a kitchen and bathroom, both old-fashioned but acceptable, then she wandered up the staircase and discovered a breathtaking bedroom with a grand piano. The room was a designer's masterpiece in blues and gold, the sort of room she had tried—and failed—to create with Graham's ill-gotten wealth before

it forced them out of city life and off to the greater gran-
deur of a ranch.

Whatever she was subconsciously seeking was not
there.

She wandered over to the bed, tested the mattress,
and was just about to explore through the other door—
which probably led to a bathroom—when the main door
closed with a click.

And there was Killer.

The last place she wanted to meet Killer was a bedroom. She moved quickly away from the bed and was
grimly aware that she had started to tremble already.

He was flushed, excited, and panting. He wore a
blood-soaked bandage over his ear, but he grinned as he
limped hurriedly toward her.

"This is a very nice room," he said, glancing around.
"Much nicer than when Jerry had it."

"You mean it has changed?" she asked, although obviously that was what he meant. Get a hold of yourself,
woman!

"I knew it quite well," he said impishly.

"You probably won't be seeing so much of it in the
future."

He put on a hurt expression and now he had reached
her and was standing too near, as usual. "That does not
sound friendly, pretty lady. I am a close friend of Jerry's
and I hope to be a close friend of yours."

"You're a little too close already, Killer," she said,
backing away. "Jerry told me that you always take no for
an answer. Is that right?"

He put on his sleepy-eyed look for a moment and
said, "You won't refuse me." He edged closer again, and
again she stepped back.

Could she? She was tensely aware of his stupendous
arrogance, the physical arrogance of a superstud, and
also a spiritual arrogance springing from his complete
lack of scruples or fear. Killer was single-minded, she
decided; when he looked at anyone, he concentrated
totally upon that person. He was hot and sweating already. She remembered their kiss after he killed the

Minotaur ... change the subject. "Did Carlo hurt you badly?"

"No. A few ribs and a cracked head. I am seeing double, but both of you are equally beautiful. You are hurting me more. You have something I want, pretty lady—something I want very much."

"No!" Damn, that was shrill, but the harsh breathing and the flushed face were unnerving her. He looked terrifyingly aroused.

He frowned in mock disapproval, advancing again. "It will make you very happy! But tell me why did you take such a terrible risk for me today? You were safe in the wagon. You must care for me greatly." He grinned hopefully.

"I'm damned if I know," she said truthfully. "Why not ask the Oracle?" She tried to side-step, and he moved to block her.

An odd look came into his eye. "The Oracle told me many strange things today. It was not for love, then?" He looked heartbroken.

"No, not for love," she said. "You're a nice guy, Killer, but . . ."

"But you love Jeremy Howard?" He smiled. "I also love him, he is strong and yet gentle. I should like to be more like him."

And Jerry Howard, she now suspected, would in some ways like to be more like Killer. She smiled also. "Are you sure of that?"

Killer nodded earnestly. "It is true. You corrected me about Clio today, and I am grateful for that, too. Would you help me more?"

Well, that was a new line! He probably had more lines than a telephone company. She would never see a telephone again.

She had not answered, and Killer reached for her hands. She backed away again and bumped against the piano. No retreat—this would be Ariadne's last stand. She wondered how long Jerry would be.

Killer took her hands in his and said, "Did you know I was an orphan?" His eyes were dancing.

Now what? He kept changing the subject. "Oh

really!" She tried to pull away, and he held tight. "Your parents have been dead for twenty-five hundred years!"

He shook his head seriously. "I always knew that Crion and Astiaspe were not my parents—they were too old. But they were good people, kind and loving parents to me. They taught me to honor the gods and serve my *polis*." For a moment he stared away over her shoulder, and his eyes misted. "They died in the year the Persians came, within two days. I saw that they had fitting rites and I spoke for them."

"Killer," she said. "I'm very tired. Please can we have this conversation another day?"

"I shall be as quick as I can!" he assured her ominously.

Then he staggered, and she grabbed his shoulders to steady him. One of his pupils was dilated...bleeding from the ear, flushed skin, loud breathing, double vision —all the symptoms!

"Heavens, boy!" she gasped. "You're running around with a fractured skull!" She guided him over to the bed, and he flopped on it. She lifted his feet up and straightened the pillow and felt his forehead—a furnace. "You lie right there, Achilles!" she ordered. "I'm going to get help and move you up to the hospital."

She had turned away and had taken two steps when he snapped, "Stop!"

She stopped.

"Come here!"

If he calls me to his bed...Almost in spite of herself she went back, trembling violently, and looked down at his grinning face.

The same smile Graham had, the straight Greek nose, Graham's bull shoulders, and the dark curls spread on the pillow...like...like Alan's. Why had she not noticed sooner? But of course she had noticed —*that* was why she had jumped to his defense, why she could not hold back when he held out his arms to her, why her own reaction had repelled her, why she had presumed to nag him about Clio...why she had wanted to spank him.

"Alan?"

"Yes, Mother."

Stunned, she sat down on the bed beside him. "How? What?"

"The Oracle told me," he said, taking her hand. "It knew that you would choose to stay and that Father would not. It forbade me to talk to him, or tell you before he had gone. I tried, but my legs and mouth wouldn't work. . . ."

They had all forgotten Alan. All the time she had been in the house of the Oracle—and when she had been talking with Graham and Maisie—none of them had remembered that there had been two children; only Lacey. More magic!

The Judgment of Solomon: Divide the children.

"I fell off in Arcady," Killer said, still grinning. "That's where my scar came from, the one that won't disappear. It's a faerie scar—I fell off, and one of the unicorn's hooves clipped me."

Achilles—Al Gillis. He had been able to tell them his name.

"Oh, my poor baby!" she said.

Killer said, "Damn right!" and smothered a giggle. "Crion had been on an embassy to Sparta; he found me and took me home. I don't remember, of course. I came here to ask a mother's blessing, Ariadne. That was all. Did you want something else?"

"Oh, *you* . . ."

You what? Obnoxious punk? Hero? Commander-in-chief?

"I . . . I am very proud of my son," she said.

He was pleased. "I'm proud to have you as a mother. The Oracle told me how you saved Jerry and the others. I am a brave fighter—I think I got my courage from you."

Graham had stayed with the women when the Merans attacked the Cretans—probably Killer did not much care that he had not been allowed to speak to his father.

Not Killer, Alan! She leaned down and hugged him, and he put his arms around her, but gently.

"And you are going to marry Jerry Howard!" he said

in her ear, and she could feel him chuckling inside. "And after that I shall always call him 'Daddy' . . . and that will annoy the everlasting piss out of him!"

"Yes," Ariadne said faintly to the pillow. "Yes, I'm sure it will."

"I always was a little devil, wasn't I?" said Killer.

AUTHOR'S NOTE

CAN ACHILLES TRULY BE ALAN GILLIS? WE HAVE only his word that the Oracle said so. If it is true, then why does he only know a few words of English and how did he get to Arcady?

A friend of mine has assured me that she spoke fluent Arabic as a child, but lost the ability through disuse. As an adult she knows no Arabic at all, so it does seem that a language can be forgotten.

The geography problem is tougher. A straight line from Crete around 2000 BC to western North America around 2000 AD does not go anywhere near central Greece in the classical period—as may be easily seen by plotting the points on four-dimensional graph paper. However, the principle authorities on migrating unicorns all insist that they normally fly a great circle route, not a straight line. Thus a pit stop in Arcady could be possible, and we should not discard Killer's statement on grounds of geography, either.

Personally, I would not argue with Killer if he claimed to be the three princesses of Serendip.

Father Julius was correct in stating that unicorns were a symbol of Christ in the early church. They were demoted from this position around the thirteenth century, but that would have been after his time.

It was my own idea to make Asterios a demon. To the

Greeks he was the perfectly normal offspring of a woman
and a bull, but he did live in the Labyrinth and he did eat
human flesh. How he managed this with bovine teeth
was never explained, but probably it was easier than di-
gesting hay in a human stomach.

The—real-world—palace at Knossos, as it has been
excavated, covered several acres and may have been as
high as five stories. It must have been very impressive
and vastly bigger than anything existing in Greece at that
time. The legend of the Labyrinth and the Minotaur may
possibly have started when some Greek tourist lost his
way in the great edifice, turned a corner, and came face
to face with a priest wearing a ceremonial bull mask. It
must have scared, in Killer's phrase, the everlasting piss
out of him, because the myth has been around for at
least four thousand years.

Asterios' mother—the lady who liked bulls—was Pasiphae, the wife of King Minos. Ariadne, who helped
Theseus kill the Minotaur, was a daughter of Minos and
Pasiphae, and therefore Asterios' half-sister. They were
an odd family.

The land of eternal youth has had so many names that
I was at a loss to know which to use. I finally coined yet
another—Mera—as an abbreviation of *chimera*. In typical Meran fashion, the dictionaries I have consulted do
not quite agree on *chimera's* meanings, but it seems to
have three.

1—In Greek mythology, *a fire-breathing monster,
part lion, part goat, and part snake*. We always get back
to Killer, don't we?

2—*A fanciful and unbelievable mixture of things*. No
comment, I'll leave that one to the critics.

3—*A mirage, and unattainable fancy*. Pity! But Jerry
said that Mera is always just out of sight. I, for one,
intend to go on looking. See you there.

D.D.

ABOUT THE AUTHOR

DAVE DUNCAN was born in Scotland in 1933 and educated at Dundee
High School and the University of St. Andrews. He moved to
Western Canada in 1955 and has lived in Calgary ever since. He
is married, with three grown-up children.

When a career in petroleum geology began to pall after thirty
years, he turned his attention to writing, first as a hobby, then part-
time. Eighteen months and nineteen thousand sheets of paper later,
he produced *A Rose-Red City*. With the oil business currently in
one of its cyclical slumps, he is now happily writing full time.

A Selection of Legend Titles

☐	Eon	Greg Bear	£4.95
☐	The Infinity Concerto	Greg Bear	£3.50
☐	Wolf in Shadow	David Gemmell	£3.50
☐	Wyrms	Orson Scott Card	£2.95
☐	Speaker for the Dead	Orson Scott Card	£2.95
☐	The Misplaced Legion	Harry Turtledove	£2.95
☐	An Emperor For the Legion	Harry Turtledove	£2.99
☐	Falcon's of Narabedla	Marion Zimmer Bradley	£2.50
☐	Dark Lady	Mike Resnick	£2.99
☐	Golden Sunlands	Christopher Rowley	£2.99
☐	This is the Way the World Ends	James Morrow	£5.50
☐	Emprise	Michael Kube-McDowell	£3.50

Prices and other details are liable to change

ARROW BOOKS, BOOKSERVICE BY POST, PO BOX 29, DOUGLAS, ISLE OF MAN, BRITISH ISLES

NAME..

ADDRESS..

....

....

Please enclose a cheque or postal order made out to Arrow Books Ltd. for the amount due and allow the following for postage and packing.

U.K. CUSTOMERS: Please allow 22p per book to a maximum of £3.00.

B.F.P.O. & EIRE: Please allow 22p per book to a maximum of £3.00

OVERSEAS CUSTOMERS: Please allow 22p per book.

Whilst every effort is made to keep prices low it is sometimes necessary to increase cover prices at short notice. Arrow Books reserve the right to show new retail prices on covers which may differ from those previously advertised in the text or elsewhere.

Bestselling SF/Horror

☐ The Labyrinth	Robert Faulcon	£2.50
☐ Night Train	Thomas F. Monteleone	£2.50
☐ Malleus Maleficarum	Montague Summers	£4.50
☐ The Devil Rides Out	Dennis Wheatley	£2.50
☐ The Shadow of the Torturer	Gene Wolfe	£2.95
☐ Contact	Carl Sagan	£3.50
☐ Cobra Strike (Venture SF 17)	Timothy Zahn	£2.95
☐ Night Visions	Campbell, Barker, Tuttle	£2.95
☐ Bones of the Moon	Jonathan Carroll	£2.50
☐ The Island	Guy N. Smith	£2.50
☐ The Hungry Moon	Ramsey Campbell	£2.95
☐ Pin	Andrew Neiderman	£1.50

Prices and other details are liable to change

ARROW BOOKS, BOOKSERVICE BY POST, PO BOX 29, DOUGLAS, ISLE OF MAN, BRITISH ISLES

NAME. . . . .

ADDRESS. . . . .

. . . .

. . . .

Please enclose a cheque or postal order made out to Arrow Books Ltd. for the amount due and allow the following for postage and packing.

U.K. CUSTOMERS: Please allow 22p per book to a maximum of £3.00.

B.F.P.O. & EIRE: Please allow 22p per book to a maximum of £3.00

OVERSEAS CUSTOMERS: Please allow 22p per book.

Whilst every effort is made to keep prices low it is sometimes necessary to increase cover prices at short notice. Arrow Books reserve the right to show new retail prices on covers which may differ from those previously advertised in the text or elsewhere.

A Selection of Arrow Bestsellers

☐ The Lilac Bus	Maeve Binchy	£2.50
☐ 500 Mile Walkies	Mark Wallington	£2.50
☐ Staying Off the Beaten Track	Elizabeth Gundrey	£5.95
☐ A Better World Than This	Marie Joseph	£2.95
☐ No Enemy But Time	Evelyn Anthony	£2.95
☐ Rates of Exchange	Malcolm Bradbury	£3.50
☐ Colours Aloft	Alexander Kent	£2.95
☐ Speaker for the Dead	Orson Scott Card	£2.95
☐ Eon	Greg Bear	£4.95
☐ Talking to Strange Men	Ruth Rendell	£5.95
☐ Heartstones	Ruth Rendell	£2.50
☐ Rosemary Conley's Hip and Thigh Diet	Rosemary Conley	£2.50
☐ Communion	Whitley Strieber	£3.50
☐ The Ladies of Missalonghi	Colleen McCullough	£2.50
☐ Erin's Child	Sheelagh Kelly	£3.99
☐ Sarum	Edward Rutherfurd	£4.50

Prices and other details are liable to change

ARROW BOOKS, BOOKSERVICE BY POST, PO BOX 29, DOUGLAS, ISLE OF MAN, BRITISH ISLES

NAME...

ADDRESS...

....

....

Please enclose a cheque or postal order made out to Arrow Books Ltd. for the amount due and allow the following for postage and packing.

U.K. CUSTOMERS: Please allow 22p per book to a maximum of £3.00.

B.F.P.O. & EIRE: Please allow 22p per book to a maximum of £3.00

OVERSEAS CUSTOMERS: Please allow 22p per book.

Whilst every effort is made to keep prices low it is sometimes necessary to increase cover prices at short notice. Arrow Books reserve the right to show new retail prices on covers which may differ from those previously advertised in the text or elsewhere.